a rebel desire novel 3

all of *you*

fabiola francisco

All of You
Fabiola Francisco
Copyright © 2018 Fabiola Francisco

This ebook is licensed for your personal enjoyment only. This ebook may not be re-sold or given away to other people. If you would like to share this book with another person, please purchase an additional copy for each recipient. If you're reading this book and did not purchase it, or it was not purchased for your use only, then please return to your favorite ebook retailer and purchase your own copy. Thank you for respecting the hard work of this author.
The characters and events portrayed in this book are fictitious. Any similarity to real persons, living or dead, is coincidental and not intended by the author.
Formatted by Integrity Formatting

Chapter 1

Jason

I THROW MY GYM BAG across the living room and slam the front door.

"Whoa!" I hear an exclamation.

I look forward. "What are you doing here?" I bite out.

"I live here," Cole, my bandmate and roommate, states.

"Doesn't seem like it lately," I mumble.

"Aw, you jealous, brother?"

"Fuck off. Not in the mood for your bullshit."

Cole takes a long, hard look at me and tilts his head. "What happened?" Gone is his mocking tone.

"Nothing."

"Suit yourself. I'm leaving for Bri's."

"See ya." *Wouldn't wanna be ya.* But I would want to be him. I thought I was on my way to having what he's found with Bri. What Cash and Olivia have. Hell, I'll even take Ryder and Jen's inappropriateness if it meant I had someone by my side. My friends all found their person, and I lost the woman I thought could be mine.

Maybe it's a good thing. With the tour having ended, it's probably for the best that I'm single again. *Again.* Was I ever not single? Not sure what I had could count as a relationship, except for me it was. I was *fooled.*

A man should have the balls to claim the woman he wants. Unless his balls were clipped and given to a cat to play with. And for what?

I sigh and stand by the glass doors leading to the patio. Staring at nothing in particular, my vision blurs until I'm watching a play by play of the last few months. I run my hand over my face and bearded jaw. *I should shave.* She loved my beard, and I need to erase her completely so I can be on top of my game to work on new music. No way am I going to be like Cash or Cole when their hearts were broken. Nah, I did enough talking to them about getting their shit together to fall down that same trap.

I move away from the living room and into the kitchen for a cold one. It's quiet in here. I got used to being crammed into a small space for months. Now I'm alone. Even though Cole has been spending more time with Bri outside of here, I had Christie to keep me company. Now I've got no one because all my friends have girlfriends and wives and I'm stuck at home with a pity party for one. It's not like I can go to Riot. That will only frustrate me more, seeing her there, probably flirting with other men as she serves them drinks.

I chug the beer and grab my guitar, playing the tunes of our newer songs. Music always takes me away. Although, at the moment, I hate the fact that I'm famous. I hate that I have the band's name tied to me.

What a bitch.

Fresh beer and guitar in hand, I get ready for a long fucking night.

“Fuck.”

“Shhh…”

I shift around, wondering who the fuck is in my room. When the whispers become louder, I groan and peel my eyes open. What the…

I turn my head and realize I’m in the living room.

“What the fuck?” I croak and clear my throat.

“You woke him up.”

I sit up and look to the left to see Bri and Cole in the kitchen. I scrub my face and look at the empty beer bottles on the coffee table. My guitar lies on the floor.

“What time is it?” I look around for my phone.

“It’s early, Jason. Go back to sleep, we’ll leave in a few,” Bri says and looks at Cole with a stern expression. I chuckle.

“It’s okay. I guess I fell asleep on the couch.”

“With a graveyard of beer bottles,” Cole juts his chin toward the coffee table. “Fuck, sorry, babe.” He looks at Bri, who smiles sadly, and hugs her to him.

I pick up the bottles and drop them in the trash. Cole whispers something to Bri and jogs up the stairs.

“What’s going on?” Bri leans against the counter and eyes me.

“Nothin.’” I shrug, demonstrating as much nonchalance as I can. I laugh as Bri squints her eyes and looks at me. “Really, I’m okay.”

“I don’t believe you. How’s Christie?” I know she’s testing me, but I groan regardless. “Oh man, Jason. Did you guys break up?"

"It's no big deal."

"Clearly, it is."

"Nah, we were only dating for a few months. Nothing serious," I wave my hand.

"It may have been a few months, but I know you really liked her. She seemed like a nice woman."

I laugh dryly. She did seem that way, until she proved otherwise. "It just didn't work out," I tell Bri.

"If you need to talk, you know we're all here for you. Hell, you were there for me when that black hole was sucking me away."

I hug Bri and thank her. She's stronger than anyone I know, to overcome the loss she did and trust life enough to find love again.

"I'm glad you're good. What are you guys up to today?"

"We're going to Pinewood Social for brunch and then some games. Do you want to come?" Her eyes light up, trying to lighten my mood.

"I'm good. Should stay home and clean up this mess and shit."

"Are you sure? We won't have to talk about… you know." She nods her head.

"I'm positive. Thanks, though. I appreciate it. And listen, if you could—"

Bri places her hand on my arm. "Your secret's safe with me."

"Thanks." I blow out a gust of air.

"They're going to figure it out soon, though."

"I know, but I want a few days to process it all," I explain.

She nods, smiling.

As soon as Cole comes back down, they leave me. Instead of staying inside the house with the same silence that led to me to drink too much and fall asleep on the couch, I get dressed and go out for a run. I need to clear my head. We've been back from tour a couple weeks, and I wish we were back on the road. I know the guys are happy to be back with their women, but having returned to the reality that waited for me sucks.

Anyone who hears my thoughts would think I'm a pussy, but I've always liked being in a relationship. Before Christie, it had been a while since I'd been in a serious relationship, with the band picking up momentum and stuff. After we became well known, it was difficult finding a woman who cared about me and not Rebel Desire or their connection to us. I thought Christie was that woman. I could see it being long term, and then she ruined everything.

No more thinking about her. I focus on my neighborhood as I jog up and down streets, sweat covering my body. A few teenagers hang outside, but overall it's quiet. Cole and I chose this place because of the tranquility and gated community. He'll probably move in with Bri soon, though. I won't be surprised when he drops that news. Since the new year started they've been spending more and more time together. Now that they've survived their first tour, it will be a matter of time. I'm happy for him, but more so for Bri. Although, that leaves me as the seventh wheel when we're all together.

Fuck that.

I hook on my headphones, turn on the music on my phone, and pick up my pace, clearing my mind for a while.

I slow my pace as the final beats of my playlist end and take in my surroundings. I ran way further than my usual route. Thankful for my phone, I check my location and find a diner half a mile away. In desperate need of water after a night of one too many beers and pushing my lungs to their limit, I find the diner and walk in, lowering my cap over my eyes to draw little attention to my identity.

The smell of stale coffee and greasy food fills me as I take a seat at the counter. This isn't like my usual eating spots, but I gladly take the cup of water the waitress places in front of me and pick up the sticky menu.

"Let me know when you're ready," she says as she leaves to take another order.

I read through each item, undecided about what to eat.

"I recommend the pancakes," the waitress returns. "Joyce makes them herself, and I don't know what she puts in the mix, but they're the best I've ever had."

"Joyce?" I look up at the waitress. I see the initial surprise in her wide eyes, but she doesn't give me away.

"The owner."

"Oh." I glance back down and put the menu flat on the counter. "I'll take an order of pancakes."

She nods and walks away to put my order in. I resist the urge to swivel on the stool as I wait for my food. Mostly truck drivers are here, probably getting in a quick bite before heading back out on the road. The red vinyl squeaks as they shift on their seats, and the once white tiles are permanently gray. I'm starting to regret the decision to eat here. Hopefully they keep the kitchen cleaner than they do the front area.

How far did I run? I've never seen a place as uncared for as this in my neighborhood. Must've taken two left turns and ended up on a different side of town.

"Can I get you anything else to drink while you wait?" the waitress, Cassidy Rae, according to her name tag, asks. I look behind her and see fresh-squeezed orange juice.

"OJ, please."

"You got it." She returns as fast as she turned away and places the cup next to my water glass. No mention of my name or the band, she just quietly drops it and goes back to work.

I watch her talk to an older woman and nod once before going into the kitchen.

Cassidy Rae. I like that name.

A few minutes later, the buttery smell of pancakes hits me and one of our songs is ringing through the speakers. Cassidy Rae hums to the song as she sets the coffee maker to brew. She's pretty, in a simplistic way. Her hair is back in a bun and her eyes a stunning green. No layers of makeup and bright lips adorning her face, unlike the fans we get at our meet and greets. I finally straighten my back and lift my head instead of hiding behind the bill of my cap.

"You like the song?" I ask her with a smirk.

"Huh? Oh, yeah." Her cheeks turn pink.

"Thanks for the recommendation, the pancakes were great." I drop a fifty on the counter and smile. "Keep the change, Cassidy Rae."

She mumbles a thanks, turning a darker shade of pink, as I stand and stretch. I take one last glance before I leave and see her gasp when she notices the big tip I left her. Grateful eyes meet mine, and I smile. Not sure what her deal is, but a job like this can't pay much. If I can pay it forward, why not?

Chapter 2

Cassidy Rae

I USED TO LONG FOR romance. I would dream of meeting someone, being courted by a man willing to accept me for who I am as we'd fall in love seamlessly. It would be gentle. Yeah, we'd have challenges, but we would come out of them with a stronger bond. Then, I woke up. I realized that love isn't the way I had portrayed it in my imagination. I was stuck on an illusion of beauty that is non-existent. Something I learned quickly. Instead, I reek of fried food and cleaning products.

I look to my right and sigh. I wouldn't trade the lifeline I'm looking at for anything, even if that kind of love existed.

I cuddle further into the couch, pulling her with me even though I should put her to sleep on the bed so she could rest more comfortably. Some days I need to hold her a little tighter to remind myself that life isn't all shitty.

Days like today, where I had to serve a handsome man, who reminded me of that lost dream. He stood out like a sore thumb between all the truckers, but when I realized who he was, my surprise was painted on me.

I sigh and look around the small space. *Our home.* Can I even call this a home? We're crammed in this mobile home, but it's the best I can do for us. One day, hopefully, I'll be able to get us a real place. A place with more than one bedroom and a decent size living room where Rae can play, maybe a desk for her to do her homework. My eyes flutter closed for a brief moment as I imagine a place like that. Unless I win the lottery, I'm not sure that will ever happen. *Can't win if you don't play.*

Rae's light breathing soothes me, and I carry her to the bed so we can rest. I'll have to be at the diner tomorrow morning, and Abigail will be here early to watch Rae for me. I've come across good things living in a not so good place. Abigail is one of them. It's a blessing she lives next door.

Holding my baby girl, I close my eyes and sleep a bit. She's growing up so fast, and I want time to slow down. She's the best thing in my life, and without her, I'm not sure where I'd be.

Every time the door opens, I look at who enters, in hopes that I'll see the same face as yesterday. It's stupid. Why would someone like him come back to a place like this? This is the best I can do, and I love working for Joyce, but this isn't the kind of place famous musicians hang out in. Hell, it's barely a place for a single mom to be a part of, but I need to survive this life. If I had gone to college and gotten a degree, I may not be here right now. Maybe I'd be living in a cushy apartment in downtown.

If that were my reality, I wouldn't have my little girl. It's bittersweet. I wouldn't trade her for all the riches in the world, but I do wish our financial situation were different. I want to offer her the best life, and right now it's subpar at best.

I wipe down the counter and refill coffee cups.

"Hey, suga, can I have a couple biscuits to take on the road?" one of the older drivers asks.

"Yup." I give the order to the kitchen and tend to a few other tables. Humming the songs that play, I think back to my upbringing. Sadness washes over me. I do miss seeing my parents every day, but it is what it is.

I take the biscuits in a to-go container to the man who ordered them, along with his check.

"How much to get you wrapped up in a container and out on the road with me to satisfy my hunger?"

I cringe at the old man's words and a shiver runs down my spine. I choose to ignore him, knowing men like this just want your attention, and walk away. As much as I love Joyce, this job doesn't pay enough to deal with people like him. Unfortunately, this is a normal occurrence. When I grab the check from his table, he boldly, and disrespectfully, grabs my behind.

Tearing away, I look at him. "I'd suggest you treat me with more respect than that or we'll have to call the authorities. We have zero tolerance to wandering hands or harassment of any type."

"What's going on, babe?" Ryan, the cook, comes out from the kitchen.

"Reminding our customers what respect is." I look at the sorry excuse for a man. Ryan looks at the man and smirks. I know that smile. It's the one he wears when he wants to kick someone's ass. I put my hand on his arm. "I think he got the message." Joyce will be pissed if Ryan gets into a fight with a customer, even if it is to defend me.

"Bullshit." He looks at the money in my hand. "If I were you, sir, I'd leave. I think leaving her your change as a tip is the least you can do after disrespecting a woman. Now, get out before I bust your ass."

Ryan waits until the man leaves. He takes his time grabbing his bag and walking out, as if Ryan's threat was a bag of shit.

"Thanks," I turn to Ryan. "But you know if you got physical Joyce would've fired you."

"She can't live without me," he jokes. "Let's get back to work." He squeezes my shoulder.

I nod and check on the other customers. I hate causing a scene, but I refuse to let men think they have more power over me because of their gender. I'm grateful Ryan has always had my back. He's the only other younger person working here, and he watches over all of us. We're a family, a small one, but it's all I need. Without them, I'd be out on the street somewhere. Thanks to Joyce, I have a job. Thanks to Maureen, another waitress, I have a place to live. It wasn't long after I started working here that she recommended the mobile home I'm living in. A friend of hers was renting it and gave me a great deal since Maureen sent me.

And some weekends, when Abigail can't babysit, I bring Rae here and she hangs out in the kitchen. It isn't ideal, but I'm grateful for it. Summer break starts soon, and I'll have Rae here more than usual.

When I'm done with my shift, I head home, eager to see Rae. I left her sleeping this morning, and I'm looking forward to spending some time with her. Maybe we can walk to the park near our house.

Opening the door, I hear Rae talking to Abigail. A smile covers my face as I hear her tell her about something that happened at school last week. At least she's having a good year in her new school. I was nervous for her to start kindergarten back in the fall, but she always proves to me how ready she is for life. She's my baby girl, but she's way too smart for her age. I don't remember being this savvy at six years old.

"Hi!" I walk in to see them.

"Mommy!" Rae jumps into my arms and I squeeze her tightly.

"Hi, sweetie."

"I missed you." She cuddles into me, nuzzling her face into my neck.

"I missed you, too. Did you have fun with Abby?"

"Yeah! We colored and played with my doll. She also brought me some cookies." Rae leans back and I'm met with a wide smile. I look over her shoulder at Abigail and mouth, *thank you.* She winks and stands from the sofa.

"We had a great day. She filled me in on what she's learning, and I helped her read her book."

"Thanks, Abby. I owe you."

"Nonsense, sweetheart. I happily do it. It's the closest thing I'll ever have to a granddaughter," she grins. Abigail and her husband never had children, although she always wanted them, so I know watching Rae is a gift for her. I only wish I could pay her, but she scolds me every time I bring it up, telling me to put the money I'd give her to treat myself to something. Instead, I split the little bit I can into a savings account for Rae and some for my parents. I want her to go to college and live out her dreams. I don't want my situation to stop her from living. Not that I resent my parents, but I wasn't able to have the support because of our circumstances.

Once Abigail leaves, I look around the home. Bless her, she cleaned for me. If she won't accept my money, I'll buy her a small gift as a thank you for all her help. She's the closest thing to family I have in this area outside of the diner. Her and Blake make sure I'm doing okay and have everything I need.

"Do you want to go to the park before the sun sets?" I ask Rae.

"Yes!" she exclaims, stating it's the best day ever. My heart flutters and tears fill my eyes. It doesn't take much to make her happy, and I try with all my being to do whatever I can for her.

Hand in hand, we walk to the nearby park. It's a blessing that there's a small park here near the mobile homes. A few of the families have children, so we have some place to take them that's safe. This area may not be the best in town, but at least the neighbors all respect each other. Outside of here, I wouldn't wander too far alone or even with company.

Rae sings as I push her on the swing. To think, I almost gave her up. I'd never have an abortion, but I did consider adoption. I knew I'd never give her the life she deserved, but after that first doctor's visit and hearing her heartbeat, I fell in love. It was instant, and I knew in that moment, I'd do anything to keep her and make a life for her.

That was when I decided to move out of my parents' house. It was too much. My pregnancy was unexpected, an irresponsible one-night-stand. I was working in a bar at the time and quit as soon as I found out I was pregnant, got a job at Joyce's Diner, and moved into the mobile home with the bit I had saved.

At first, my dad said we would make it work, but when I told him my reasons, he respected my decision. He did make me promise I wouldn't disappear on them. I could never do that to them. My mom's disease was too advanced for her to notice.

"Mommy, look!" Rae interrupts my thoughts, and I clap loudly as she goes down the slide.

"Great job, baby," I praise and wrap her in my arms when she runs up for a hug. I look at her wavy, blonde hair and big brown eyes. People say she looks exactly like me, but I wouldn't know if she looked more like me or her father. The eyes aren't mine, so they must be his.

After swinging a little longer, we head back home and lock ourselves inside.

I stir the mac and cheese as it cooks, and Rae watches cartoons on the local channel. I serve our dinner and sit with her on the sofa.

"Tomorrow's a school day, so once we're done eating you have to clean up and get ready for bed." It's the last week of school, but I'm still maintaining a strict sleep routine.

"Okay. Can I take one of the cookies Abby brought for snack tomorrow? They're really yummy." She folds her hands with a wide grin.

"Of course you can. Do you want me to ask her where she bought them? Or do you prefer we bake some next weekend?"

"Bake! I want to be a baker when I grow up."

I giggle and pull her to my side. "You can be anything you want." I kiss the top of her head.

"Did you always want to work at a diner?"

"Not really, but I do love it."

"What did you want to be when you grow up?" I love her innocence.

"When I was your age, I wanted to be a dancer."

Rae's eyes light up. "Like a ballerina?"

"Yeah. I always thought they were so pretty," I smile, remembering the photograph of a ballet dancer I had in my room.

"They are pretty. You woulda been a great ballerina." She scoots closer to me and hugs my arm. "When are we gonna see Grandma and Grandpa again? I miss them."

"I miss them, too, sweetie. I'll talk to Grandpa so we can go soon."

My mom was diagnosed with Alzheimer's right before I graduated high school, and it devastated my father. For years it was just the two of them. When they thought they couldn't conceive, *bam*, I came along. They were always much older than my friends' parents, and I worked a lot to help them pay for the doctors and medicines. My mom doesn't recognize me anymore, but I help as much as I can. Although my dad refuses when I give him money, saying I need to save for Rae's college fund, I slip a little bit of money into his room every time I go.

It's hard for Rae to understand the complexity of the disease, but she's a champ. When we go and visit, she takes on the role of caregiver the same as my dad and me. She lightens up the house with her energy and chatter.

"Time for bed," I announce, before she falls asleep on the couch.

"Okay." Rae goes to wash up while I wash the dishes. I'm lucky she's so well behaved. Her teacher also praises her.

"I'm ready, mommy," she yells from the room.

"Want me to read you a story?" I peek into the room.

Her enthusiastic nod brightens my mood. Cuddled together, I read her favorite book until her eyes shut and her breathing slows.

Chapter 3

Jason

"YOU'VE RISEN IN THE RANKS with your new album, hitting the top ten. Your fans are excited about this album and the infamous bonus track written by Cole. Great choice to add that in. It's hooked them to buy it," Vivian, our publicist, informs us. I listen as much as possible, but my mind is elsewhere.

Christie called me last night and I ignored it, and the text message she sent afterward. It's over, and I made that crystal clear when we last spoke.

"You have a few interviews and photo shoots. Cash, you and Olivia also have the interview with People Magazine. They'll be shooting photos in your house," Vivian continues.

"We're ready," Cash replies.

After sorting out a few more things, we practice and work on the songs we wrote while on the bus. We've recently welcomed Hunter Daniels, a new songwriter, to work with us. His songs are on point, and Cash and him mesh. He's coming by today to check out our recent work.

I strum the bass, keeping in rhythm, as my mind wanders to the green eyes I met Saturday. Met is a stretch, we barely spoke. I still have no idea how I ended up in that part of town, but I want to make it back and see her again. *Cassidy Rae*. Although, I don't need any distractions right now.

"Jason, are you with us?" Cash calls out.

"Yeah, sorry. Spaced out for a sec."

"No shit," Cole says.

I run my hand through my hair. "What's going on?"

"Ryder was suggesting a riff between the second verse and chorus."

"That works," I reply.

"Are you sure you're okay?" Ryder stares at me.

"Yeah."

"Did something happen with Christie?" Cash asks.

I groan, tugging my hair. "I don't wanna talk about it."

"You sure?"

"I'm positive. We broke up, that's it. Nothing else to tell." I clench my jaw. I don't want to go into the reason why we broke up. "Are we going to keep practicing?" We get back to work and I let out my emotions on my instrument of choice.

"Okay, now tell us what happened." Ryder props his elbows on the desk of our office after we finish working on the music to the new songs. We still have a while to go before they're perfect, but we got a good chunk accomplished.

"Nothing to tell. I already told you."

"Something happened." Cole crosses his arms.

I roll my eyes and look at the three of them. Sighing, I confess. "While we were on tour, she showed up at the label saying I recommended she go talk to Carl."

"Why?" Cash interrupts.

"Looks like she had an agenda. She waited for me to leave to try to worm her way into the business. I never thought about it before, but I looked her up on the internet after we broke up. She has a YouTube channel, singing covers of some of the hottest country songs.

"I got a call from Carl asking about her and I was confused when he said he met her. I confronted her when we got back. She told me it wasn't a big deal, and she thought I'd help her get a meeting so she could share her talents with the label."

"Fuck," Cole murmurs.

"I know."

"I really thought she was honest. One of the good ones."

"Me, too." Cole interacted with her the most since she'd come over. I know he wasn't expecting this.

"Damn. Sorry, Jason."

"It's okay, Cash. I told her it was over and moved on. This is my career. I can't have anyone coming in and trying to manipulate me or my bosses."

"Yeah, but it's still hard," Cash crosses his arms. I nod and lean back on the chair.

"How about we all have dinner at the house tonight? We can order food and have it delivered by the time we get there. I'll let Liv know," Cash says.

"Sure," we all agree.

I watch as the three of them send messages to their significant others and inwardly growl. I've always been a black or white guy, but this is gray matter and driving me insane.

I cared about her. I saw a future for us. I shared everything with her, while she withheld who she really was. The next woman I meet will have a requirement of questions to answer. I'll definitely research her, too. I refuse to get used again.

"It's settled. Dinner tonight," Cash announces as if there were ever a possibility Olivia would say no. She loves having us over.

Using the location from my Uber app, I type in the address to my Maps app and follow the directions. You bet your ass I wasn't walking back home after that long run out there. The front of the diner is familiar, although I've only been here once. *Joyce's Diner*. I'll remember next time.

The paint on the siding is peeling and the tin roof is rusted. I count the number of trucks parked, stalling. This is probably a bad idea.

I'm here because I keep thinking about the way she hummed our song as she worked. And the way she gasped when she recognized me, but was kind enough to keep my secret. The way she blushed when I caught her singing.

I check the time. I have about thirty minutes before I need to go to the studio, enough time for a glass of fresh OJ served by her, hopefully. I bring the cap down, shading my face, and hop out of my car.

As I open the door, chimes ring above my head. I've always hated chimes on doors. It doesn't allow for any privacy. Every time you walk in somewhere, people are aware of your presence. Right now though, I'm glad for them, because they've given me the opportunity to see her green eyes light up a bit upon seeing me. I smirk, walking over to the counter and take a seat.

"Mornin.'"

"Good morning." She wipes the same spot incessantly.

"Can I have an OJ please?"

"Oh, yeah. Sorry." She bites her lip, causing me to chuckle. "Would you like anything else?"

"That's all for today. Thanks. Best OJ I've had in a long time." I hold the cup up and take a sip.

"I doubt that," she laughs and crosses her arms, the towel she was using hanging from her hand.

"I mean it. Doesn't hurt that it's served by a beautiful woman." This gets me an eye roll.

"Nice try, but I'm not interested in being any groupie," she hushes so no one else hears her.

"That's not—"

"Save it for someone else." She walks away, leaving me to scold myself for being a jackass. Scratching my chin, I try to think of anything to let her know I didn't mean any offense by it.

I try to wave her down to pay her, but she's ignoring me harder than I ignore the paparazzi. I drop a twenty on the counter, leaving her the change for her tip. As I walk to the door, I hear someone call out, "Mommy." I turn to see a little girl with a head of curls skip to Cassidy Rae.

The wide green eyes tell me she didn't want me to know she has a child. Fuck, I didn't mean to offend her if she's with someone, but I didn't see a ring. Although, I should know that it doesn't take marriage to be committed to someone. Any type of relationship is to be respected.

I leave, wondering what kind of man allows his wife to

work in a dump like this. Maybe they really need the money and it was the best she could find. Hell, I don't know, but she's not for me to take care of.

Lately, I've been a fucking disaster, flirting with a woman I don't even know because I want more than my current situation. I want what my friends have, but I'm a loser if I think that will happen magically. *Grow some balls.*

This is my problem. I see a woman, think she's beautiful, and pursue her. I did that with Christie. She was kind, normal, sweet. I could've fallen in love with her. I take a deep breath and exhale all memories of her. She's not worth my time.

"Do we still want to perform at Riot while we're in town?" Cash asks as the photographer positions him.

"Why not?" Ryder styles his hair with his fingers.

We're taking pictures for one of our interviews, mostly questions about our recent tour, our latest album and our reaction to the quick success it's had. Some days I wake up in disbelief that this is my life. We all do. We hang out with people I admired for years. I never, in a million years, would've imagined talking to Garth Brooks, and we met him at one of the awards shows we went to last year. Hell, we've had writing sessions with some of the biggest names in the industry.

"Jason?" Cash calls me.

"Huh?"

"Riot?"

"Oh, whatever you guys want. I'm not gonna fuck up our career because she works there."

"Fuck that. Grab another chick and make her jealous. You don't need that kinda bullshit in your life." Ryder's words of wisdom even make the photographer pause and stare.

"Thanks, Ryder, but I'm good. Really. Let's do what we always do and forget about my personal life. I can keep things professional." As much as I was pissed and hurt Christie did that, I meant it when I told her I was done.

Cassidy Rae's offended face from a couple days ago comes to mind. I'm going to have to apologize. *Any excuse to see her again.* The more I think about her, the less I think she's married. Something doesn't add up, but that could be a gut feeling.

"I know we don't make anything performing at Riot, but I like that we go in when we have some free time," Cole says.

"Honestly, I'm good with it. I won't be going for pleasure any time soon, but I'm okay with performing there," I reassure them.

"Great. I'll call them and set something up," Cash smiles, speaking, but staring at the camera. It's as if he's always posed for pictures.

When the photographer is done with Cash, she calls the rest of us one by one before she takes group photos.

As we finish up, the anxiety to go to the diner and see Cassidy Rae to tell her I'm sorry is making me restless. It's late afternoon already, and I'm not sure if she'll be there but it's worth a shot. For whatever reason, I feel the need to explain myself. I don't want my reputation to be what it's not.

We finish up with the photographer, and I tell the guys I'll see them tomorrow. They all have women to go visit, and I have one green-eyed beauty I want a glimpse of. Something tells me I should go straight home, but I ignore the rational part of my brain and head to Joyce's Diner.

I'm surprised by the amount of trucks parked, but I guess truck drivers don't follow a set schedule. *What do I know?*

I shield my eyes from the sun and duck into the diner. I look around, finding mostly men and some couples. There are more people than the two mornings I've come by. I guess some people are eating an early supper.

I look around and don't see Cassidy Rae, but I sit at the counter anyway. Maybe she's in the kitchen. I look at the menu for no other reason than I need some distraction so I don't look like some idiot staring around the entire place looking for her.

"Sor–What are you doing here?"

I smirk. "Hi. I was craving pancakes and was told the ones here were amazing."

Cassidy Rae rolls her eyes. "Is that all?" She raises her eyebrows.

"Actually, the real reason I'm here is to apologize. I feel like a jackass for what happened the other day. I promise I wasn't just flirtin' for the fun of it. I meant what I said. You are beautiful, but I don't want you to think I'm a jerk who hits on women all the time."

"Okay."

"Okay? That's it?"

"Well, yeah, what do you want me to say? It's okay. You really didn't have to drive out here to tell me that."

"I wanted to."

"That's nice of you. Do you want anything else?"

"Just the pancakes and a coke please."

She nods and walks away, dropping my order off in the kitchen before tending the other tables. I watch her interact with the customers and clean up the tables. Every so often she'll look my way, and I smile. No pretending

I'm not looking at her. I'm here for her, after all.

She drops off my coke with the same expression she gives everyone. A part of me was expecting a little more after my apology.

"Don't get mad, sweetheart. It's not like I grabbed your pussy." My head whips to the left. What the actual fuck did I just hear? I turn to see a fuming woman and make my way to her.

"What'd you tell her?" I stare at the smug man sitting comfortably in his spot. *Fucker.*

"Are you her baby daddy?" The guy snickers. I look between him and Cassidy Rae.

"No, but that doesn't mean I'm gonna let you disrespect her." I take a step forward, ready to kill the man.

"It's okay," Cassidy Rae places her hand on my arm, but I scoff.

"The fuck it is. He just touched you without permission. I'll be damned if he lays another hand on a woman without her consent. Wouldn't mind breaking all the bones in his arms."

"Mommy?" I hear the soft voice calling. *Shit.* I wouldn't want any child seeing someone treat their mom that way.

"It's okay, baby. Go to the kitchen with Ryan." Cassidy Rae pleads with her eyes that I drop it. I breathe deeply and rake my hand through my hair.

"Is he?"

"No, sweetheart." Her daughter's eyes drop to the floor.

I look at Cassidy Rae and her daughter. This confirms what I was thinking. The girl doesn't know her father.

"I suggest you get your ass up and leave before I beat

you so hard you can't sit on that piece of shit truck long enough to finish your trek," I growl at the man.

Cassidy Rae ushers her daughter back into the kitchen and the other people eating here are staring. I don't give a shit. No one else stood up for a woman who was obviously in an uncomfortable position. This is what's wrong in today's world—a lot of closet preachers with no intention of ever standing up for what they believe in.

I finally take my seat again, no longer hungry. I could use a beer right about now instead of this coke. Hearing that bastard talk to Cassidy Rae that way lit something inside of me.

"Thanks," she whispers when she drops my pancakes.

"You're welcome. I wish I could've kicked his ass. Are you okay?"

"Yeah," she nods.

"How's your daughter?"

"She's okay. She didn't hear everything."

"I'm glad. At what time do you get off?"

"In about an hour."

"Okay, I'll wait for you to be done and make sure you make it out safely."

"Oh, no. You don't have to. Ryan will take me home."

"Ryan?" I cock an eyebrow.

"Our cook. He's a friend. He'll give me a ride home." She hooks her finger over her shoulder in the kitchen's direction.

"If he's the cook, he's probably here til closing time."

"Yeah, but we'll be okay."

"I'll take you home," I offer.

"It's really okay. We can wait."

"I'm taking you," I say with finality.

When the hour is up, I stand and wait for her. No way I'm going to let her get away. If she doesn't have her own car, I'll be dead before I let her walk home with her daughter by herself. It'll be late before they close the kitchen and her child needs to have a routine.

"Ready?" I ask her when she comes back out.

I lead them out to my car. Her daughter is quiet, eying me as we walk out. After opening the door for the both of them, I go to the driver's side and ask her for directions.

"What's your name?" Cassidy Rae's daughter asks.

"I'm Jason. What's your name?" I look at her through the rearview mirror.

"Rae, like my mommy," she smiles proudly.

"It's a beautiful name."

"Thanks. Do you and my mommy know each other? I've never seen you before."

She's perceptive for a little girl, but I wouldn't know much about kids.

"We met the other day, baby," Cassidy Rae responds before I can.

Following the directions Cassidy Rae tells me, I end up by a bunch of mobile homes.

"This is perfect. Thanks. You didn't have to drive us, but I do appreciate it so Rae can get to bed on time."

"I'm glad I was able to drive you." I look around the area. It's definitely a part of town I'm not familiar with.

I open the door for Rae. Her mom jumped out as soon as the car was put in park.

"Thanks again," Cassidy Rae says.

"My pleasure." I look down a beat. "Maybe we can get together?"

"I'm not sure. My life is a little different than yours."

"That's a sorry ass excuse," I tell her.

She glares at me. "I appreciate your help today and driving us, but I'm not interested in more."

I've never been shut down so bluntly.

"I think you're pretending you don't. Think about it. I'll be around the diner soon."

She rolls her eyes, her grip tight on Rae's hand. I look around assessing the area and it seems safe enough at the moment.

"I'll walk you to your door. Lead the way."

"We can go alone. I don't want to take up more of your evening."

"Just walk, or I'll ask Rae to tell me." I look down. "Rae, you want to lead us to your house so I can make sure you get there safely?"

The little girl blushes and nods.

"Please, don't use my daughter." Cassidy Rae shakes her head.

"I'm not. I mean it; I want to walk you to your door. Let me."

Cassidy Rae sighs and walks toward one of the mobile homes. From the bits I've seen, she's working that job to afford the minimum for her and her daughter. We stop in front of a white door.

"This is us. Thanks."

"You're welcome. Think about it. I'd love to get to know you." I smile at Rae. "Nice to meet you."

"Me, too," she responds.

I walk away as she opens the door, but keep an eye close to them until they're inside. Rae tells her mom something, but I can't hear it. I take one last glance around the trailer park and wonder what the hell leads a woman to live here with her daughter. It can't be the safest of places, but probably the most affordable in this area.

Seeing this gives me more of Cassidy Rae, and now I want to know the rest that she's keeping to herself.

Chapter 4

Cassidy Rae

"HEY, MOM, CAN I LICK the spoon after we finish?" Rae looks at me with puppy-dog eyes. I chuckle and wipe the side of her mouth.

"Looks like you already did."

Her eyes wander all over the tiny space as she holds in her smile. "Busted," she whispers.

Laughing, I hug her. "I love you, baby girl."

"I love you, Mommy. Thanks for making cookies with me." She squeezes me tightly before letting go and returning to her task of measuring the chocolate chips necessary for the recipe Joyce shared with us.

"I'd do anything for you." It's the truth. I would sacrifice anything to make Rae smile. She's my life, and the hardships I've encountered since having her erase the moment I see her smile light up her face.

When Joyce overheard me ask Ryan if he could take me by the market, she insisted I take all the ingredients to make cookies, including her family recipe. I tried to say no, but that woman is intimidating when she's stern. I'm grateful, though. That means I can put a little extra into Rae's savings this month. I was going to use the excessive tips Jason has left to buy what we needed, but I'll happily add it to her savings account.

"Are you ready to stir in the chocolate chips?" I ask her. She eagerly nods her head and dumps my favorite part of the cookies into the bowl. I hand her the wooden spoon to mix.

"Do you think we'll see Jason again?" Rae surprises me with her question.

"What?"

"He looked nice." She shrugs as she rakes through the dough, incorporating the chocolate into the cookie mix.

Jason dropped us off at home a couple days ago, much to my dismay. I freaked when he realized Rae was my daughter, but nothing prepared me for his offer to drive us home. I'm embarrassed about my situation and not being able to offer my daughter a better life. Someone like him, who is used to fancy things, would look down on this trailer park.

"Can we make the cookies into shapes?" Rae interrupts my thoughts.

"We don't have cookie cutters." I purse my lips.

"That's okay. It's like play dough. Watch."

I stare at my daughter as she grabs a piece of cookie dough and rolls it out under her little hands. Hands that used to wrap around my finger when she was a baby. She shapes the long roll and beams. "You see!" I look at the cookie sheet, and sure enough, she made a heart out of the dough.

"That's perfect," I tell her, admiring her creativity. I didn't have much growing up, we were always tight on money, but my parents were able to buy me cookie cutters.

"Let's make more. What shape are you going to make?"

Cheering up, thanks to Rae, I think for a second and smile. Silently, I roll out the dough the way she just did and twist it.

"Ta-da!" I exclaim.

"A star!" Rae jumps up and down. "I love stars."

We finish making shapes out of the cookie dough and wait for the cookies to bake. Every few minutes Rae peaks through the oven glass to see if the cookies are done. *I like them soft*, she said as I had set the timer.

"Ready?" I ask her, grinning at how she's hopping up and down. Her eagerness is contagious and even I want to binge cookies and milk.

"Come on, Mom!"

I chuckle and stop teasing her. I carefully take out the cookies, place them on the trivet, and inhale the sweet scent.

"It smells so good," I comment.

"I know." Rae licks her lips. "I can't wait to try one."

"We'll let them cool and then we can eat them."

I rush into the back door of the diner, Rae's hand tight in mine. She gave me a hard time leaving, begging to go with me so she can personally deliver cookies to Joyce. Abigail was there to watch her, but the six-year-old in her came out with a vengeance, tantrum and all. I finally conceded, knowing if I didn't I would be late to work, and if I left her, I'd feel guilty the entire shift.

I try to avoid bringing Rae to the diner when I work the later shift. It's not a place I want her roaming around in without real supervision and she gets to bed way past her bedtime.

"Hi, Joyce." I make quick work of putting my purse away and tying my apron.

"We brought you cookies!" Rae yells, jumping up and down with a sealed ziplock in her hands. She put them in the bag herself, saying these were special for Joyce from her.

"Sorry," I whisper. "She wouldn't let me leave without her."

"Don't you dare apologize. You know I love that little girl almost as much as you do."

I smile gratefully and thank her.

"Someone was asking for you," Joyce whispers back.

"Who?" My stomach drops.

"Go out there and see for yourself." Joyce smiles and winks before taking Rae's hand and asking her about the cookies.

I creak the door open a sliver and peek out to see who's waiting for me. I catch his baby blues and he smiles. *Busted.* I chuckle to myself as I repeat the same phrase my daughter did earlier this morning. Seeing me laugh, Jason sits taller and his smile widens. I frown, realizing he thinks I'm happy to see him.

I walk out into the diner and begin to work, taking orders from the customers waiting to eat or drink something.

"Hey," Jason calls out. "You gonna serve me?" His smirk is adorable.

"I thought Joyce had already taken your order."

"Nah. I was waiting for you."

I sigh and take his order. My life isn't a romantic comedy movie, where the handsome man falls for the poor, single mom. And I'm not talking poor as in, *poor me.* I mean poor as in I can barely afford to buy my daughter clothes. I depend on thrift stores and donations from a local church, but I hate pity and it seems like a lot of people around me like to give it.

I drop Jason's plate where he's seated in his usual spot at the counter and look around. Everyone seems to be okay for now so I go check on Rae, but before I can open the door Jason speaks.

"How are you?"

I close my eyes and turn around. He wants to chat. "Good and you?"

"Great." His smirk tilts up to one side. "Do you work everyday?"

"Yes."

"Maybe we can—"

"Hey, doll face," a customer interrupts Jason. I see him tense, his fingers curling into his hands.

"It's okay," I whisper. The last thing I need is for him to think he needs to stand up for me when it's no big deal. This man isn't trouble like the asshole from the other night.

I walk over, see what he wants, and when I turn around Rae is talking to Jason. I pause a second, watching her short legs swing from the stool as she talks up a storm. I can only see their profiles, but it looks like they're smiling. I walk around the counter and face them.

"Rae, please let our customers eat without interruptions."

"I just wanted to say hi and give him a cookie."

"It's okay," Jason says. "She came by to say hi and we started talking. I couldn't turn down the cookie, either. Delicious." He smiles at Rae and for a brief moment I imagine what it would be like if she had a father, or a father figure, in her life.

"We made the shapes ourselves, like with play dough," Rae explains to Jason.

"Well, you're quite the artist then. I loved the star."

"My mommy made that one," Rae's toothless grin is mischievous. If I didn't know any better, I'd think my daughter is playing matchmaker. My six-year-old daughter. I roll my eyes and tell her to get back in the kitchen.

"But I want to stay out here for a while. Jason even gave me a nickname. Can I talk to him a little longer? Pleeassse." She links her hands together and begs. "I'll use my indoor voice." Her voice lowers a bit when she says this.

Jason chuckles. "She can stay. I'm having fun talkin' to her."

"Okay, but you have to behave and be respectful." I'm more concerned about leaving her sitting next to a man we barely know, but I'll be right here watching them.

"I promise." Jason places his hand over his heart.

I giggle. "I was talking to Rae, but you, too." My daughter's entire face lights up like a Christmas tree. I leave the two of them talking so I can keep working, wondering what the hell is going on.

A couple hours later, Rae is sitting in the same spot, an empty bowl of ice cream, and still talking to Jason. I have no idea what all he has to talk to a six-year-old about, but she always finds anything to talk about once she likes a person. She only got up a few times for quick bathroom breaks, making Jason promise he wouldn't leave while she was in there.

Observing this worries me. She's so young, and I don't want her to get attached to someone who isn't a part of our lives. Jason is a musician. He's part of a band. People like him are busy and move around a lot.

"Mommy?" Rae walks up to me while I sit in the pantry a moment to rest.

"Yeah?" I smile despite the pain in my feet.

"Are you almost done?" She climbs on my lap and hugs me, sneaking her face in my neck.

"I still have a little bit left. Did Jason leave?"

She shakes her head against my neck. I shiver as it tickles, but squeeze her tighter. In a few years she won't want to spend time with me like this. "He says he wants to drive us home again."

"Ryan can take us."

"I really want Jason to. He's nice. I like him."

Sighing, I pull her back. "We don't even know him, baby girl."

"You don't, but I do. I've talked to him all afternoon. He even told me about his band. Did you know a bass isn't the same thing in music like in baseball?"

My body shakes with laughter. "They're different, but do sound the same. The bass is a guitar."

"Yeah, Jason told me. So, can he drive us home?"

"Maybe. Right now I need to get back to work."

Rae wraps her arms around my neck tightly and kisses my cheek. "I love you, Mommy. You're da best."

"I love you, too, sweetheart. So, so much." Being

exhausted from work is worth it to see her happy.

We walk back out into the front of the diner and Rae takes her seat next to Jason, who smiles and winks at me. The last two hours of work are going to be long. It's been distracting enough watching him interact with my daughter as if it were second nature to him. His smile has wrapped me up and transported me to a life where I could've had it all. But I know I don't. Simply because Jason is here, trying to get my attention for who knows what reason, doesn't mean we'll suddenly live a happily ever after a la Cinderella (minus the evil stepfamily).

"That boy has eyes for you."

"Oh please, Joyce." I'm surprised she's remained quiet about Jason this long.

"He does. Anyone can see that. He's been here since this morning waiting for you, and now he's becoming best friends with your daughter. He's a looker, too. Doesn't hurt."

Ignoring her, I walk up to Jason and Rae to let them know I'm done.

"We're leaving?" Rae squeals. Her and Jason stand.

"Sorry if she bothered you too much today."

"No way. She's a great kid."

"Thanks. I know she can be a bit much when she's excited."

"Nah. She's funny." He smiles down at Rae. "Can I drive you home?"

"It's really okay. You don't have to."

"I want to."

"Come on, Mommy. I'm tired. He already knows where we live." She smirks at Jason, an accomplice to his plan.

"Fine." Because who am I to say no to a handsome

man? I should, but I'm too caught up in his eyes to turn him down. Instead, I follow him to his car and climb in.

"Have you eaten dinner?" Jason asks.

"No. I'll have something at home."

"We'll stop somewhere and eat."

"No, really. It's okay. It's late, and I'm tired."

"I'm hungry," Rae says from the back seat. I look back at her and scowl.

"We'll eat at home, Rae. Besides, you ate mac and cheese for dinner."

"That was like two hours ago." Jason snickers on the driver's seat. "My teacher taught me how to tell time."

"You said you were tired," I tell her.

"But I'm hungrier. If I don't eat something, I won't fall asleep."

"Rae, I'll give you a snack at home," I snap, embarrassed that Jason is witnessing this. Why is Rae being so difficult today? I throw my head back on the headrest and exhale.

"We won't take long. A quick bite to eat and I'll have you home, safe and sound. Promise."

"It's not that." I look out the window.

"I want to invite you and Rae to eat. Hell, she'll probably guide the entire conversation."

I giggle because it's true. She will talk us all under the table.

"Is that a yes?" He looks at me with a smile.

"I smell like food and I'm tired and I don't know what you expect from me." No reason to pretend.

"I think you're pretty. You're a good mom. I don't know much else, but I want to. Zero expectations. I want to get to know you. I have nothing else to go by except the bit I've seen from watching you work, and it's not enough."

Our hushed voices finally catch Rae's attention when she says, "Are we gonna go 'nywhere?"

"We are, Rae Rae," Jason cheers and Rae squeals.

What does he want from us? What does he want from me? I don't understand what appeal a broke, single mom has, or why he even tries coming around the diner to see me. He's handsome, successful, and obviously sweet, so why is he trusting of me? For all he knows, I'd try to take his money and run.

He parallel parks his car and turns off the engine. Before I can react, he's opening my door and Rae's. I undo my ponytail and brush out my hair with my fingers. My heart is beating fast, threatening to drown all other sound from my ears. I notice Jason lowers his cap to cover more of his face and wonder if people recognizing him is a nuisance.

"This place is good and low-key. They also have the best ice cream sundae," he winks at Rae. Her eyes widen with excitement and her hand squeezes mine. My normally calm and quiet girl is smitten with the bass player of Rebel Desire, and I know I'm going to have to talk her down later.

"Hey, Maya," Jason speaks to the hostess.

"Hi, Jason. I don't have you on the reservation list," the pretty blonde smiles.

"It was a last minute thing. Any chance you have a table away from the crowd?"

"Let me check."

"Thanks."

Jason turns around and smiles. "They usually have some tables that are more isolated."

"What does isolated mean?" Rae looks up at him.

"That they're separate from everyone else."

"Why do we need a separate table?"

"Because I don't want people coming up to me and interrupting our dinner asking for autographs or pictures."

"So you're like really famous?" Rae's round eyes look at me.

"Yeah, baby girl, he is." I squeeze her hand and hope no one recognizes him for the sake of my daughter. The last thing I want is someone mentioning her in some gossip magazine, or the two of us getting pulled into some celebrity drama. Usually Rebel Desire is scandal-free, but it takes one single mother to change that. My daughter doesn't need that kind of attention.

"You're in luck. We have a small table. Not your usual spot, but it's private enough."

"Perfect. We'll take it."

"Great. How many?"

"Just us three," Jason looks at Rae and me.

"You got it," the hostess smiles and leads us to our table.

I self-consciously look at the people enjoying their dinner, all dressed up for a Saturday night with friends or partners, while I'm wearing old jeans and a gray tee shirt that has seen better days. We take a seat, Jason being a gentleman and holding a chair for Rae and myself. Menus in hand, I scout the options for the cheapest item. Rae is coloring on the kids menu after deciding she wants chicken nuggets with fries.

"The burgers are great here," Jason says.

"I can't believe so many people are still here." It's not that late, but I'm so used to town being on the quiet end by nine at night.

"It's not too late and it is the weekend."

"Yeah, I guess." I wouldn't know. It's been years since I've been out on the weekend enjoying some free time.

"Do you know what you want?"

"I think a burger, since you so highly recommended them."

"Good choice. I'm having one, too." He smiles.

I take him in for a second, eyes blue as the summer sky and honest grin. The dark blond hair hidden beneath his ball cap. "I'd normally not eat with a cap on, but I don't want anyone coming and interrupting."

"It's okay. I get it."

An awkward silence falls around us until the waitress comes and takes our orders.

"What are you working on, Rae Rae?" Jason asks. I can tell he purposefully uses her nickname because she likes it.

"I'm connecting the numbers to make this house." She holds up her menu to show us. "Oh! My mom needs a nickname too. I'm Rae Rae, and she could be...."

"Hmmm... What do you think?"

"How about Crae?"

Jason and I both laugh at her suggestions. Rae frowns at us.

"Nope. That means crazy to some people," I explain.

"It does?" Rae scrunches up her now. "You're not crazy, Mommy."

"Cassie?" Jason asks.

"Mmm... That's what my Grandpa calls her. She needs something new. Caz? With a Z so it sounds cool."

Jason tilts his head and Rae imitates him. "Do you

think she looks like a Caz?" Jason asks her. I feel awkward having him stare at me, coming up with nicknames for me with my daughter, who he only got to have a real conversation with this afternoon. They're both so comfortable with each other, I'm starting to feel as if I'm the one who missed some kind of memo.

"Yeah!"

"Shhh, Rae. Not so loud." I look around and smile apologetically to anyone watching us, which fortunately we are pretty secluded from the crowd.

After dinner, Jason drives us back to our home.

"I'm glad you decided to say yes to dinner," he whispers.

"I didn't have much of a choice. Rae was already emotional this morning. Had I said no, the tantrum would've been brutal." Rae isn't the only one who wanted to have dinner. I was curious about what sitting at a table across from Jason would be like.

"Well, I'm glad, regardless. She had a blast, too." He peeks at her through the rearview mirror. As soon as he put the car in *drive*, Rae fell asleep.

"Thank you," I say honestly.

"I want to do this again. Take you out to dinner or whatever you want to do. Rae, too."

"I don't know." We both have such different lives, but I'd be lying if I said I wasn't the teeny bit curious about him.

"Think about it. I want you to know where I stand."

"All you know about me is that I'm a broke, single mom, living in a mobile home. You know where I work. That's all. I wouldn't fit in."

"Don't even say that. I didn't get to where I am

because I had connections. The band and I worked hard, but we didn't always have the abundance we have now. Cash makes sure to remind us every now and again, so our egos don't inflate. But deep down, I'm a southern boy, born and raised in Tennessee, that worked hard to achieve his dreams."

"I was born and raised in Tennessee, too," I offer a bit more about myself.

Jason gives me a lopsided grin. "What are you dreams?"

It's obvious my dream isn't working seven days a week at a diner. To be honest, I've never put much thought into my dreams. I always worked to help my parents. I look back at my sleeping daughter and smile.

"Giving her the best life I can and making sure she has the opportunity to do anything she wants. If she wants to do ballet, be able to give that to her. Or art class. Basically, get her out of this cycle." I sigh and turn back around, looking out the windshield.

"I think you're already working on that. What about *you*? Dreams for yourself?"

I shake my head. I haven't had dreams for myself in years. First, it was make sure my mom had all the care she needed. Then, I had Rae to think about. Now, I have to keep a roof over my head and sneak trips to my parents' house a couple times a month when my schedule allows for it. Getting my own place wasn't an easy decision, but I needed my own space to raise my daughter, even if that space is a trailer park in a shitty part of Nashville.

Fortunately, we pull up to our row of homes and I get out of the car before Jason can open my door. I pick Rae up out of the car and carefully walk her to the door.

"Hey," Jason calls out, catching up to me. I turn

around and meet his frown. "I want to walk you to your door." He places his hand on the small of my back and walks with me. Careful not to wake Rae, I try to fish out the keys from my purse, but I carried her on the side of my purse, making it almost impossible.

"Want me to hold her?" Jason offers. I look at him. He spent the entire day with Rae and I know he's one of the good guys, but the idea of him holding my daughter as she sleeps… I don't know. It's too much for one day.

"Do you mind grabbing the keys from my purse as I lift her a bit?"

"Sure." He reaches in and finds them right away. Not much in there to hide my set of keys anyway.

"Thanks." He goes as far as unlocking the house for me. When our eyes meet, he brushes a few strands of hair that have swept over my face and places them behind my shoulder. His fingers ghost down my face as he does this, covering me in chills.

"You're welcome. You should get her to bed."

I nod and walk into my house, turning back once more to look at him.

"I'm going to see you again, Cassidy Rae," he calls out. I bite down my smile and shut the door.

After setting Rae down in bed, I take a quick shower to wash away the day and diner smell. This is my alone time. A moment where I can relax and reflect. Normally I reflect on work, helping my parents, and saving money. Tonight, I'm thinking about sky blue eyes that have an extraordinary shine and the sensation I felt when he touched me. Dinner was so relaxing, with Rae leading most of the conversation, I felt normal for a while. Albeit, self-conscious about being seen, especially with Jason, but there was a normalcy about going to dinner on a Saturday night that I haven't felt since I was in high school.

One other night felt normal, but the result of that night was a shock that began this whirlwind chaos that is now my life. I love Rae more than anything, but finding out I was pregnant hit the pause button on my life.

I dry off, and thoughts of Jason's hand touching my face follow me to bed. I've been a mother for so long that I've forgotten what it feels like to be a woman.

Chapter 5

Cassidy Rae

A BREAK IN ROUTINE THROWS me off. It always has. After last night, I woke up disoriented, worked the morning and afternoon shift in some kind of loopy state, and got home with my eyes barely open. I'm glad I worked the earlier shift, so I could relax the rest of the day. Even Rae was asleep when I left for work.

"Mommy," she screams as I walk in the door. Her daily greeting always expands my heart.

"Hey, baby."

"It's Rae Rae," her eyes light up. I sigh and give her my best smile.

"That's right. Rae Rae," I relent.

Abigail looks at me from her spot on the couch and I shake my head. As I sit next to her, she leans in and whispers, "She told me all about him."

I close my eyes and throw my head back against the top of the couch.

"I don't want her to get attached," I murmur to Abigail.

She places her hand on my knee. "She may already have. You know how kids are. Rae has always wanted to know her father, and in her young mind, this may be the closest thing she'll have."

Tears blur my vision. "I don't want her to get hurt. She's too young to understand how this works."

"She is, yet all she did today was talk about him and dinner. She even drew him a picture to give him the next time she sees him."

I look at Abigail, the closest friend I have, and a few tears roll down my cheeks. "And if we never see him again? What am I supposed to do? I've tried to avoid this exact situation."

"Maybe stop avoiding it. You can try to do something, but it doesn't mean you are actually doing it. I also think you need to talk to her. Rae is mature enough that you can have a heart to heart with her and explain some things."

"But she's still a child."

"Yes, but have a little faith in her," Abigail pauses, "and a little faith in him. The Lord had you cross paths for a reason." Abigail has always kept her faith throughout her entire life. Every time things get difficult, she brings in the Lord and His love into her situation. I admire her for that, and I can't say I've always had the same belief.

"I'll talk to her."

"Good." She kisses my cheek. "Holler if you need anything." I watch Abigail leave, knowing I won't have any buffer for this conversation with Rae.

"How was your day?" I look over at Rae, lying on the

floor as she colors. It's her favorite place to color, despite having a small table in the kitchen she can use.

"Good. Abby played with me."

"Did you wake up late?" I ask.

"Kinda." She shrugs. "I'm not sure, but Abby made me pancakes." Her focus is on coloring, so I decide a shower first and conversation later.

"I'm going to take a quick shower, okay? Remember, don't open the door to anyone, even if it's Abigail."

"Okay, Mom."

I double check the door is locked and hop in for a quick wash. I go over possible ways to bring up the conversation and which direction I want to take. I haven't exactly told my daughter she was created out of a one-night-stand—she wouldn't even understand that—but I know this will bring up the topic of her father again. The last thing I'd want is for her to think she was unwanted.

I walk out, combing my hair and sit on the floor with her. "What's this?" I ask about a drawing lying next to her. Maybe this is what she made for Jason, and I can bring him up that way.

"It's a guitar. I drew it for Jason. When will we see him again, so I can give it to him?"

"I don't know." I breathe in courage and exhale the truth. "Rae, Jason is someone we just met. We don't really know him, and…" This isn't off to a great start.

"What I mean is, he has a life and a band that he works very hard on. He's nice, but I don't know when we will see him again, or if we will."

"But he told me yesterday he would." Rae's little mouth twists with a pout.

"I know it's difficult to understand, but adults are different than kids. We have responsibilities and lives that come first."

"I like him," she whines. This is exactly what I wanted to avoid.

"I know you do, baby. I just don't want you to have expectations for him. He's not responsible for us, only we are responsible for ourselves. I promise, I will always protect you and love you. You're my number one."

"I want him with us. If I can't have a dad, I want Jason." Tears gush from her eyes and my heart is slowly breaking.

"You have a father."

She shakes her head furiously. "No. I don't know him, so I don't have a dad. If I did, he'd come to my shows at school."

I pull her into me and hold her tight. "I'm sorry." It's my fault she doesn't know her father. I could've looked for him, but what man would want to get pinged for a one-night-stand? I wouldn't even have known where to look for him. We were young and drunk.

"You have Ryan and Blake," I say, adding Abigail's husband, and hoping that she realizes she does have two men in her life she can count on.

"It's not the same. They're friends, not my dad."

"Neither is Jason."

"Yeah, but he could be. He likes us."

"It's not that simple, Rae. You don't just become a dad because you like someone. That's not how it works."

"You could marry him. Then he'll be like my dad."

There's no winning with this girl. "I can't just marry him. I don't even know him. People don't just get married the first time they meet. First they get to know each other and make sure they want to spend their lives with them."

"Okay, so do that."

I squeeze her and pull her onto my lap. Children don't see the complications in situations, or maybe we adults make things more complicated than they are.

Rae cries a little longer, asking questions as she does. Mainly begging me to see Jason again. My heart shatters upon hearing her, realizing that despite the amount of money I save or hard work I do to offer her the best, she'll never have what she truly needs.

After she calms down, I let her choose what she wants for dinner, and promise her a special dessert, too. We make due with the life we have, but I want her to be happy. After tossing out dinner ideas and getting rejected, Rae finally announces she wants pizza for dinner. Then, she grabs the cake mix in the cupboard and says she wants that for dessert.

I tie her apron around her and then put on mine before we get to work making pizza dough and mixing the cake ingredients.

The sound of a knock interrupts our cooking and alerts us of an unannounced visitor.

"I'll answer it!" Rae yells and runs to the door.

"Not without me!" I holler and follow behind her.

"It's Jason," she exclaims after peeking through the window near the door.

"What?" I screech, quickly twirling my ponytail to make it more presentable as Rae swings the door open.

"Hi!" Her squeal is deafening.

"Hey," Jason laughs. She hugs him, gaining herself a megawatt smile from the handsome man, who showed up at my house unannounced.

"I made you something." Rae runs to the drawing—still on the floor—and hands it to him. "It's a guitar," she explains before he has a chance to analyze it.

"I love it. Thanks, Rae Rae." He musses her hair, causing her to laugh.

"We're making pizza and cake for dinner. Do you want to eat with us?"

"Rae, I'm sure Jason has plans."

"Actually," he looks at me, "I'm free as a bird and hoping you two are as well. I do love homemade pizza and cake." He winks at me.

"Awesome." Rae bounces the short space back into the kitchen. "Mommy was just letting me lick the spoon." The corners of her mouth are full of chocolate cake and we both laugh at her.

"I never would've guessed," Jason replies. He looks at me and smiles softly. "Hey."

"Hi." I glance around the house to make sure it's not too much of a mess. Fortunately, Rae is a pretty neat kid, and the only stuff lying around are her crayons and coloring book.

"You left your hair tie in my car. I went to the diner, but Joyce told me you were already home."

"So you came all the way over here to bring it?"

He shrugs. "I was already in the neighborhood."

"That's a sorry excuse."

"Well, I know how much these things mean to girls." He holds up the black hair tie. "My sisters used to flip when they would misplace theirs."

"Sisters?"

"Yup, I've got two of them, both younger than me."

"Oh." Using a hair tie is a sorry excuse, and I'm sure he knows it. I have more than one, and while I hate losing them, his visit isn't about a hair tie.

"So, what can I do? I love cooking." He rubs his hands

together and stands next to Rae, taking instructions from her on how to roll out the dough. I stand, dumbfounded and in disbelief, as I watch them interact. I see why she wants him around. Their bond has been instant. What happens when he moves on with his life and leaves us behind? No way he actually wants a relationship with me.

We sit at the small, round table in the kitchen with pizza on our plates and a cooling cake on the counter next to the sink. The smell of pizza and sweetness lingers in the air.

"Do you like the pizza?" Rae asks Jason. Since he's arrived, I've been the background music to the tune these two play.

"It's delicious. You're going to make a great chef one day," he compliments.

"Yeah. I want to have my own restaurant like Joyce. Mommy and me can work together."

"That would be fun," I tell her. This is the first time she brings up that dream. She always says she wants to be a baker, but never mentioned owning a restaurant.

"I'm sure you two would have the most popular place in town. You don't find pizza like this just anywhere."

I look at Jason and smile gratefully. He winks again and takes a bite of his pizza.

"Rae, use your napkin," I remind her. She grabs her napkin and runs it across her mouth. Pizza is always messy with her. I giggle as she smiles in victory, but still has a spot of sauce on her cheek. "Here," I say, and wipe it off.

"I'm glad you came. Mommy said we wouldn't see you again, but she was wrong."

I shut my eyes and frown. Kids have no filter.

"I'd like to see you again, but that's something your

mommy and I will talk about. Adults are different than kids."

I smile in gratitude at his response, somehow backing up what I told her earlier.

"That's what she said." Rae pushes her plate, leaving the crusts uneaten.

Once we finish eating, Rae cuts the cake into uneven chunks and I help her serve it on plates.

"We didn't have any frosting, but we'll have some next time," she hands Jason a plate.

"This is perfect. Frosting is too sweet sometimes and I like tasting the cake." He takes a spoonful and says, "Yum. You're definitely going to be the best baker in town."

Rae laughs at his words, but her smile shows me that she is happier than a pig in mud at his compliment. Is this what having a family would be like? We wouldn't be living in a trailer park, that's for sure. Should I have searched and told Rae's father I was pregnant? I wouldn't have even known where to begin. His face is a blur from that night, no recognition to hold him accountable. Besides, I've never believed staying with someone because of a pregnancy was the right choice, especially when you're strangers.

"Do you like it?" Rae asks me.

"Yeah. The cake is delicious. You did good, baby girl."

"It's Rae Rae," she reminds me. I sigh and Jason laughs. "And you're Caz," she points at me. I feel as if no matter what happens, Jason's memory is already woven into our lives.

After dinner, Rae colors a little longer while Jason helps me clean up the kitchen.

"You don't have to help."

"I want to." Jason stands next to me as I wash the

plates and he dries them for me. "I know I kinda showed up here and interrupted your dinner. Sorry about that."

"Kinda showed up? More like you did show up," I tease.

"Potato, potahto. But, I can't stop thinking about you. This isn't a line I grabbed from some cheesy movie. I know, I know, I don't even know you," he chuckles when I raise an eyebrow. "But I've seen enough to know I want to. I want to help you discover what your dreams are and watch you offer your daughter the best life she can have."

"It's complicated with her around. She already expects to see you everyday, and this is only the third time she's seen you. I always thought if I ever met someone, and that was a big if, I'd get to know the man really well first, before introducing him to my daughter. This is backwards. It's almost as if she's gotten to know you before I have. It's confusing for her."

"So let me get to know you." He angles his body toward me. "Let me show you who I am. It's easy with her because she came right up to me, offered me a cookie, and started talking as if I was her best friend. I guess kids are less guarded in that sense." He casts his eyes down a moment. I place my hand over his.

"They've got it easy, don't they?" I ask him, trying to lighten the mood.

"Yup." Jason continues drying the plate he was working on.

I'm not the only one with a past.

Rae falls asleep on the couch after showing us all the drawings she can make and then asking Jason a ton of questions about his guitar. I come back into the living room after laying her down in bed and find that Jason is still sitting comfortably on the couch.

"Sorry if she asked you way more questions than necessary."

"Don't apologize. I love talking about music. She's a great girl, Caz." The use of the nickname Rae and him came up with catches me off guard. I sit next to him, unsure of what to do now. I'll admit, it's easier when Rae is around because I can take a step back and not interact with him as much. Now I have no choice.

Jason turns toward me. "I know this isn't how you imagined meeting someone, but give me a chance. I'm not some crazy musician. I'm homegrown and like to keep it that way."

"Why?" I fold my hands together and look at him.

"Because from that first moment I saw you singing one of our songs, I knew there was something about you that I wanted to get to know." He holds my hand. "I'm old enough to know what I want, but I'll take my time for the right woman."

My throat runs dry. I clear it, staring at him. "I've got nothing to offer you."

Jason shakes his head. "What I'm looking for isn't material. You gotta get rid of that self-judgment."

"Can we start as friends? That may not be what you have in mind, but I need to go slow, especially for Rae's sake. She's already attached to you and she just met you."

"Well, we bonded a lot yesterday while you worked."

"I know." My breath slips from my lips.

"You're right, I'm interested in more, but I'm willing to get to know you without the pressure of that."

I nod, seeing a gentle side to him that I've missed before.

"So, where are you from?" he starts off the

conversation.

"Pleasant View, not too far from here. Are you from Nashville?"

"Yeah. I've lived here my whole life, except for my four years of college when I lived in Knoxville. That's where I met Cash."

"That's really cool. I moved here after my twenty-first birthday. I was pregnant with Rae and got hired at the diner immediately. Joyce didn't care that I would have to go on maternity leave, she just wanted to help me."

"You look younger than twenty-eight."

"You're quick at math," I counter.

Jason shrugs. "I majored in accounting."

"Did you really?" I ask, surprised.

"Yup. Helped a lot in the beginning with the band, before we got signed with the label."

"I'm sure it did."

"Do your parents still live in Pleasant View?"

"Yeah." I swallow the lump in my throat and go for it, ready for the judgment. "My parents are older. I was a miracle child since they were never able to conceive. They raised me as best they could and loved me, but right before I graduated high school my mom got diagnosed with Alzheimer's.

"It was a shock to all of us. The symptoms were there, and my dad and I recognized them after we got the news. I got a job at a bar and my dad worked as hard as he could. When he wasn't at work, he was taking care of my mom. I'd watch her while he worked during the day, and I'd leave at night to work at the bar." I rush through the facts.

"I'm sorry about your mom." He squeezes my fingers.

"That's life. When I found out I was pregnant, I moved out. I couldn't add more stress to my dad."

"What about Rae's father?"

I shake my head. "He doesn't know about her. It was a one-night-stand. Not my proudest moment, but I would never regret having her. She's the best thing I've done in this life." It's a challenge to look him in the eyes as I tell him this, but if he wants to know me, then this is part of who I am. I rather lay it out all in the open and let him decide if he truly wants to spend time with me.

"Anyway, what about you? You said you have two sisters."

"I do. They're younger than me. They used to drive me crazy when we were growing up, but I love them. My parents are divorced, but they have a good relationship. My mom got remarried while I was in college. We're all pretty low-key, honestly."

"Besides the fact that you're part of a famous band," I chuckle.

"That's my career, and yeah, it's different than had I been an accountant, but it's only part of who I am. I love what I do, and my bandmates are my brothers, but at the end of the day, I'm just Jason Stone. I'm a regular guy who likes college football way too much, and playing the guitar on my downtime."

"Do you write the songs on your albums?"

"Not really. Cash is the biggest songwriter. There's something inside of him that causes him to spit out songs by the dozen. I don't know how he does it. Cole recently wrote a song that's a bonus track on our album for his girlfriend, Bri. Ryder and I give out ideas, but we're better at brainstorming than actual writing. We can all sing, though."

"That's cool. How long have you been playing?"

"Since I was a kid. I always dreamed of being a

musician, but that's not an easy goal to achieve. I played on and off with some random bands when they needed a bass player during high school and some in college until Cash told me he wanted to start a band."

"Accounting was your back-up plan? They're such different career choices."

"They are, but I like math and I'm good at it."

"I never went to college," I get that information out of the way. "I'm not even sure what I would've studied. I always liked history, but I never pegged that as a career. The only thing I could do with that is teach, and teaching was never something I was passionate about."

"Was there ever a career that felt impossible, but you would've liked? How music was for me, and I got blessed to be able to make it happen."

"I guess archaeology. It sounds dorky, but I'd love to travel the world digging up old artifacts."

"Like a sexy, female version of Indiana Jones."

I laugh at the absurdity of that. "Not quite."

Jason cups my cheek and smiles. "I feel like you're finally loosening up."

I freeze and wait, wondering if he's going to kiss me or just hold me. His thumb rubs my cheek and he releases my face and holds my hand again. "Where would you like to excavate?"

"Somewhere in Europe or Africa. There's so much history there, ancient civilizations that are yet to be discovered or pieced together."

"You do have dreams. You just needed to relax a bit to rediscover them." He leans back on the couch with a triumphant smile.

A yawn interrupts the smile covering my face. "Sorry," I say as I cover my mouth.

"You're tired. I'll get going, but I'm glad I came by. Thanks for letting me crash your dinner. I like you, Caz. We can be friends, but I'm definitely hoping that builds the foundation for a lot more."

Speechless, I walk him to the door. Jason kisses me on the cheek and promises to be in touch this week. I have no idea how since he doesn't have a way of contacting me. Apparently, he likes showing up in places instead of calling.

Chapter 6

Jason

I'VE HAD CASSIDY RAE ON my mind all day. From the songs we worked on, to the proofs from the photo shoot we received, she's been on my mind. The songs make me think of her, the kinda romance I want. The photos had me wondering if she'd like them. If she'd have a favorite.

I've only seen her three times—two of those times can actually be called interaction—and I already have this feeling. God, when did I become a romantic like Cash? A part of me was always like that. I wasn't ready to settle down before now, I guess. The women I'd meet all had an agenda. A quick fuck with the Rebel Desire band member. Being the only single one left leaves me as a more open target for bullshit.

"Hey, you going home or to Bri's tonight?" I ask Cole.

"Going home. What's up?"

"Wanna grab a beer?"

"Fuck. Yeah. Is everything okay?"

I've known Cole the longest, and being roommates adds more to our friendship. When he first started making rounds on Bri, I gave him shit for it and told him to back off. Now I'm making rounds on another woman, and although their situations are different, their guard might be similar. I'm prepared for him to give me the same advice I gave him, but keeping hope that love has changed him.

"Yeah, just wanna talk about something."

"Let's go to Tap for beers," Cole suggests.

The drive to Tap has me wondering what the hell I'm even going to talk to Cole about. Seems like all four of us are hooked on the women we want. The only problem is that I met Cassidy Rae a few days ago. No way can I be hooked on her, yet. There is something about her simplicity, her heart, that shines around her like the aura my sisters are always talking about. Maybe I should talk to them instead.

I park my car in the lot near Tap and meet Cole at the entrance, both clad in caps.

"What's going on?" Cole asks once we have pints of beer in hand.

"I met someone." Cole cocks an eyebrow. "It's complicated, though."

He chuckles and takes a drink of beer. "When's it not?"

"No, this is real complicated. Almost Bri complicated."

That stops Cole. He tilts his head and asks, "Who is she?"

I shake my head. "You don't know her. I met her by coincidence. Although, I'm starting to think there was some kind of divine intervention."

"What makes it complicated?"

"Brother, you have no idea. That day you and Bri went to Pinewood Social, I went out for a jog. I was so in my head thinking about Christie that I somehow ended on the wrong side of town. I found a nearby diner on my phone and jogged over for some water and to figure out where the hell I was. This waitress was cute, humming one of our songs. When she realized who I was, she blanched, but then kept my secret. After pancakes and fresh OJ, I knew her name based on her nametag and that's it.

"I couldn't get her out of my mind, so I looked up the diner and drove over one morning before work. I've been showing up randomly since then, driving her home. We had dinner the other night, and the following night I showed up at her place with the sorry ass excuse she left her hair tie in my car. She was making dinner and I stayed." I breathe heavily.

"Okay. Why is it complicated?" Cole furrows his eyebrows.

"She has a kid."

"Fuck, bro." He runs his hand up and down his face.

"I know, I know, but she's not like that."

"How do you know? Where does she live?"

"On the north side, in a trailer park." Might as well tell him everything.

Cole shakes his head. "Let her go. This smells like trouble, and you don't need that. Remember what Christie did."

"Right, but she's so different from Christie. She wants to be friends, take things slow. Her daughter is awesome."

"Fuck, Jason. You met the girl?"

"She was at the diner one night and came out while some douche was harassing Cassidy Rae. I went up to defend her, and the man said some insulting things. Her daughter came out. I'm not sure what she heard, but that's the night I confirmed Cassidy Rae was a single mom."

"Cassidy Rae? You have a thing for Cs?" Cole tries to joke.

"Apparently." I chuckle and chug the rest of my beer, motioning for another round to the waiter a few feet away.

"So she's a single mom, who works at a diner and lives in a trailer. Does she have family?"

I tell Cole everything I know about her. I tell him about dinner, her insecurities, and my feelings. Three beers in, I'm more honest than I intended to be.

"I want to advise you stay away, but I can tell that won't happen. I don't even know what to tell you. A kid is a whole different ball game. By the sound of it, the girl likes you a lot, but that's different. How do you know she's not going to try to lasso you in for money?"

"She won't. I know it. Don't ask me how, but I know those aren't her intentions. My worry is that she realizes she wants nothing to do with me and leaves me. She's so insecure in her role. I'd miss Cassidy Rae. I'd miss Rae. I want to give her a better life."

"Dude, you just met her."

"Right? I'm insane. I have no idea what's taken over me."

"I wish I had some inspiring words to share with you, but right now all I can do is sit here with you and drink some beers."

"Fuck, I'm down for that."

Cole waves down our waiter and orders a pitcher of beer and food. At the rate we're going, we're going to need to Uber our asses home.

By the time we finish eating, we're sober enough to

drive, but I have no real grasp on the situation with Cassidy Rae.

"We're playing at Riot this weekend."

"Don't remind me," I respond, walking out of Tap. I told Cash I could keep things professional, and I can, but I have no desire to see Christie ever again.

Since I spoke to Cole a couple days ago, I've resisted showing up at the diner or Cassidy Rae's house. I want to give her time to rest and spend with Rae. I know she works a lot, and I don't want to disrupt the routine she has. That's not to say I haven't considered saying *fuck it* and showing up at her place.

I have to be patient. I promised her that much. Tomorrow, I'll stop by in the morning for some OJ and pancakes and hope that she's working the early shift. With Rae on summer break, I'd assume she'd work the morning as much as possible to enjoy the afternoon with her daughter. My plan is to ask her out to dinner. Not some dinner plans on a whim, as I take her home from work. I want to pick her up and take her out. I know her neighbor watches Rae while she works. Maybe she'll be willing to keep an eye on her at night, too. Or Rae can come.

"Well, if it isn't our big bro." I turn around as I walk out of the store I was shopping in.

I smile at my two sisters approaching me. "What are you guys doing here?"

"We were shopping," Reese, the older of the two, holds up shopping bags.

"Good to see you're using your hard-earned money on things you like."

"What's up?" Taylor, my youngest sister, asks.

"Was getting ready to head home. I was checking out a few things at Threads." I hold up my own bag.

"Wanna grab dinner?" Taylor asks.

"Sure."

We walk into a small restaurant a few doors down from Threads and are seated immediately.

"What's going on in your life? We've only seen you once since you came back from tour. Are you too cool for us now? Because we have baby pics we can blast," Reese laughs.

"Never too cool for you two. I've been busy. We came back and went straight to work. I've been meaning to call."

"Yeah, yeah. Yadda, yadda, yadda," Reese teases as she rolls her eyes.

"Have you seen Christie again?" Taylor leans on her elbows and whispers. She's the more sensitive one.

"Nope. That's done with."

"Good," she leans back. "Don't give her a second chance."

"Whore bag," Reese mumbles.

I can't help but laugh at them. Despite being the older brother, those two are mighty protective of me. Our age difference means nothing when it comes to us.

"How are things with you?" I ask both of them.

"I got a promotion at work last week, hence the shopping spree," Reese informs me. She works in advertising for a big firm in downtown. "She's still dating Mike," she tilts her head to Taylor.

I cross my arms on the table and lean forward. "Are you two serious?"

"I guess." Taylor shrugs indifferently, but I know

better.

"He seems like a cool dude. Why don't you guys come to Riot on Saturday to watch us play?"

"You're still playing there?" They both exchange a look.

"Yeah. I told Cash it'd be okay. Business is business."

"Good for you. Show her who the bigger person is," Reese nods in approval.

Our conversation follows a similar flow throughout dinner. Once we're done, my sisters promise to go to Riot, for moral support and all that, and I hug them goodbye. Cash and Cole have brothers and Ryder is an only child, so they don't always get the bond I have with my sisters, but they treat Reese and Taylor as if they're their own blood.

The chime goes off when I walk into Joyce's Diner and I curse that damn thing. Immediately, Cassidy Rae's eyes land on me and widen. I sit at the counter and wait for her to come over.

"Hey," I grin when she finally makes her way to me.

"Hi," she bites her lip. "What can I get ya?"

"For starters, a dinner date," I smile. "We can discuss my breakfast after."

Cassidy Rae rolls her eyes. "Jason," she warns.

Joking aside, I whisper, "I've been wanting to come by and see you, but didn't want to get in the way our your job or routine with Rae. I also want to respect the pace you want to lead."

She doodles on her notepad as she thinks. When she looks up at me, her eyes are small. "So far, you've proven to be a nice guy. My daughter is crazy about you. But truth is, we don't know you and I can't fathom why she's already so attached to you. It scares me, because she's a little girl and vulnerable. In her eyes, you're a hero."

"What about you? I want to hear what you feel. Right now, I want to talk about Jason and Cassidy Rae."

A light blush covers her cheeks before she speaks. "I don't know. Confusion? I don't have much to offer, and Rae is my number one priority. Then, my mom's health. I'm not sure I'll have time to date anyone, let alone someone with such a hectic career."

"I'm home for a while as we work on music. Maybe a few trips here and there, but it will give us time to get to know each other." I grasp on to anything that will convince her to give me a chance.

"Why are you so persistent? I'm not about the chasing game." She crosses her arms.

"This has nothing to do with that. I can't quite tell you why, except that I feel it. All I ask is for dinner. Hell, if you want to bring Rae, we'll get a table for three."

She looks me over closely, searching my face. "Can I let you know about Rae? I don't want her getting used to late nights."

"Does that mean you're saying yes?"

Cassidy Rae nods.

"Tonight? Tomorrow? When are you free?" I know I sound desperate, but my self-respect walked out the door the minute that chime rang.

"How's tomorrow?"

"Perfect." I grin and squeeze her fingers. It's paying off, showing up here. Happy, I order my usual and watch Cassidy Rae work.

We talk a bit in between customers when she's behind the counter and confesses she's also been thinking about me. I ask her how Rae is doing, and make sure she tells her I say hi. I don't want Rae thinking I've just up and disappeared on them.

My phone buzzes with a message from Cash asking where I am. *Shit.* I got caught up staring at Cassidy Rae. I type out a quick, 'on my way,' and ask for the check.

"I'm late for work, but any chance you'll give me your number?"

Cassidy Rae scribbles on a piece of paper and hands it to me. I stare that the number and the way her name is written out in cursive.

"Don't forget to tell Rae I said hi. I'll pick you up tomorrow at seven. Does that work?"

"Yeah," she smiles.

As I walk out of the diner I hear, "That boy's taken by you." I chuckle all the way to my car. Hell yeah, I'm taken by her.

Chapter 7

Cassidy Rae

"THAT BOY'S TAKEN BY YOU," Joyce says, the corners of her eyes crinkling.

"Come on, Joyce," I wave her off.

"Take it from someone older and wiser, who's been around the block a couple times," she winks, and I laugh. "That boy there," she hooks her thumb over her shoulder, "is smitten with you and that daughter of yours. No man would come to a rinky dinky diner like this if he can afford to eat anywhere else."

"He wants to take me to dinner tomorrow."

"I thought you told him yes."

I raise my eyebrows and smile. Joyce knows everything that goes on in her diner. "I did, but—"

"Don't you dare make up excuses. I've known you for seven years, since that baby girl was still in here," she pats my stomach. "You've never had a moment for yourself.

You live for that girl, and that's okay, but it's time you start having some fun again. You're still young, and one day that daughter of yours is going to go away and live her life. You don't want to be left alone, do ya?"

"God, Joyce. No need for dramatics." She has a point, though.

"Well, I need something that will shake the dust off ya and have some fun. If a boy like him were making rounds on me, I'd already have surrendered to him."

"I'm worried I'm not enough."

"Nonsense. That's all up here." She taps my temple. "A woman like you has a lot to offer. You're smart, beautiful, and selfless. Hell, I'd date you if I were a man, or swung that way," she winks.

I burst out laughing. "Thanks." I hug her and get back to work, my mind swimming with Jason's smile.

I unlock the door to my home and find Abigail and Rae on the couch reading. I stop and listen to Rae sound out words from her book until she sees me.

"Mom," she jumps up and hugs me. Her excitement to see me every day is something I live for. I pray she's always this way with me.

"How was your day?"

"Great. Abigail and I went to the park for a really long time. Then we came home, ate lunch, and practiced my reading."

"Sounds like a fun day." I smile at Abigail. "Thank you."

"You know you don't gotta thank me every day."

"I know, but I will anyway."

"Did Jason go by the diner?" Rae stands in front of me, brown eyes framed by a mess of blonde waves.

"She's been talking about him," Abigail murmurs.

"He did, actually. He wanted to make sure I tell you that he said hi. He's been busy with work, but I'm sure we'll see him soon."

Rae's eyes light up. "Yippee!" She jumps with her hands clenched tightly in the air.

Abigail looks at me. "Why don't you go take a bath, baby girl," I tell Rae.

While Rae is in the shower, I turn to Abigail. "He came by today and asked me to dinner. He said I could take Rae if I want, but…" How do I say this without sounding like a terrible mother? I'm already worried Rae is going to get upset she won't go to dinner.

"Say no more. I'll watch her."

"Should I take her? He did offer."

"It's important you have adult time. If this man is serious about getting to know you, then spend time with him as a woman. When Rae's around, you're a mother. You know I love that little girl, but I love you, too and want to see you have fun."

"Thanks, Abigail." I hug her. "Not sure how I'm gonna break the news to her."

"Blake and I will take her to have ice cream. That should make it a little bit better."

"I'll talk to her today, too and explain as much as I can."

"She'll understand. I can come over tomorrow and take her next door to our house."

"I appreciate it, Abby."

"I'd do anything for you two." She smiles and kisses me on the cheek before going home. I'm blessed to have people around me that care as much as they do. Not just for me, but for Rae, too.

While Rae finishes up in the shower, I call my dad to see how he and my mom are doing while I start cooking the ground beef for our taco dinner. I try to keep our meals fun, so she eats everything I serve her. Since she likes to cook, it helps to keep her excited for our meals.

Rae tumbles into the kitchen and sniffs. "What are you making?"

"Tacos," I reply.

"Yummy. Can I help?"

"Sure can. Just spoke to Grandpa. He says hi and he misses you. I'll see if we can make a trip there soon. Maybe one morning on a day I work the night shift." I try to visit them during the day, because there is no way I'm taking the bus back at night with Rae alone.

"Yay!"

While I finish the beef, Rae puts some cheese in a dish and washes lettuce. I'm grateful food stamps helps cover most of our groceries, so I can buy some healthier options and vegetables. Some weeks are a mac and cheese kind of week, but other times we can get creative and have fun.

"Did Jason really say hi?" Rae asks.

"Of course he did. He came by the diner for breakfast and asked about you."

"I really like him, Mommy."

"I know, sweetie. I do, too. Actually," I pause. This is the perfect time to bring up tomorrow's date. "He asked me to go to dinner with him tomorrow night."

Rae's head whips toward me. "He did?" Her eyes widen.

"Yeah."

"Are you gonna go?"

"I am. I wasn't sure at first, but he seems like a nice person."

"He does," she sighs.

"Are you okay with that?"

"Is this just for adults? Like a date?"

I laugh, surprised she knows that term. "How do you know what a date is?"

"We've talked about it at school. Jessy's mom went on a date and we talked about it."

"You and her mom?" I furrow my eyebrows.

"No, silly. Jessy and me. She wondered if he would be her new dad, and since her and I don't really have dads, we talk about that."

"You're only six."

"Six and a half," she smiles with pride.

"So you're okay with me going to dinner with Jason? I want to make sure you're okay with this."

"I am. Maybe you'll get married one day and he'll be my daddy."

My breath catches in my throat. I close my eyes for a brief moment. "It doesn't work like that."

"Why not? If you like him and he likes you, and you both like me, why can't he be my dad?"

I lower the heat on the stove and look at Rae, standing on the small step I have for her to cook on. "First, we need to make sure we like each other and want to spend a lot of time together. People need to fall in love before they get married because that's a big step. If that were to happen, he'd be your stepdad, not your real dad."

"I know he isn't my real dad, but he would act like it. If you got married he'd always be around, eat dinner with us, play with me. Maybe teach me to play the guitar. I want a daddy."

My heart breaks for my little girl, because it's my fault

she doesn't have one. Had she been born in different circumstances, or I would've tried to find her father, maybe she'd have what she so badly desires. However, I couldn't give her up when I went to my first sonogram. Adoption was an option, but she became my whole world the moment I heard her heartbeat for the first time.

"How about I go to dinner with him tomorrow and then we go from there?" She's so wise. I always knew she was an old soul, and each day she proves it more and more to me.

"Okay. Maybe another day he can come over and I can see him?"

"Sounds good. Would you like to be here when he picks me up, so you can say hi, and I'll walk you over to Abigail's house?"

"Yes!" Her face lights up.

Everything is going to be okay. As long as Rae and I can talk things out, my life is on track.

I look at myself in the mirror and blow out air. I'm nervous about tonight. I've been home for an hour, showered and hair done. Rae is picking out my outfit, and I've resorted to digging out older clothes from my pre-Rae era. I have no idea where we're going, or what to wear.

"How come you never wear this?" Rae is holding up a blue dress.

I shrug. "I don't have anywhere to wear that to. Jeans are more comfortable."

"I think you should wear it."

"I don't know." Rae waves the loose-fitting dress with thin straps and a V-cut neckline both in the front and back. It's been years since I've worn anything like that.

"Try it on." Rae hands me the dress and sits on the bed, waiting to judge the look for herself. As I put on the dress, I'm reminded of the stretch marks I was analyzing in the shower. I'm nowhere near being sexy. I'm thin, because of my situation in life, but I'm not fit or toned.

I'm not like these super stars who have children and are a size zero the next day. I mean, that's not real life. Except, that is Jason's real life. He's surrounded by people like this. Women like this. It began to stress me out in the shower at the thought of the possibility of ever sleeping with Jason and him seeing my flawed skin.

"You look beautiful," Rae exclaims. "You should wear that."

"Are you sure? It's not too short?" I twirl around, trying to catch glimpses of myself in the mirror. Times like this call for a full-length mirror. I'm sure I can find a cheap one at Wal-Mart.

"No. You look so pretty. You're always pretty, but this dress makes you look different. I think Jason will like it."

God bless the love of a daughter.

I smirk and ask her which shoes I should wear. After she chooses nude sandals, I take a step back and ask her what she thinks.

"Perfect," she grins.

My accessories are limited, but I find small earrings and a bangle bracelet. *Thank goodness I didn't get rid of all this when I moved.*

"Can I put on lipstick, too?" Rae looks up at me.

Normally, I'd say no. She's too young and beautiful to cover up her face, but I'm having mother's guilt for not including her tonight, so I nod and bend down. "Just a bit." I add a thin layer of the blush color on her lips.

"Now I'll look just like you." She skips out of the

room.

I take a few deep breaths as I look around the room Rae and I share. This is our sanctuary. It isn't fancy or spacious, but it's our safe place.

A knock at the door distracts me.

"He's here!" Rae yells from the living space.

My heart is racing, and nausea is consuming me as I walk out of the room. Rae is by the door, ready to open as soon as I give her the okay.

"Hi," she squeals.

"Hey, Rae Rae. What's up?" Jason's voice reaches me before I see him. The thumping in my ears is frustrating me. This isn't the first time we spend time together. He had dinner here the other night for goodness sake. *But Rae was always there to buffer the conversation.*

"Hi," he stops and looks at me.

"Hi."

"Doesn't she look pretty?" Rae tugs on Jason's hand and pulls him in. I roll my eyes at her question. She's not discreet at all.

"She sure does," Jason responds.

"And she let me put on some lipstick, although I'm just staying at Abby's house. I wanted to look like my mommy. Do you like it?"

Jason squats down to look at Rae. "Yeah, but you're too pretty to wear makeup."

"You're right." Rae swipes her lips with the back of her hand, causing me to laugh. Go figure. Then she giggles when Jason whispers something in her ear, turning to look at me. "He likes you." She points at me.

Shifting on my feet, I cross my arms and say, "Okay. Let's get you to Abigail's." I hold Rae's hand as Jason leads us out of our home with his hand in the small of my back. Thoughts of what if consume me as I imagine what it would be like had we met in a different situation. What could we be if we drop our guards and give this a shot? Is he more smitten with my daughter than actually having a relationship with me?

"Hey, Abby," I say as she opens the door.

"Hi."

"This is Jason. Jason, this is Abigail." I introduce them, and Rae runs into her house as if she owns the place.

"Bye, Rae," I call out.

"Bye, Mommy." She runs back and hugs my waist. "Bye, Jason."

As we turn to walk to his car, Jason holds my hand. I look down at our interlocked fingers and up at him. His grin is the only reaction I get, and when he opens the car door for me and I slide in, I miss the feel of his hand in mine.

I sound like some desperate teen infatuated with the popular jock. He's so handsome, it's only natural I'd feel this way.

"Am I dressed okay for where we're going?" I can't stand the silence anymore.

"Perfect." He turns to look at me before driving. "You look stunning." He runs his fingers down my cheek before cupping my face. "Shall we go?"

I nod and watch him as he drives to our destination. His plaid shirt is rolled up just below his elbows, and the blue in it brightens his eyes even more. His dirty blond hair looks as if he brushed it with his fingers on the way out of the shower, and the woman in me desires to comb my fingers through it and tug. Life was simpler when I was just a woman. Now I'm a mother. A mother on a date with a hot musician. I must be insane. This can't be real life.

"You're thinking real hard there."

"Huh? Oh, sorry. I guess I got quiet."

"Relax. Tonight is about having fun and getting to know each other. We'll take it slow." He reaches for my hand again.

"Okay." I breathe out slowly.

"How was work?" he asks.

"Not much changes in a diner," I tease.

"Anyone else bother you?"

I shake my head. "No. You don't have to worry about that. If that happens, Ryan is usually out of the kitchen before anyone can get too far."

"Is Ryan just a friend or…"

"Just a friend," I say quickly. I chuckle at his not so subtle way of asking.

"A guy needs to know what he's up against," he defends.

"You're not up against anything or anyone." We make eye contact for a brief moment. Jason squeezes my hand and a smile covers his face.

Chapter 8

Cassidy Rae

As Jason opens the door for me, he explains Pinewood Social and the hangout concept. Apparently, it offers everything anyone could want—coffee, dining, bowling, Bocce ball, a pool.

"I thought we could eat dinner and then we could bowl."

"That sounds like fun."

We walk in to see a wall of people. Jason shakes some hands and smiles at others, always holding my hand and keeping me by his side. The hostess walks us to our table, and I smile when it's a booth to the back of the restaurant. I'm sure Jason requested that.

"What do you think?"

I look around the huge industrial space. "So many people are here."

"Yeah. It's kind of a hip place. Their brunch is good,

too."

"Cool." I look around, observing the crowd and décor. It's simple; some walls with exposed, whitewashed brick and different types of lighting. I see the bowling alleys from our booth and hear the people cheering as they play.

I realize how much I've secluded myself from the world by working and being a mother. It's hard to balance a social life when money is very tight and you have a daughter to care for. I didn't even know this place existed, but then again, I don't run in this circle.

"Hey, I feel like I keep losing you," Jason dips his head to make eye contact.

"Sorry. If I can be honest—"

"Yes. I want you to be one-hundred-percent honest with me." Jason's shoulders slump a bit.

"I'm realizing how removed I am from this." I wave my hand around the space. "I know nothing about any of this. I can't even remember the last time I bowled."

"It's a good thing I'm an excellent teacher then," Jason's smile is mischievous and his eyes twinkle.

"I don't remember the last time I was on a date. Way before Rae was born. Maybe high school or right after graduation?"

"That doesn't matter. Relax and enjoy the experience."

"Hi, I'm Mandy. I'll be your server today. Can I get you something to drink while you browse the menu?" a chirpy brunette with a wavy bob says.

"Do you know what you want to drink?" Jason asks.

I quickly scan the drink portion of the menu. "I'll have a sangria."

"Awesome choice. How about you?" She looks at Jason.

"The Top Hop IPA."

"I'll be right back with your drinks. If you have any questions about our menu, I'm here to help."

"Thanks," Jason replies as our waitress walks away.

"She didn't say anything about who you are."

Jason shakes his head. "We come here often, and the staff is used to seeing us. Quite a few well-known musicians stop by as well, so the staff is trained to treat us like everyone else. Besides, I'm not that popular."

I raise an eyebrow and lean back in the booth. "Really?"

Jason laughs. "Not like Cash."

"You're all popular. If I recognized you, everyone else here would."

"Tonight's about us, though."

The side of my mouth tilts into a smile. "Okay."

The waitress serves our drinks and takes our dinner order. Jason holds his beer up once she walks away. "Cheers." I raise my glass to his, feeling silly. "To new beginnings."

"Cheers." I tap my glass with his and take a sip of the fruity, wine cocktail.

"How's the sangria?"

"Delicious. It's been so long since I've had a cocktail. I may need to limit myself to one. I'm lame."

"You're not. You're a responsible parent, who loves her daughter."

"More like a single mom trying to make ends meet so her daughter has a place to sleep." *Why did I just say that?* "Sorry."

Jason reaches for my hand across the table and smiles. "Don't apologize. I admire you. Anyone else would've given her up or terminated the pregnancy. You're a fighter, Cassidy Rae. You're brave."

"Thanks," my voice is hushed.

"What was your favorite cocktail before you had Rae?"

"I'd have to say Jack and Coke. I'm simple like that."

"Jack and Coke is always a good choice. What's something you love to do?"

"I love dancing. It was so invigorating to step out onto a dance floor and let loose. After high school, I got a job at a bar to help my parents with their bills. My mom had to quit working when she got sick, and it was too much for my dad to handle on his own. Bartending paid well enough, but I loved watching people dance and let go of their shields for a little while. Alcohol does that, make you less guarded."

"I'm a great dancer," Jason winks.

"Really?"

"Yup. I can put Luke Bryan's moves to shame."

I laugh until I snort and cover my face.

"That was cute."

"Oh yeah, because sounding like a pig is adorable."

"Nah, you didn't sound like a pig. It's nice to see you laugh openly. I know I've only seen you a few times, and you're different around Rae, but I like seeing you like this. I like sitting across from you, holding your hand, and learning about the woman behind the mom."

"I'm so used to being that mom. Are you even sure you want to get involved with a mom? It's not easy, and it's definitely not the same as dating someone who has no attachments."

"I like you, Caz. Relationships don't come with a checklist. Sure, I can have an idea of the woman I want in my life, but I'm not going to throw away a chance with that woman because she has a daughter. That's not a deal breaker for me."

We're talking as if we were more serious than we actually are. He mentions an *us* as if we've been steady. How is he so sure?

"You don't even know me."

"You gotta stop with that excuse. No one knows anyone until they take the time to get to know them. I watch you. I'm an observer by nature. When I sit at Joyce's Diner, I take you in. The way you interact with your customers, how you cross your arms when you're uncomfortable, and the way you giggle when one of your regulars teases you. I see it. I see the way you look at Rae as if she's the only light in your world. I'm sure she is, but I want a piece of that light."

I stare at Jason, my heart racing. I used to believe in love like this, but I stopped believing a long time ago. Is it possible to have someone in my life who would care about me *and* Rae?

"I know I need to stop with that excuse. I keep telling myself to get over that, but it's hard to. The last time I dated someone for more than a few weeks was when I was in high school. I asked to take things slow because I have no idea how to do this. I haven't been out with anyone since I got pregnant. I get that this sounds repetitive, but it has nothing to do with you."

"Caz," Jason laces our fingers. "I get it. I was seeing someone and I didn't click with her the way I'm clicking with you from the start. Yeah, we got along really well, but the beginning was a chase. I hate games, and I thought she was different, but all she wanted was to use me to get to the big names in the music industry. I got played, and it sucks. I want to put that out in the open because I'm about honesty. If you're honest with me, tell me what you're really feeling, we can make this work."

"Am I a rebound?" I blurt out.

"Hell, no. I wouldn't work this hard for a rebound. Ever since I saw you that first day, I liked you. It was a combination of things. When I found out you had a daughter I tried to stay away because I assumed you were married or with the father. But trust me, never did a rebound cross my mind."

I nod. "I want to have fun tonight. Get to know you, too. Can we start over?"

Jason shakes his head. "I like that we talked this out. How about we order another round and kick off the conversation in a different direction."

"I like that plan."

Jason and I eat and talk. Although I told him I would only have one sangria, I'm enjoying the second one mighty well.

"So you were homecoming queen?" Jason asks.

"Yeah." I think back to that night. I was one of the popular girls in high school, and I was nice. Everyone liked me. Back then I didn't think I'd end up where I am now, but I am a fighter, like Jason said.

"Who was the king?"

"Typical—captain of the football team. We were friends, so I was happy with that choice."

"I never won anything cool like that in high school," Jason pouts.

"Who you are in high school doesn't define who you'll be. I never thought I'd have a child so young. It wasn't in my plans. I remember telling my friends it'd be a long time, if ever, that I'd have a kid. And bam, three years later I get pregnant."

Jason nods as he listens to me speak. "Anyway, did you play any sports?"

"Not in high school. I played baseball when I was younger."

"The All-American sport. I used to watch when I was a kid."

"You know, Cole's girlfriend, Bri, works for the Sounds. Maybe we can go to a game one day and take Rae."

I bite my lip and smile, nodding. Could this actually be real?

After dinner, we head to the bowling lanes. It's an odd feeling being taken care of and have someone pay for my meal. Jason does it so nonchalantly.

He's barely released by hand, and I can't hide the joy that gives me. After we laid everything out on the table, our conversation flowed. Jason told me about his sisters and his parents. They've both remarried, and he gets on well with their spouses.

"I know you said you haven't bowled in a while, so I'm ready to teach you anything you need." Jason's eyes twinkle with a naughty gleam as he pulls me to him by my hand, resting his other one on my waist.

"I only have one condition for our game tonight."

"What?" I breathe out.

"You have fun." This is the closest we've been. I can see a ring of gray around his pupils.

"I can live with that." Jason chuckles at my reaction and kisses my forehead.

I pull in a gulp of air. All those romantic movies I used to watch and love showed forehead kisses, and I always thought the woman's reaction was exaggerated. It's so not.

"Come on."

We put on the bowling shoes and settle into our lane.

I decline the offer of another sangria, knowing two is my limit for tonight. I don't want a headache at work tomorrow and I want to be in control. I still have Rae to think about, even if I'm here having fun with Jason.

"Anything else to drink?"

"Water would be great." I check my phone to make sure Abigail hasn't called while Jason grabs our drinks. Thank goodness for inexpensive phone plans. The data isn't the best, but I don't use it for anything other than calls.

"Everything okay?" Jason asks as he returns.

I put my phone back in my purse and smile. "Yeah. I wanted to make sure I didn't miss a call from Abigail."

"Good. Now get ready to learn from the pro."

I giggle. "I never said I don't know how to bowl. I said it's been years."

"Let me have this moment," he jokes.

When he walks up to me, my breath catches. The closeness accelerates my heart. There's an intimacy involved.

"Besides, I keep thinking about holding you close as I help you throw the ball." My eyes flutter closed for a brief second. "You feel it, too."

I nod and wonder how his short beard would feel as he kisses me. I dare touch his face, my fingers barely touching his skin to see if it's pinchy or soft. Jason stares at me as I explore. His beard is soft, framing his face flawlessly.

"Jason," someone calls out. We both jump back as if we've been caught in a secret rendezvous. "I didn't mean to interrupt." I turn to look at the man speaking, sheepish shrug taking over his body.

"Hey, Tyler. No interruptions. What's good? This is

Cassidy Rae. Caz, this is Tyler Hunt."

"It's nice to meet you, Caz. I'm here celebrating my latest album. Just wanted to say hi. I'll leave you two alone."

"Congrats, brother. Tell Mikayla I say hi."

"Will do," Tyler waves over his shoulder.

"Thanks to him, we got our big break in this industry," Jason tells me. "He took us on tour as his opening act a few years ago, and his label signed us on after that."

"I love his music," I say, a little starstruck.

"Let's play." Jason smirks and grabs my hand, guiding me to the lane.

As we take turns bowling, Jason tells me about his career. I ask him a lot more questions than I mean to, but the more he speaks, the more curious I become about the music industry and how it all works.

"It sounds fascinating," I say as I stand next to him while he gears up to bowl.

"It is." He looks at me and winks. "Strike," he exclaims.

I groan jokingly.

"Come here." He beckons me with his hand. "Stand here. Tilt your body like this." He grabs my hips, shifting me a tiny bit to the right. "Now, you're going to wind your arm back, and when you swing, put your body into it."

I hold the ball as I'm supposed to, and Jason stands behind me. One hand is on my hip, the other holding my bowling arm. We move together, him guiding my body to propel forward enough to release the ball with force. His body is warm against mine, and when I release the ball, the hand at the hip moves toward my stomach and hugs me.

"Excellent," he whispers in my ear.

I'm frozen. Who knew bowling could be sexy? I never imagined being out like this. Not even in my wildest dreams did I think I'd be out on a date again, especially with someone like Jason. The most attention I've gotten is from perverted truck drivers.

I shiver.

"Are you cold?" Jason asks.

"No." I turn around to face him.

We're paused in this moment as I look into the eyes of a man that's supposed to be a stranger, yet feels more real than most things in my life. It's a glimpse of the life I could've had if not for that one-night-stand. Would I still have had a daughter like Rae with a man like Jason?

He clears his throat and looks at the scoreboard. "You knocked down almost all the pins."

"Now it's game on," I joke. I go for the second round and knock down another two pins.

"Good job. Now watch the pro."

By the time the game is over, my laughter is heard by everyone near us. Some people stare, others laugh with me. Jason is being silly. Each time it's his turn to bowl, he shakes his behind, reminding me he could put Luke Bryan to shame with the dancing.

He dances his way up to me, making a fool of himself, but everyone around us seems to enjoy it as they cheer him on. I cover my face, my stomach cramping as I snort.

"Oh, God." I say and Jason laughs.

"I think it's adorable." He stands me up from the chair and continues to dance to whatever song is playing in the building. I'm too embarrassed to notice. A few people whistle and cheer. I bury my face into Jason's shoulder.

When the song ends, Jason hugs me. "Are you having fun?"

"Yes," I look up at him.

"Good. I've accomplished my job."

When Jason drops me off at home, he helps me carry Rae in and waits for me to lay her in bed.

"I had a great time tonight, Caz."

"Are you always going to call me that now?"

"Rae came up with it, and she's a girl you don't go against."

"You're right about that. Thank you for tonight, Jason. I had fun."

"I'm so glad you did. I want to see you again."

"Okay." My stomach flutters.

"Tell me when, and I'll be free." He brushes my hair away from my face, inching in as if waiting for me to reject his descending lips. When they finally touch mine, I sigh. Jason cradles my face with both hands and holds me to him as his lips kiss mine. The tip of his tongue teases mine, but he doesn't take it any further. His forehead leans on mine, his eyes closed.

"I know you want to take things slow, but I've been itching to kiss you all night. Every time I held you close, I wanted to taste your lips."

"You're not the only one," I whisper.

"We're playing at Riot tomorrow night, but I'll call you before. Get rest for tomorrow."

I watch Jason walk to his car before locking the door and leaning against it. Tonight I felt like a true twenty-eight year old woman on a date.

Once in bed, I toss and turn to get comfortable, hoping I don't wake Rae. Finally in a comfortable position, my phone makes a sound. I furrow my eyebrows and stand to grab it from my purse.

Jason: Goodnight, beautiful

I smile and internally squeal. I've never been a big texter. I'm more old school. Give me conversation instead of half-written words and images, but this message went straight to my heart.

Chapter 9

Jason

"HEARD YOU WERE OUT ON a cozy date," Cash greets me as I walk into the studio before we go to Riot for our show.

"Damn Tyler," I mumble.

"Date? You're not back with Christie, right?" Ryder looks up from tuning his guitar.

"Nope. She wasn't Christie," Cash smirks. *Fucker.*

"Is it impossible to have privacy in this town?"

"Only if you're home with the blinds shut," Ryder laughs. "Who is she?"

I look at Cole, who has remained silent. He shrugs, letting me know they won't let it go.

"Listen, guys, it's kinda complicated and I'm not ready to talk about it."

"You shoulda thought about that before you put on a show in Pinewood Social," Cash arches an eyebrow.

"What?"

He holds his phone up so I can see a picture of me bent, in what can only be booty dancing, and Cassidy Rae in the corner of the picture laughing.

"Fuck. I was messing around trying to make her laugh."

"You know better than that, though."

"I honestly was so into the date I didn't think anyone would notice who I was. It's not like I'm you," I point to Cash.

"They know who we all are. So tell us, who is she?" Cash leans back against a desk.

"I met her a couple weeks ago. It's not that simple with her, and I don't want to hear a lecture."

"Stop stalling." Ryder rubs his hands together.

"What the fuck? Are you that excited?"

"Yeah. After being the last one to find out about this asshole's love for Bri, I'm glad to be included in this one."

I roll my eyes. We're a bunch of chicks when it comes to relationships.

"Here's the thing, she's a single mom." Rip off the bandaid.

"A kid?"

"Usually when you're a mom, that's what you have." I look at Ryder.

"No shit, jackass. Are you ready for that?"

I shrug. "Yeah, I guess."

"There's no guessing when it comes to a child," Cash, the levelheaded one, says. "It makes the attachment different."

"I know." I go into detail about how I met Cassidy Rae and Rae as they listen intently. They give me the time to speak it all out.

"How long have you known her?" Cash asks.

"Maybe a couple weeks? Yesterday was our first date."

"You better be sure, because from the sound of it, that little girl's ready for you to play daddy."

"Come on, Cash."

"I'm calling it how it is. If you're sure, then great, but don't hurt the girl or the woman," he warns.

Cole has been sitting in the background listening. No words have come from him, and I wonder if he still thinks Cassidy Rae is a bad idea.

"Just make sure you're protecting yourself as well. After what happened with Christie, I'd hate to see you go through something similar for different reasons," Ryder crosses his arms.

"I get where you're coming from. Cole told me the same thing, but this is different. I don't know."

"Well, I'll be damned. Mr. Get Over It and Move On is hooked on a woman." Cash's smile annoys me.

"You were acting like a pussy," I defend. When things between Cash and Olivia weren't hot, I may have told him to get over her and fuck someone else. Something along those lines. My memory is blurry after some years. In my defense, he was moping and acting like a dick.

"I get it. I'm the guy usually telling you fools to man up and see things clearly. Call this karma or payback or whatever you want, but this woman is special."

"Is she coming tonight?" Ryder asks.

"She has a kid. She can't just up and leave her to go to some bar downtown."

"So you didn't ask her," Cole finally speaks up.

"She wants to take things slow. She has a routine with

Rae, and Rae is used to having her around all the time. Besides," I pause. "I don't want any drama with Christie. She's still been trying to contact me, and that's not an ideal situation."

"I think that's smart," Cash nods.

We get to work on what we need to review and prep for the show. Having played at Riot hundreds of times, we don't even do sound check anymore. The stage is always ready for us. I do dread running into Christie. If she's been trying to contact me and she knows we'll be playing, she may try to come in from the outside bar and talk to me. Fuck that.

Our set played out flawlessly, fans singing along with Cash. I kept thinking about Cassidy Rae while I was up there. What she'd think watching me play. Would she sing along and dance, or shy away by the bar? She mentioned she loves dancing, so I need to make it a point to get her on a dance floor. The idea of moving my body with hers excites me.

Holding her close last night gave me a taste of what it would be like to keep her in my arms for a while. The kiss wasn't nearly long enough, but I knew if I started, I wouldn't stop. Her daughter was sleeping in her room.

I enjoyed every second with Cassidy Rae. When she finally relaxed, I saw a glimpse of who she truly is.

"Hey." I clench my teeth and close my eyes.

"What do you want?" I don't turn around to look at her.

"You guys did good tonight."

"Christie, I'm going to ask you nicely to leave me alone. I'm not interested in listening to what you have to say."

"Can you please look at me?"

I sigh and turn around. Arching an eyebrow, I say, "What?"

"I wanted to apologize. What I did was fucked up and I ruined a good thing because of my selfishness. I should've talked to you about it."

"You used me. Plain and simple."

"And I'm sorry. We had a good thing going." I flinch when she touches my bicep. "Can we at least have dinner sometime to talk?"

"I accept your apology, but we're done. Forever. I'm not interested. Once someone breaks my trust, they're dead to me."

Christie's eyes widen. "But…"

I shake my head, stopping her. "No buts. It's over. You signed an NDA, remember," I warn.

"I wouldn't share anything."

"That's not what your actions have proven. Now, I think you have work to do," I dismiss her. The hurt in her brown eyes is evident, but I don't give a fuck. I opened up to her and she betrayed me. You don't come back from doing that, with your tail between your legs, expecting me to forgive and forget. I can be the bigger person and forgive her, but I sure as hell don't have room for her in my life.

Another woman has invaded my space and I welcome her warmth. As much as I want to rush, I need things to go at Cassidy Rae's pace. After what happened with Christie, it's probably for my own good, too. I'm hoping after last night, she'll be more open to the idea of us. We still have a lot to learn about each other, but I have no doubt I'd like everything else about her, as well.

And there's Rae. That girl wrapped me up the moment

she sat next to me and offered me a cookie. Chocolate chip is my favorite. Next time, a trip to the zoo will be fun. I wonder if Cassidy Rae can get a day off from work. Hell, I'll pay her the daily wage, although I know she'd be pissed if I even offered that.

"Hey!" Reese calls out.

"Hey guys, I didn't see you."

"No shit, you were deep in thought. We were talking to the guys, waiting for you to show up and you didn't.

"Sorry about that. I came to grab a beer and Christie came up to me."

"What did she say?" Taylor rolls her eyes.

"Nothing important. Hey, Mike." I shake Taylor's boyfriend's hand and head over to the where the guys are with my sisters.

I'm glad my sisters came tonight, and I can spend time with them. However, I keep thinking about Cassidy Rae. When I called her earlier she was still at work. I may have to show up there tomorrow. See her in the flesh and maybe kiss her again.

I've got it bad.

"Let me guess. You'll have an OJ and order of pancakes, but you don't want me to serve it. You want the young lady over there." Joyce's eyes gleam. I want her in more ways than just my waitress.

I smirk and shrug. "Can't blame me."

"No, boy, I can't. I will tell ya, it's pretty obvious you're smitten with her, and if she's blind to it, then the girl won't see nothing no matter how bright the sun shines on it."

I lean forward on my elbows, but she keeps talking.

"But, you better treat her right. Just cuz she's workin'

at my shitty diner don't mean she deserves a *boy* instead of a man. You got me?"

"I sure do, ma'am. I have every intention of proving to her that she's worthy. Full respect."

"Good. After all, no way you'd be coming here all these days if all ya wanted was to stick your thing in a hole." She waves her pointer finger in the direction of my pants. I cough back my laugh.

"I promise I'll do right by her and her daughter."

"Atta boy. Now let me tell that stubborn blonde that a customer is waiting for her." I smile and chuckle as she walks away. *My thing in her hole.* I guess that's better than hearing an older woman say dick and pussy.

"Hi."

I look up from the menu to find my gorgeous girl. A slow smile creeps on my face. "Hey."

"I was told you needed some attention." Her cheeks turn pink despite the teasing tone.

"I do. I wanted to see you. Couldn't think of anywhere better for Sunday brunch than here."

"I doubt that." Cassidy Rae crosses her arms.

"You're here, so that's all I care about. Can't stop thinking about you," I confess.

Her eyes soften and she bites her lip. Lips that I want to taste for myself. "I've thought about you, too."

"And what exactly were you thinking about?" I waggle my eyebrows.

"Ugh, not like that. Just stuff."

"Good stuff or bad stuff? We had a great time on Friday, we like each other, and we sealed the night with a kiss." I wink.

"I did have a great time." She fidgets with the pockets

of her apron.

"How's Rae?" I lighten the subject.

"Great. She asked about you yesterday," Cassidy Rae smirks.

"Tell her I say hi. I was actually wondering if you'd like to go to the zoo with her some day soon. I get to spend more time with you and it will be fun for Rae."

"She'd love that, but I'm not sure when. I work every day, so my schedule is pretty busy."

"Can you ask for a day off?"

Cassidy Rae shakes her head, but I think it's more for a financial reason than Joyce not willing to give her the day.

"I want to spend time with you. I want to get to know you and Rae better. Maybe one morning when you do the evening shift? I'll stay here while you work and drive you home." I wish the counter wasn't in the way, so I could hold her hand, reassure her somehow.

"Hey, sweetheart, can I get some attention, too?" I clench my jaw as I hear some asshole call out across the diner. Before I can stand, Cassidy Rae puts her hand on my arm. I look at her, nostrils flared. People have no fucking respect.

"Relax. Best thing to do is ignore it."

"I can't."

"Please," she begs with her eyes.

"For you." I inhale ragged breaths. I was always taught to respect people no matter where they came from, what they looked like, or what gender they were. Having two sisters, I respected women even more. I can't stand when men treat women the way these asshole customers treat Cassidy Rae.

"I'll be right back and bring you a glass of orange

juice."

I turn on the stool and watch her in case that douche wants to get fresh with her. I won't let anyone think she's less significant because she works at a diner.

Once she heads back from his table, she places a cup of orange juice in front of me and smiles.

"Pancakes?" she asks.

"If I keep eating pancakes, I'm going to need to work out twice a day." Cassidy Rae rolls her eyes. "How's the ham and cheese omelet?"

"It's good if you like eggs."

I raise my eyebrows. "You don't like eggs?"

"They're not my favorite," she shrugs.

"I'm not sure this is going to work." As soon as I say the words, Cassidy Rae's eyes widen for a second. "I'm joking. You not liking eggs isn't a deal breaker." I chuckle.

"Oh."

"I'm trying really hard not to walk around the back of this counter and pull you into me. You're making it even more difficult with that cute expression."

"I'm at work," she whispers hurriedly.

"Go to the zoo with me." There's a sentence I never thought I'd tell a woman.

"I work, Jason. I'll be back with your omelet."

Cassidy Rae walks away and into the kitchen. I check my phone while my food is getting prepared, but nothing interesting catches my attention.

"Out." I look up to see what's going on in the kitchen. That didn't sound like Cassidy Rae.

Then, I see her walking out of the chase door, hiking her purse on her shoulder. She stops in front of me, angry as hell.

"Let's go."

"What?"

"We're leaving," she sneers.

"Okay," I furrow my eyebrows.

"Joyce overheard our conversation. I was instructed to leave with you and take Rae to the zoo." Cassidy Rae crosses her arms.

I can't help the laugh that takes over.

"It's not funny, Jason. I got kicked out of my own job, a job I've had for seven years," she leans around me to stare at Joyce. "So that I can go on a date with you."

"Well, damn, your boss must suck," I tease. Turning around, I offer Joyce a grateful smile.

"Have fun," Joyce calls out.

Cassidy Rae huffs and puffs all the way to the car. Her tantrum is adorable. Before I open the car door for her, I encase her against it with my arms on either side of her. Her eyes widen in surprise, and I lean in to kiss her. Fuck skirting around so she feels comfortable with the pace. I know she does. She's feeling what I'm feeling.

She relaxes as she kisses me back. My dick springs to life, and I mentally curse when she pulls me closer to her. A soft moan leaves her lips as I end the kiss and lean my forehead against hers. Her chest rises rapidly, mine mimicking it.

When I lean back to look at her, she's staring at me with intensity. Her eyes shut for a beat, allowing me to take in her subtle beauty. I cup the side of her face with my hand and rub my thumb across her cheek.

"I could do that all day, but we've got a little girl to pick up and some animals to visit."

Cassidy Rae is silent on the short drive to her place.

I'm still feeling the effects of the kiss, and I hope she's thinking about it. I know it's different when Rae is around, but I want to show her we could be a couple while she's still a mom. There's no reason it has to be one or the other.

She's a woman and deserves to be treated as one. Her life doesn't have to end because she's a mom.

"Do you think Rae is going to be excited?" I ask.

"Excited? She's going to flip. Ever since she went to the zoo on a field trip this past school year, she's been begging me to go back."

"Awesome," I smile, proud of my plan.

Once I park the car, Cassidy Rae leads the way to her house and unlocks the door.

"Mommy?" Rae asks before her eyes widen. "Jason!" She runs up to me and hugs my side. "What are you doing here?"

Cassidy Rae bends to talk to her, not giving me a chance to explain.

"Hey baby, Jason came by work today and asked if we wanted to go to the zoo. Joyce gave me the day off so we could take you."

"Really?" Her voice screeches, and she looks between us. I nod, smiling.

"This is the best day ever!" she exclaims as she jumps up and down and runs around.

"Hey, Abigail," Cassidy Rae says. They talk for a few minutes before Abigail leaves, a huge smile plastered on her face. Seems as if everyone in Cassidy Rae's life is cheering me on. I'll gladly take their cheers and run with them in the direction of the woman currently staring at me.

"I'm going to change a minute and I'll be good to go."

"No rush." I sit on the couch and Rae plants herself right next to me.

"I love the zoo. We went on a field trip and it was so much fun. My mommy couldn't go because she was working, but my teacher took pictures and showed them to her that afternoon. We saw monkeys and giraffes and a lion and a zebra. My favorite was the giraffe. What's your favorite animal?" She gasps for air as she finishes. That girl speed talks when she's excited.

"I'm glad you're excited. My favorite is the lion."

"What's your favorite, Mommy?"

I look up to see Cassidy Rae looking at us in a fresh pair of jeans and a tee shirt. "Ready," she says.

"What's your favorite animal?" Rae repeats her question.

"The elephant." Cassidy Rae smiles. She should wear that smile every damn day, and I want her to do so because of me.

"Are we ready?" I ask, smiling.

"Yes!" Rae yells.

We head out to my car and drive to the zoo, a chattering Rae in the back seat. My gaze wanders to the woman next to me every time my car is stopped in traffic or at a light. When her eyes meet mine, I feel her gaze in my chest. I'm ready to move forward with her, no matter what.

Chapter 10

Cassidy Rae

JASON SMILES AT ME AS Rae runs up to the railing where the giraffes are. This was our first stop since it's her favorite animal.

"They're so beautiful." Her face is bright when she looks back at us. I've never seen her this happy. I work tirelessly to make her happy, but this is a different level of joy. It's obvious Jason is the reason for that. Not that he brought us here, but that he's here at all.

"They are," I call back as I watch her stare off in hopes that one of those giants comes up to her. "She's so happy. Thank you," I turn to look at Jason.

"You don't need to thank me. I'm happy, too. Bringing you two here and being a part of this. I know you want to take things slow, and I respect that, but this feels a lot more than it should."

"I can't imagine what it will do to Rae if we decide

down the road that we're better off as friends or just acquaintances. She already likes you so much. If you suddenly disappear because we didn't work out, she'll be devastated. She's asking questions. As mature as she seems, she's still a little girl." Rae is already seeing Jason in our lives for the long run.

"I don't see this changing on my end."

"You don't know me. You don't know if I smoke, if I'm psycho, if I'm extremely jealous." My hands are everywhere as I speak.

He grabs my hands and holds them. "Are you those things?" Jason tilts his head, removing his sunglasses to look at me.

"No, but—"

"Caz, the only thing I see happening in the future is me falling real hard for you." His hands land on my hips, the distance still between us, but it doesn't help my racing heart from slowing down.

"We'll go slow," he promises. With a peck on my forehead, he joins Rae by the railing.

I look on for a minute as he interacts with my daughter. No reservations or awkwardness, he's all in with her. I'm a stupid, stupid woman to turn away a man like him.

As I approach them, Rae says, "We can do that?"

I look between them. "Do what?"

"Feed the giraffes!" Rae is dancing around.

"We don't have to," I whisper to Jason. Guilt washes over me as he pays for all of this. I know he says he wants to, but a small part of me feels like a user. I've never been one to use anyone for anything, and I don't want to do that now.

"Are you kidding me? Look at her. Hell, I want to feed the giraffes."

"I just feel…" How do I say it without sounding offensive or ungrateful? "Never mind," I shake my head. That's a conversation for another time. I do want to let him know I don't expect any of this from him.

"Loosen up," he whispers in my ear, his breath chilling me. "Now, let's go feed these animals."

"Yes!" Rae exclaims, her little fist pumped at her side, as she celebrates.

Jason holds my hand, and before I can reach for Rae's, she's already skipped to Jason's other side. *She's such a flirt.*

We walk back to the ticket booth where Jason purchases three tickets for a tour that includes feeding giraffes. While we wait for that to begin, Rae plays on the jungle gym.

"Thank you, Jason. I don't mean to sound ungrateful. I do think we have a few things to discuss. Nothing major, it's just something I need to get off my chest before anything moves forward."

"Okay."

"Not now, but soon?" I grin in what I hope is reassurance.

"Yeah." Jason squeezes my fingers before we call Rae to head back to the meeting point for the tour.

The tour is educational, and Rae is eating up every second of it. She'll be talking about animal conservation and care for a long time.

"Okay, now are you ready for the fun part?" The tour guide leads us around the giraffe barn. With bags of green vegetables in hand, he leads us to the ramp where we will feed them. Knowingly, the giraffes begin to approach us.

With it being summer break and a Sunday, our tour size is significant, but we all take turns. Rae laughs as their long tongues sweep the lettuce from her hand.

"Mommy, you have to try it!" She hands me a leaf of collard greens and pushes me forward. Smiling, I wait for the animal to grab the leaf and giggle just like Rae did.

"That tickled," I turn around to face them.

"Your turn, Jason." Rae pushes him like she did to me. He winks at me and approaches the giraffe.

As we finish the tour, Rae asks the guide where the elephants are. "They're my mommy's favorite."

"Actually, we had to move the elephants due to construction. They're in The Elephant Sanctuary in Hohenwald."

"Oh," Rae looks down.

"It's okay, baby girl." I thank the guide. "I had so much fun feeding the giraffes, I almost forgot about the elephants." Rae pouts.

"How about we have lunch and then we can see a few more animals that weren't on our tour and maybe play a little more on the jungle gym?" Jason asks.

"I think that's a good idea," I respond.

"Okay," Rae grins.

Jason holds out chairs for both Rae and me when we get to the cafe.

"What was your favorite part besides feeding the giraffes?" Jason asks Rae.

"I liked learning all the cool stuff about the animals. Maybe I want to work at a zoo when I grow up."

"I thought you wanted to be a baker?" I look at her.

"Yeah, that too. I can do both things. You always say I can do whatever I want," she shrugs and sucks her apple juice from the straw.

I giggle and kiss the top of her head. "I do say that."

"I think both jobs would be fun," Jason chimes in.

"Yeah. I could work at the zoo during the day and bake at night. It'd be fun."

"Are you ready to order?" Our college-aged waitress asks. This must be her summer job. Rae could probably do something like that. *Too soon.* I don't want to think about her going off to college.

"Do you know what you want?" I ask Rae.

"Mac and cheese, please."

"Great. How about you two?" she asks Jason and me.

"I'll have the burger." Jason keeps his head down, shielding his face with his cap.

"Me, too." I hand the waitress the menus and smile.

"I'll be back with your food shortly." She bounces away to check on another table.

Jason smirks, probably proud no one recognized him. I never thought band members besides the lead singer were so popular, but Rebel Desire is treated as one. Every time I've heard people talk about it, all members are mentioned.

"What was your favorite part?" Rae asks Jason.

"Seeing the lions and the rhinoceros hornbill."

"Was that the bird with the upside-down beak on its forehead?" Rae laughs.

"Yes. It's a horn."

"That was a weird one."

Jason nods.

"How about you?" Jason looks at me.

"They didn't have your elephants," Rae's bottom lip curls down.

"I also liked feeding the giraffes. The tortoise was cool."

"How about that weird lizard," Rae comments.

"No." I shake my head. "I did not like that one." I shudder.

Jason and Rae both laugh at my reaction. As soon as I saw that odd creature, I hid behind Jason and tried to race out of that area despite it being very well locked up.

"We know you didn't like that one," Rae laughs. Her fit of hysterics makes me laugh. She's my wild girl, careless and happy.

Anyone on the outside looking in would think we're the perfect family. Little do they know, we're nowhere near being a family, but sitting here after the day we've spent makes me want that.

"I guess we wore her out," Jason whispers as he parks the car near my house.

"I'm pretty sure the sugar in the cotton candy after lunch did the trick." Rae got extremely hyper after eating most of the cotton candy, causing a crash once she sat in the car.

"Yeah. She was on fast forward after she ate that."

"Welcome to a child's sugar rush. It's a real thing."

"Is she going to wake up and be up all night?" Jason asks.

"She'll probably wake up in an hour or so. Won't be too bad."

"I'll help you take her in," he offers.

"You don't have to." I go to open the door, but Jason stops me by placing his hand on my knee.

"I want to." His eyes widen with meaning. "Let me." He's asking for permission, and I nod. This might be a good time to have that conversation I brought up earlier, if he's not in a rush to get somewhere.

Jason carries Rae into the house and lays her down on the bed. It's the first time he sees all of our tiny space. If he didn't assume it before, he now knows we share a bedroom.

Watching him lay her down with such care and a big smile swells my heart. She's not even his to be proud about, but the way he looks at her tells a different story. I wonder if he's always wanted children. He'd make a great father one day, that's been proven over and over again.

"Are you in a rush?" I ask.

"Got nowhere to be, Caz."

"Can we talk?"

"Sure." He takes a seat on the couch. I fidget and wring my fingers together as I look at him.

"Do you want something to drink? Coffee? Water? OJ?" I smirk.

"Come sit next to me. I'm okay." He pats the cushion next to him.

I sit, tucking my legs under me and turn toward him. I take him in. His long lashes and blue eyes staring at me, waiting. The furrow in his eyebrows tells me he's nervous about what I'm going to say. He finally took off the cap in the car, leaving his hair a mess.

I run my finger around his face, outlining the shape of his eyebrows and down the side of is face. He sits still, letting me touch him. His short beard tickles my finger and I shiver.

Jason grabs my hand when I pull away and places it back on his face. "Don't stop."

I keep creating a path on his face as I begin speaking.

"Let me start by saying thank you. I'm not sure you realize how special today was for Rae. For me." I look down at my lap. "But I need to say this before anything more can happen. For years it's been just us two. I've supported her the best I can, making sure she's in a decent school, meeting with teachers, working hard to put money into a savings account her for. Now, you come into our lives and in the short time you've known us, you've taken us out three times. I appreciate it and have had fun—"

"But?" Jason interrupts me. "And I said don't stop." He moves my hand across his beard.

"Don't interrupt me."

"Yes, ma'am."

I move my fingers again, smiling, and continue my speech. I'm not sure I'm getting my point across. "What I'm trying to say is that I don't want you to feel like you have to pay for us. We've gotten by, albeit without extras, like trips to the zoo and cotton candy. I like you. Rae obviously likes you. But I don't like you for your money. I know I'm a struggling single mom, but I don't want it to seem like I'm using you for fancy meals and fun trips.

"I've never used anyone for anything, and it's not my style. Call it my insecurity; call it my guard, but I don't want to come off that way. I need you to know that I don't expect you to suddenly take care of us."

"Cassidy," he holds my hands, leaving half my name out. "I don't feel as if you're using me. I want to be here. I want to spend time with you. If I didn't, I wouldn't. Trust me. I can be very cut and dry. But you bring out something else in me. A need to take care of you. I was always tough on the guys because they were whipped when they met their women. Now, they're laughing at me.

"The last thing I want is for you to feel as if you're some kind of charity work. You're not. Rae is not. I've always been more of a relationship guy, and I've taken my sweet time making sure the woman I was seeing was who I wanted in my life. With you, it's like fuck the rules. I'm careful, even more so now because of my career, but I know you're not the type to come after me for my name or my money."

"It's different. I've never been involved with someone like you."

"Caz, I'm a normal guy. I grew up with a normal life. I struck a lucky chord and joined a band, but there's nothing spectacular about me. God, I'm really not selling myself right now." Jason places his forehead on my shoulder, and my body shakes with laughter.

"I love that sound," he looks up at me. "This is what a gentleman does. He takes care of the woman in his life."

"I scratched off the idea of a relationship from my bucket list a long time ago," I confess.

"It's a good thing I like a challenge. Before you know what's happened, I'll have you believing in fairytales." I roll my eyes. "A country fairytale instead of princes and princesses. We wear cowboy boots instead of glass heels and polished dress shoes."

"I don't own boots," I challenge.

"That's a quick fix," Jason shrugs.

"Don't you dare," I warn. I don't need him buying me any shoes.

"So, you like me?" He changes the subject, a confident smile now adorning his face.

"Slick," I arch an eyebrow.

Jason leans in and kisses me. His hands wrap around my back, holding me in place, as his lips taste mine. I sigh into him, wrapping my arms around his neck. I surrender to the feelings circulating inside me and remove my mind from the situation. I told him my concerns, and he listened. He knows where I stand.

I sigh as we end the kiss and look into those baby blues

that mesmerize me.

"I don't want to leave."

"Then don't." His smile lights up his eyes. "The space is small, but we can hang out." I roll my eyes. I sound like an idiot.

"I wouldn't want to be anywhere else."

I sit back and finally relax. Jason tells me about his show last night at Riot. He also talks more about his sisters, which is nice to hear. Being an only child, I've always wondered how I'd get along with a sibling.

"My parents couldn't have more kids after me. I was a miracle as it is, but my mom struggled with the pregnancy and they did a hysterectomy."

"How is she doing?"

"Okay." I shrug, unsure of how to respond. Alzheimer's isn't something you ever recuperate from.

"Have you spoken to your parents?"

"I spoke to my dad the other night." I frown. "He says she's the same, whatever that means."

"You can visit soon. Rae can see her grandparents."

"I was thinking I could go soon when I work a late shift. I don't like taking the bus back when it's late. I could ask Abigail also, but I'd hate putting her in that position."

"I'll take you."

"No, Jason. You don't have to."

"Caz, I'd be more than happy to take you and pick you up when you're ready to go see them again." Jason moves closer to me and brushes my hair behind my shoulder.

"Some days it's hard to go and see how the disease has affected my mom." My vulnerability shows with my statement.

"I'm sure it is, but I know you'd want to be there with

them. When was the last time you saw them?"

"A few weeks ago." I lean back and look at him.

"You let me know, and I'll be available to take you. No way you're taking the bus if I can help it."

I place my head on his shoulder. "Thank you," I whisper. Jason's hand wanders to mine and holds on tight.

The sunlight peeks in through the window, casting shadows around the living room and illuminating other parts. It's beautiful if you stop to look at it. I never stop to take it in.

"Mommy?" My head snaps up as I hear Rae's voice.

"Yeah, baby girl?" She walks toward us, rubbing her eyes. A shy smile follows as she looks at Jason and climbs on my lap.

"You're still here."

"I am. Your mommy and I were talking."

"Thank you for taking me to the zoo today." She reaches over and hugs Jason. "I had the best day." She looks tiny wrapped in a hug with Jason and tears threaten to betray my cool.

"What time is it?" she asks as she settles on my lap.

I check the clock hanging over the television. "It's just after six. Are you hungry?"

"Yeah."

"Do you want tacos since you had mac and cheese for lunch?" Rae nods. "You're more than welcome to stay for supper," I tell Jason.

"How about I take y'all out? I know this place I think Rae would love."

"Are you sure?" My eyebrows knit together.

"Positive." A gentle hand squeezes my fingers.

"Do you want to go?" I ask Rae, who seems like she's

still waking up from her nap.

"What is it?" she asks as if that would change her mind. I know my daughter, and she'd go anywhere.

"It's a treehouse restaurant." Jason winks.

"That's so cool. I want to go." She turns to look at me, a soft grin and messy hair staring back at me.

"Go take a bath. Are you okay waiting a few minutes?" I ask Jason.

"Of course I am." Rae runs to the bathroom.

"She's a good kid, Caz."

"Thanks. She's what I'm proudest of."

"As you should be." He kisses my temple and I sigh. I've never had a man care about me like this. Then again, I've never dated a man. All my prior relationships were pre-Rae, and you can't call an early 20s guy a man.

Chapter 11

Jason

ONCE RAE IS READY, WE go to dinner at Tree Tops, a treehouse inspired restaurant.

"Wow," Rae whispers as her wide eyes stare at the structure.

After we climb the ladder, Cassidy Rae looks at me. "This place is amazing." Her head spins around the space. "It even has kids' drawings."

"Yeah, I knew y'all would love it."

"It's so, so cool, Jason. I want a treehouse," Rae is beside herself with excitement, floating on cloud nine as she takes it all in.

Seeing her excitement makes me so happy. These two ladies have suddenly become my sole focus. I want to treat them right and give them so many experiences, especially Rae. She's still young. There are so many things in life for her to enjoy. I've always wanted kids, but I never thought

I'd meet someone who already has a child. I thought I'd be crazy jealous because the child wasn't mine. I'm not though. Instead, I want to offer her everything I can.

I've got all these feelings way too fast, and my brain is struggling to catch up. All I know is that I need both of these people in my life, permanently.

After a long wait, we're finally seated.

"Will you play word search with me?" Rae asks, holding a crayon up.

"You got it." I look for food related words on the kid's menu as I sneak peeks at Cassidy Rae. She watches us with bright eyes. I wink at her before continuing to search for the word *hamburger*.

"We got them all," Rae shouts.

"Rae," Cassidy Rae warns, and we both laugh.

"It's a big deal to find all the words in a word search game," I tell her. "Besides, it's loud enough here that people didn't notice."

"Yeah, what Jason said." Rae hooks her thumb in my direction.

Now Cassidy Rae and I laugh. The mood is light, different than at the zoo, and I'm glad Cassidy Rae and I spoke this afternoon. I understand her concern and appreciate her bringing it up. As wrong as I was about Christie, I know I'm right about Cassidy Rae. She's worried about seeming like she's mooching off of me, and I don't see it that way.

We place our drink orders when the waitress comes by, thankfully interrupting my thoughts. Once she returns with them, the three of us toast—Rae with her apple juice, Cassidy Rae with the sangria I insisted she order, and me with a beer.

"To awesome Sundays and the best two ladies I

know," I smile as I clink my glass with theirs.

"And to the best boy we know," Rae adds. I chuckle and take a sip of my beer.

It's an odd feeling, being this proud when I'm not her father and I haven't know them for too long. I think the Man Upstairs is telling me to eat my words. Nothing is black and white when it comes to the heart.

"What do you do with your band?" Rae asks.

"We make music. We write songs and add sound to it. Then, we record it. We also do a lot of other stuff, like interviews, small shows in Nashville, and other stuff that aren't as fun."

"I think anything that has to do with being in a band is fun."

"When it comes to the music, yes." No six-year-old will understand the business aspect of the industry.

"Do you have a song you can sing me?" I look into big brown eyes.

"How about in the car? Like that you can hear me," I suggest.

"Okay." She nods her head quickly. Maybe one day I'll teach her to play the guitar. I'm sure she'd love that.

"At what time do you work tomorrow?" I ask Cassidy Rae.

"Early afternoon, so I'll be able to rest in the morning."

"Good. May need to stop by for a late OJ drink."

"You don't have to."

"I know." I don't have to, but I'd use any excuse to see that woman, even if it's glimpses of her as she tends tables and wipes the counter.

"Can I go to work with you?" Rae asks.

"You're staying with Abby. I think she's going to take

you to the park."

"But I want to be there if Jason stops by." Rae leans back and crosses her arms, her eyebrows pulled in.

"He may not be able to. He works, too. We'll figure something out." Cassidy Rae peeks up at me.

"Yeah, kiddo. It depends what my boss needs me to do tomorrow, but I'll see you again soon."

"You will?" Rae looks at me with stubborn tears in her eyes. Damn. I run a hand through my messy hair.

"Of course. Who else am I going to play word search with?" I hold up the crayon. "Are you any good at tic-tac-toe?"

"Yes!" Just like that, tomorrow is forgotten and we're back to enjoying our dinner.

"You're a natural," Cassidy Rea mouths, and I wink at her.

Three games in, our food arrives and I'm losing to Rae. I didn't even let her win. She's that good at tic-tac-toe.

Rae digs into her chicken nuggets almost immediately after Cassidy Rae pours ketchup on the side of her plate. Cassidy Rae stares at her plate of tacos while I cut my steak and take a bite.

"This looks great." She takes a bite and moans. I wish I were what she was tasting. Then I look at Rae and rein in my thoughts.

"Good?" I raise my eyebrows.

"Delicious." She blushes and wipes her mouth with her napkin.

"I'm glad you're enjoying it." I crave to taste her lips again, and so much more. She's my ideal woman—humble, caring, and brutally honest.

Having spent almost all weekend with Cassidy Rae has shown me exactly how much she's sheltered herself and made Rae a priority. Not to say I wouldn't do the same in her situation, but she has to learn to live again and I want to teach her how.

We're waiting for Peyton to meet us in the studio, and I missed my chance to stop by the diner. I called Cassidy Rae to let her know I wouldn't make it, but she must've been working already since I got her generic voicemail. I'll call her when I leave work and make some real plans. Date number three, just her and I, and hopefully more of her lips.

"Hey, sorry I'm late." Peyton takes a seat at the table and shuffles some papers. "We got a call from a music director working on a new film. The story is about a prisoner of war, who finds himself free and trying to find his way back to the States after his family and friends declared him dead. It touches up on the struggles of being deployed, the risks, and the weight families and friends carry." Peyton looks up from the paper he's holding, most likely notes from the director.

"Anyway, they want you to be a part of the soundtrack. They're interested in original music, which will be used for promos as well."

"Okay," Cash says, looking at us and stopping to look at Cole. "You good with this?"

"More than good. I think this is a great opportunity." With Bri's past, I understand why Cash is making sure Cole is on board. Not that we doubt he wouldn't be. He would probably be proud to do something like this. Who knew underneath the provocative man-whore was someone capable of settling down.

"Great. We'll get more details from the director. Your buddy, Ronan Connolly, is actually one of the stars,"

Peyton tells Cash. Cash and Ronan bonded over their love of country music some time ago and have kept in touch ever since then.

"Cool." Cash smiles.

We go over more business before we work on our current music. The day is slow moving since the one thing I want to do is not possible while I'm working. As much as I love music and playing, thoughts of Cassidy Rae have taken over. Everything I thought I'd never be, she destroyed with the force of a wrecking ball. It's true I've always been more of a relationship guy, but I've been careful with that. Calculating, to a certain degree. Now I'm acting like damn Cash when he met Olivia. The last thing I need to do is call Cassidy Rae up on stage in front of a crowd of thousands.

"Bro." I shake my head when I feel something hit me. I was lost in thought, daydreaming about the blonde beauty that's slowly opening up to me.

"What the fuck?" I look at the three, all with suspecting smiles.

"Wake up. We wanted to know what you thought about this," Cash laughs. He and Ryder both play their guitars as Cash sings part of the chorus, a change in beat that I clearly missed.

I listen intently and mark the change. I like it. It gives the song more of a homegrown vibe.

"That works."

"What do you think, Scott?" Cash calls to one of our producers.

"Sounds good here. Let me hear it from the top." We play the song, tweaking to the new sound that was just implemented and wait for Scott to respond.

"Sounds good, boys."

As much as I'd like to say that working on a song is something we do in a few hours, realistically it can take up to a few days or a week. Usually the lyrics come in fast if Cash is writing and Olivia's inspired him, but adding music is a different story.

After work, I call Cassidy Rae. Hearing her voice would satisfy me at the moment until I can see her again. I check the time when she doesn't answer and realize she must be putting Rae to bed. I shoot her a quick text asking her to call me when she's free, and I impatiently wait for her call.

Cole is already home when I walk in through the door.

"Hey, I was waiting for you to get home to order takeout."

"What were you thinking?" I plant my ass next to him on the couch and lift one foot on the ottoman.

"I was just looking through the Eatery app to see which places had the shortest delivery wait."

"Thank God for technology and its ample restaurant choices."

"Yeah. No way I'm going out now," Cole leans back on the couch and scans his phone. "You wanna just get pizza?" He asks after spending a few minutes scrolling through the options. I've been staring at my phone willing Cassidy Rae to call me.

"Sure."

"It's the one with the shortest wait time."

"Works for me. I'm always game for pizza."

Cole orders and brings us both beers. "I actually wanted to talk to you about something," he looks around the living room.

"Okay?"

"Bri and I were talking, and, um…" I raise my eyebrows waiting for Cole to finish. "We're gonna move in together."

"That's great. Congrats, brother." I pat him on the shoulder.

"Thanks. I wanted to make sure you're okay, though. I mean, I know you recently met Cassidy Rae and all, but you good?"

"Yeah, I'm good. You're over at Bri's place half the time chasing her," I joke. "Seriously, I'm happy for you both."

"I'll still pay for my half of the bills this month."

"Relax. It's okay." Cole and I had an agreement from the beginning. If one of us was moving out for whatever reason, particularly one like Cole's, the other could stay in the house and become sole owner, or we'd sell it and split the profit. I want to stay, and I've been expecting for this day to come for a long time.

"You're staying in her apartment?"

"Until her lease is up. Then, we'll figure out where we want to live."

"Make sense. I'm sure you'll want a bigger place by then."

"How are things with Cassidy Rae?" He switches the subject.

I rub my face and chug what's left of my beer. "Honestly, I'm not sure. Friday night was great. It was her and I alone, so I got to spend time with her. Her daughter is amazing, but I want a relationship with Cassidy Rae, and alone time is needed for that.

"I've never been in a situation like this, but I like her. A whole damn lot. I like her daughter. We went to the zoo yesterday and then I took them to Tree Tops. You should've seen that girl's face when she saw the treehouse. Cassidy Rae's wasn't too far off."

"Sounds to me like you've got your hands full."

"It's weird, but I'd be ready to make things official today if she'd let me."

"Welcome to the club," Cole chuckles and slaps my shoulder once.

My eyebrows furrow. "Club?"

"The pussy-whipped club. I felt the same way about Bri, and Cash had to burst my hopes by telling me she was taken then." Cole looks down a moment. Knowing him as well as I do, he's probably sending a quick prayer for Josh. "Anyway, when you feel it, it's impossible to get rid of it."

"I've turned into Cash, haven't I?"

Cole laughs and points at me. "We all have, he was always in tune with it. I will say, I'm surprised about you. You're so straight-laced when it comes to situations like this. I don't know why. Let loose, brother, and if you want her to become your woman, make her yours."

The doorbell rings along with the meaning of Cole's words. He stands, grabbing his wallet from the console table, and gets our dinner.

Fuck. He's right. If I want Cassidy Rae to be mine, I have to make sure I prove to her how good we are together.

After dinner, I stop feeling sorry for myself and call Cassidy Rae again.

"Hey, sorry I haven't called you back," she answers, breathless.

"Is everything okay?" I hear a door close.

"Yes. No. I mean, yeah."

"What's going on?" I sit straighter on my bed, ready to go to her if I need to. "I can be there in a few."

"No, no, you stay where you are. It's not like that. Rae

woke up sick, so it's been a little busy around here between work and taking care of her. She's been attached to me since I got home this evening."

I sigh and lean back. "What does she have?"

"I think it's just a cold. No big deal, but she has some body aches, and that always makes her more needy."

"Her momma makes her feel better," I state.

"Yup." Cassidy Rae yawns. "Sorry."

"No need to be. I wanted to hear your voice, but you're tired. Get some rest in case Rae needs you at some point in the night."

"No, I'm okay. It's still early." I hear a pause and then, "Oh, maybe not that early." She stifles another yawn.

"Get rest, babe. I'll call you in the morning."

"Okay."

"Night, Caz."

"Goodnight, Jason. Thanks for calling." I smirk at her sleep-induced voice and wish I were holding her tight through the night. Cole is right; I've joined the pussy-whipped club.

Chapter 12

Cassidy Rae

THIS WEEK HAS BEEN CHAOTIC with Rae having a random cold in the middle of summer, work's picked up, and Jason has been calling. I appreciate his concerns and attention. I'm not ungrateful, but having conversations with him on the phone proves to me how much I like him. He even talked to Rae last night, since she was feeling better. She giggled the entire time and asked when she'd see him again.

She's not the only one who wants to see him again.

"Mommy," I look over at Rae, who is coloring at the small kitchen table.

"Yes, baby?"

"Are you and Jason boyfriend and girlfriend?" Her focus is on her paper, as if this conversation is as casual as asking for a glass of water.

"Ummm… no." I shake my head although she's not

looking at me.

"Why not?" Her head snaps up and her brown eyes are full of questions.

"Things don't work that way."

"But he takes you out. He plays with me. He likes us, and we like him. He's nice to us." This right here is a six-year-old's guide to relationships.

"Well, it's about more than that." A sneeze interrupts me.

"Bless you."

"Thanks. Anyway, before adults get in a serious relationship, they have to know who the person is. You know, make sure they really like them."

"Don't you really like Jason?"

"I think so. Yeah."

"So?"

"Well, we haven't really spent a lot of time together. Sure, we've gone out a couple of times, but adults need more time to talk and have adult conversations."

"Okay, so go out with him again."

"You wouldn't mind?"

"Nope." Her hands are crossed over her paper. "If that will make him your boyfriend, I want you to."

"You really are okay with Jason being in our lives." She's so smart about some things it surprises me. I guess when I was her age, I knew what a boyfriend was. To a certain extent.

"I know he's not my daddy," her eyes cast downward. "But he can kinda be like one."

I stand and walk toward her, crouching next to her and moving her body so she's facing me. "I know you wish your dad was around. I'm sorry he's not."

Rae sniffles and looks at me with thick tears in her eyes. "Oh, baby girl." I pull her to me. I have no idea how to make this right. She's too young to understand, but I know that spending time with Jason has emphasized her need for a father figure.

I hold her to me and hum in her ear. Her small hands grip my back with force. "It's okay. It seems like things with Jason are going well. Maybe he will become my boyfriend." I realize I'm saying it to comfort both her and I. I may have thought my chances of finding someone who would accept Rae and I were slim, but Jason may be the odd man who does.

Once Rae is tucked in bed for the evening, I see the message Jason sent an hour ago asking if I were free to talk. I begin to type my response and delete it. Instead, I call him. I want him to know I'm interested and being confident is attractive. It's silly to send him a text message saying I can talk just for him to call me. I put on my big girl panties and hit call on my phone.

"Hey, beautiful." His voice vibrates happiness as he answers the call.

"Hey." I curl on the couch and smile.

"How are you? How's Rae feeling?"

"We're good. She's much better. Almost one hundred percent."

"Good. Being sick sucks, I can imagine it's harder on a little kid."

"You have no idea."

"How was your day?" Jason asks. His voice is soft.

"Busy, but that means better tips." I shrug as if he were here. I wish he were. "I'm happy Rae is feeling like herself again. How was your day?"

"Good. We got asked to work on a song for the soundtrack of a new movie. We're waiting on more details, but it's a cool honor."

"That is really cool. What movie?"

"Peyton didn't tell us the title, but we know it's a war movie. We'll get more details from the music producer of the film soon."

"Well, look at you being all popular and stuff," I tease.

Jason chuckles. "People like our music."

"They should. You guys are talented," I compliment.

"Thanks. So, I was wondering if you're free tomorrow night. I want to take you out."

I sneeze before I can respond. "Bless you," Jason says. "Are you getting sick?"

"Thanks. No, it was just a sneeze." I don't have time to get sick. I sneeze again, causing Jason to go into protective mode.

"Yes, you are. I'm coming over and I'm bringing medicine and a few other things."

"You don't have to, Jason. I'm sure I have something here I can take." Truth is, I have all the medicine required for any child's sickness, but I don't buy medicine for adults. It's not often I get sick, and I do believe this is just the sniffles.

"You can argue with me, but I'm coming anyway. I'll see you in a bit, stay where you are."

Where the hell am I going to go?

I don't have a chance to respond because Jason hangs up on me. I sigh and lean into the couch. He's worried over nothing. A cold is nothing I can't deal with.

I turn on the TV and watch reruns of Friends. Thankfully, I don't need cable to watch this. It could be worse; I could have no TV and no entertainment. Internet is a luxury, and it's not like I have a computer anyway. What would I even search?

I'm half way through the second episode of Friends when Jason knocks on my door. I open to find his brows furrowed and his hands full of bags.

Laughing, I say, "You're ridiculous. You didn't have to come."

"I wanted to. You take care of Rae, but who takes care of you?" His question is full of meaning, and I stare at him, speechless. "Come on."

He walks in, setting the bags he brought on the kitchen table. "I bought cold medicine, Emergen-C, cough drops, and chicken soup."

"How much medicine did you buy?" I look through the bag.

"I didn't know exactly how bad it was, so I got enough for each symptom."

"You're insane." I shake my head. "I promise I'm okay."

"I want to take care of you. Let me." He inches closer, the plead evident in his voice.

I smile and relax. "Thank you. I do appreciate it." It will take some getting used to, having someone around to take care of me.

"Now, what do you want to drink first?"

"How about Emergen-C since the only symptom I have is a sneeze. It will help build my immune system."

Jason nods as I grab a glass of water and empty the vitamin into it. "Do you want something to drink?"

"Water would be great."

Cups in hand, we sit on the couch. I cringe a little when I drink the liquid and Jason laughs.

"It's not that bad."

"I hate taking any sort of medicine, even if it is a vitamin."

"Well, I want you healthy." He pulls me into him with his arm around my shoulder. I relax, placing my head on the crook of his neck. He's comfortable. He's what I would imagine my future looking like, minus the famous status.

I exhale. "Thank you for coming." The only bad thing about this cold is I can't visit my parents until Rae and I are both completely healthy.

"You're welcome." Jason kisses the top of my head. I have no idea what he's thinking, but by the way he's holding me, I can assume his thoughts are similar to mine. I briefly know what happened with his ex-girlfriend, and I can take away from that conversation that he isn't one to succumb to games. I'm glad about that, because with Rae in my life, games are a hard limit.

We stay like this for a bit, silence surrounding us except for the beating of our hearts. I could get used to this—always having Jason around.

"I guess if you're sick, tomorrow night would be a no-go." Jason's fingers tickle my arm as he runs them over my skin. I shiver as my skin becomes covered in goosebumps.

"You act as if I'm dying." I peek up at him.

"Don't joke that way." The panic in his voice makes me laugh and warms my heart. I sit up and look at him. I hold his face and stare into those blue orbs I love.

"It's a measly cold. What did you have in mind?"

"I wanted to cook dinner for you at my place." I tense for a moment. "Don't worry, that's not code word for Netflix and chill." I raise my eyebrows, confused. "You know, Netflix and *chill.* Never mind." Jason shakes his head.

"No, now I want to know."

"What I'm saying is nothing has to happen just because I want you to come over. I want to spend time with you, and I hope my cooking skills sway you more in the direction of team Jason."

I laugh at his big puppy dog eyes. "I can handle that. I'd just want to double check with Abigail and make sure she can watch Rae."

"You let me know." He leans in and kisses my lips. Before he can pull away, my hands reach around the back of his head, and I kiss him back. It's a TV appropriate kiss, but it's more satisfying than the soft peck.

Jason grins with an arched brow. I smile as a blush creeps up my neck. I've always hated that I turn pink immediately. Jason rubs his thumb against my cheek saying, "So beautiful." He gives me a peck on the lips. Now I'm sure my smile is matching his.

"Cole is moving in with Bri. He told me today."

"That's good, right?" I tilt my head and look up at him.

"It is. I'm happy for them. We had an agreement that if either of us wanted to move, the other could take over the ownership or sell."

"What are you going to do?" My eyes wander across his face for any signs of an answer.

"I love my house. I'm not moving." He pulls me closer.

"Tell me about your friends," I request.

"Well, you know about Cole and Bri. Cash and Olivia have been married for a few years. I'm sure you know that. Honestly, they're some of the best people I know. Ryder is inappropriate at times, but his wife is equally inappropriate, so they work."

"Sounds like a great group of friends." I yawn and wiggle closer to Jason.

He chuckles and holds me tighter. "They are."

"Thank you again so much, Abby." I hug her. "I owe you."

"You don't owe me anything. Have fun tonight," she winks.

I bend down to give Rae a hug and kiss. "See ya later." I pull her in tightly.

"Have fun, Mommy."

"I will, baby. Behave and listen to what Abby and Blake say, okay?" I know she will, but it's the mandatory parent speech. She was so excited when I told her this morning I was going out with Jason. Our talk yesterday afternoon helped clear the air.

I give her one last hug and kiss before walking back to my house. Jason should be here soon to pick me up. I won't tell him, but I woke up feeling a little sick, so I've moved up to cold medicine instead of vitamins only. He'd probably cancel our plans if he knew, and I want to see him. Last night was nice. It was… I'm not sure I have a word for it, but I wanted more of that feeling.

Back at my place, I make sure I have what I need in my purse and check the time. I scheduled my medicine intake so that I would be able to take another dose right before our date.

I finish drinking my water as a knock vibrates around my home. It's odd he drove this way to pick me up to go back to his house, but there's also a romantic feel to it.

"Hi," Jason looks at me with appreciation when I open the door. I'm not sure why. My outfit is simple—jeans, a faux silk black tank, and black sandals.

"Hey." I smile and hold in my sneeze. I know you're not supposed to, but sneezing right now would break this greeting.

"Gorgeous," Jason whispers and leans in to kiss my cheek. "Is Rae already over at Abigail's?" I love that he asks.

"I dropped her off a little while ago."

"Was she upset or okay?"

"She's okay. We actually had a conversation yesterday afternoon, which helped her to kinda understand this dynamic."

Jason nods. "Ready to go then?"

When he pulls up to his house, I try not to stare. It's beautiful, though. The porch is big, leading up to it are three brick steps. The cream siding gives it an airy feel from the outside. Despite being a famous musician, the home is relatively modest. I was expecting bigger and flashier, although after getting to know Jason, I should know better than to think that.

"It's a beautiful house," I tell him as he opens my door.

"Thank you. We didn't need much when we were looking to buy. This place has everything we need, plus I love the amount of land we have. I hate having neighbors so close to me.

I look around, taking in the surrounding area as the sun sets. It's probably about an acre of land in total. The front driveway has a decent amount of space, but I'm guessing most of the land is in the back.

As soon as Jason opens the door for me, the smell of garlic and herbs hits me. If he wanted to impress me with his cooking, he's off to a great start. He holds my hand as he leads me further into his house. I look around, taking it all in. It's modern, yet cozy, with warm tones. This is definitely not what I was expecting.

"Do you want the tour now or after we eat?" Jason interrupts my observation.

"Either way. Smells good."

"Thanks. It's almost ready. I'm making chicken in a creamed herb sauce and mashed potatoes. The chicken is cooked and so are the mashed potatoes. I'll just need to warm up the potatoes and make the cream sauce."

"That sounds great." We walk into his kitchen. Granite countertops and stainless-steel appliances adorn it, but what catches my eye is the plate setting. He already has everything set up on the kitchen bar that extends like a peninsula. He even used place mats, and a candle and vase of flowers are set in the center.

"Wow," I whisper. This is a first for me.

"Do you like it?" He hugs me from behind.

I nod. "It's beautiful."

"I'm glad you think so." He kisses my cheek and turns on the candle. "Take a seat and I'll make the sauce. I have white wine chilled, and red in the wine fridge. Which do you prefer?"

"White would be great." I sit on the stool, in awe of the trouble he's going through for a dinner. Is this what people do on dates? Maybe it's not trouble to him.

Jason winks as he serves me a glass of wine. With the medicine I'm drinking, I should limit myself to this one glass.

He cooks, and I watch him. When I asked if he needed help he shook his head and told me to stay put. We talk about everything, including where I grew up. I've opened up to him, feeling as if I can trust him with anything.

As I stare at the setting on the counter, I take in the details. The plates are ceramic, not paper, the silverware is also real, and there's even a spoon for dessert. He's thought of everything, and the food smells delicious.

"Who taught you to cook?"

"We grew up helping my momma in the kitchen. She always made it a family event. My sisters and I would fight about who would make what, but being the oldest usually helped in getting the fun responsibilities, like chopping."

"That sounds like fun." My mom and I used to bake when I was younger, but once she got sick that ended. It's why I like to involve Rae in the kitchen and love when she says she wants to bake for a living. It brings back memories.

"Do you like cooking? I mean, I've seen you cook, but do you enjoy it?"

"I do. I was just remembering when my mom and I used to bake when I was a child. I try to keep that going with Rae. She loves being a part of our meal preps. She even has a step-stool, so she can reach the countertop."

"I think it's great you implement your own memories into her upbringing. How's your mom?"

"My dad says she's okay. He always says that. I told him once Rae and I got over our cold we'd go visit. It's been longer than usual between visits." My mom has outlived the original span they gave her when she was diagnosed. She's going on ten years, and every time I call my dad I dread hearing him say she's worsened.

"That's a good idea. I'm sure your dad would love to see the both of you. Although your mom may not recognize you or her, I'm sure somewhere inside she'd feel your presence."

My stomach grumbles as I inhale the smell coming

from the stove. Whatever Jason is putting in that sauce must taste as good as it smells. I watch as he stirs the pot, adding ingredients. His confidence spreads through the kitchen as he moves with ease and knowingness.

"Dinner is almost ready. Do you want another glass of wine?"

"I'm okay for now. Still got some in here." I raise my glass to show him. When he frowns, I say, "I'm taking it slow since I took some of the medicine you brought me."

"Are you feeling worse?"

"No, no," I fib. "More as preventative care."

Jason squints his eyes as he scans my face. "If you say so, but I'll take you home at any time if you feel sick."

I tilt my head and look at him. "I'm okay. I want to be here." He groans and tilts his head back.

"I want you here." He stands on the opposite side of the counter, leaning into it as his hands hold the edge. That one sentence expresses more meaning, but I don't dwell on it. We're starting off, and we have time for everything else a relationship entails.

Is it crazy of me to envision Rae and I here, with him, living as a family? It totally is. I drink the contents of my glass and Jason lifts his brows in my direction.

"Thirsty," I shrug.

He turns to the stove with a proud smile and flips the chicken breasts, pouring some of the sauce over them. "This is ready." Jason plates the chicken and mashed potatoes, drizzling sauce over them. He moves around the peninsula and takes the stool next to mine, refilling both of our glasses with white wine.

"Cheers," he raises his glass. "To the gorgeous woman sitting with me tonight and that I get lucky enough to have more nights like this."

"Cheers." He's such a sap, but the romantic in me chewed it all up.

I take a bit of the chicken, savoring all the flavors. "This is delicious, Jason."

"Thanks. I'm glad you like it. It's one of my favorite recipes."

The flavors in the food pop with each bite I take. This is by far one of the best meals I've ever had.

"Which is your favorite recipe?" I ask him, curious about the extent of his cooking skills, although this is impressive.

"Actually, my favorite thing to do is grill. There's not much to it, but I enjoy the whole process."

"My favorite thing to cook is chicken Alfredo. I love the creaminess of homemade Alfredo sauce."

"I make a mean Alfredo sauce. Next time you come over, we'll cook that."

I envision Jason and I cooking in the kitchen together like a real couple. A more intimate couple.

When we finish eating, Jason clears the setting without letting me help. He said I'm a guest in his home and he's trying to woo me. Little does he know I'm beyond wooed. Never has anyone done something like this.

"I confess, I didn't make dessert. This is store bought, but I can guarantee it's as good as homemade." He pulls out a foil container from the warming drawer. "Peach cobbler."

"Oh."

He frowns. "You don't like peach cobbler?"

"I'm allergic to peach." I bite down my lip.

"What? Shit, I should've asked before. I just didn't think… I've never met anyone allergic to peach." His hand attacks his hair as he speaks. When he looks up at me, my attempt to bite back my smile fails. "You're shitting me, aren't you?"

I throw my head back and laugh. "You… should've seen… oh my God, that was funny." I gasp for air.

He stalks toward me and turns my stool. "Funny?"

I wipe tears from my eyes and look at him. "So funny."

"I thought I had screwed up the entire evening."

I drape my arms around his neck. "Even if I were allergic, this is still the sweetest thing anyone has ever done for me. Thank you, Jason."

"Sweeter than peach cobbler?"

"So much sweeter." He leans down and kisses me, careful at first until I sigh, opening my mouth. His tongue sweeps mine, and I lean into him.

"Let's have dessert," his voice is hoarse.

"I do love peach cobbler," I tell him.

"I freaked."

"So much." I laugh again. Being here tonight has been a salvation. I'm free to be the person I was, the person I thought I could no longer be because I am a mom now.

Chapter 13

Jason

I STARE AT THE WOMAN next to me, her braid a little mussed from leaning her head against the couch. She let me pick the movie, but my attention is fully on her. I couldn't care less about the jokes the actors are saying. Instead, I admire her laugh as she shifts on the sofa, getting more comfortable. I want to pull her closer to me, hold her and make her feel cherished.

As soon as she walked into my house, I could picture her and Rae here, spending Sundays with me, grilling out in the yard. I know her life hasn't been ideal, and I noticed how she looked around my house. It's modest, considering my income, but it's fancier than she's used to. As I gave her a tour after dinner, she commented on the decor and expressed her amazement at how tied together it all looks considering we are guys.

I wanted to offer her the entire space for her to do with what she wants. Clearly, I'm insane when it comes to this woman.

I smile to myself as she snorts at something the woman in the movie says. Cassidy Rae covers her mouth and looks at me. I kiss her cheek and grin. "You're adorable."

"That's embarrassing," she says.

"Don't be. I love to hear you laugh." I take advantage and pull her into my side.

She shifts her head on my shoulder until she's comfortable.

"Are you watching the movie?" She looks up at me.

"I rather look at you."

"Smooth," she teases. Cassidy Rae leans up and turns to me. "Do you want to watch something else?"

"This is perfect." I hold her hand.

"I don't mind." Her smile is easy. Being with her is easy. Cassidy Rae is Sunday mornings when I've been stuck in an endless cycle of crappy Saturday nights. She's the woman I want in my life permanently.

"Let's talk," I suggest. Movies can be replayed, but time like this can't.

"I feel as if I don't have much to tell because my life has been exactly how you see it for the past few years."

"I want to know who you are beyond that stuff. What's your favorite movie?"

"Umm…" she pauses and looks up at my ceiling. "I'm not a big movie fan," she shrugs.

"What?" My eyes grow big. I wave at my movie collection. "We have to find a favorite movie for you." Movie buff or not, everyone has to have a favorite movie.

"I'm more of a TV show person. Friends, Big Bang Theory, stuff like that. I used to watch, like, silly romance movies a long time ago, but nothing worth mentioning."

I shake my head. "I'm on a mission now. What kind of storylines do you like? Romantic? Comedy? Horror?" I wouldn't mind showing her a horror film so she scoots real close to me and I can hold her.

"No horror," she shakes her head, her big, green eyes begging me. "Romantic or comedy. I can't deal with the anxiety of a horror film."

"And here I thought I'd be able to hold you through a scary movie."

She smirks and rolls her eyes. The more time we spend together, the more I see the woman in Cassidy Rae. She exposes her, almost as if she's remembering who she is and becoming her again.

"I like you, Jason." Her expression is serious. I lean in and kiss her, showing her how I feel, instead of telling her.

"I like you, too, Cassidy Rae. A whole lot." I touch her lips with mine again. I'm impatient. I want to move time forward, to a place where she and I have known each other longer. I want forever with this woman that I've just recently met, and I don't understand how or why. The craziest part is that I don't even care that it's fast. The usually measured man is wiping his ass with the rules and diving head first into a romance with a single mom, and fuck if I don't want to drown in her.

I tug her braid and she looks at me, a brow arched. I grab her hands from her lap and kiss her fingertips.

"What do I need to do to make you officially mine?"

Her eyes soften, and her shoulders relax. "Yours?"

"My girl. I want you in my life more than a few dates and phone calls. I'm working hard to prove to you I'll take care of you and Rae. I want a real chance at us." I feel like a teen all over again, asking the girl I like to be my girlfriend.

"Okay."

"Seriously? You don't want to think about it or talk to Rae?" I sound like an idiot.

"Rae and I have already spoken about it. She actually asked me yesterday if you were my boyfriend."

"She's too smart for her age."

"I know," Cassidy Rae shakes her head.

"So, we makin' this official?" I drawl. As soon as Cassidy Rae smiles and nods, I cradle her face and kiss her hard, tumbling onto her. She lets out a loud laugh as I crush my lips on hers.

I've totally turned into a pussy-whipped guy like my friends, and she's so worth it.

Cassidy Rae grips the back of my shirt, her laugh intensifying as my lips move to her cheeks, neck, and then back to her lips. My breathing is labored as I stare down at her, her eyes bright.

"My cheeks hurt." She tries to relax them, but the smile covering her face is more powerful. I love seeing her like this.

"You proved me wrong," her voice is barely above a whisper.

"How's that?" I lean up enough so that my weight isn't on her, but she's still caged beneath me.

"You showed me fairytales do exist." She looks to her right as much as she can. "No one has ever prepared a dinner like that for me or cared about me and Rae this much. We have our few friends, but this is different." Her hand touches my cheek and I close my eyes. I grab her hand and kiss her palm.

"We've got our own southern fairytale." I wink. I kiss her hard one more time before lifting myself off of her.

The movie long forgotten, Cassidy Rae and I talk until

I need to take her back home.

I woke up feeling sick after our date last night. Thankfully, we're not performing at Riot tonight. I wanted to spend another day with Cassidy Rae, but when I called her she sounded about as bad as I do. So I do what any kind and caring boyfriend would do, I pick up lunch and head to her place.

I knock on the door and wait for her to answer. I can hear Rae calling my name from inside and grin.

"Hey." I look at Cassidy Rae–red nose, messy hair, and a fist full of tissues.

"Hey, babe." I kiss her cheek.

"You didn't have to come. You should be home resting." Her eyes travel all over my face. "How do you still look handsome while sick?"

I chuckle, which ends in a cough. "You're gorgeous, no matter what."

"Hi, Jason!" Rae shouts.

I lean back. "Hey, kiddo. How are you?"

"Good. My mommy's sick, though. She said you were, too."

"Yeah. I woke up feeling under the weather today. I brought lunch, though. Chicken nuggets and mac and cheese for the best girl I know," I hold up a paper bag. "And freshly made chicken soup for your mom and me."

"Thank you," Cassidy Rae smiles. I help her set the table and we eat. Sick or not, I'd rather be here than anywhere else. Rae tells us about what she learned on a TV show she watched last night at Abigail's house and all the arts and crafts they did.

"After we eat, I'll show you some of it," she says,

enjoying her lunch. I look over at Cassidy Rae. Her eyes are sunken and barely staying open.

"Was Joyce okay with you not going to work?" I ask, knowing missing work is difficult for her.

"Yeah. She told me to take the weekend off, so I can recuperate."

"Hey, it's okay." I reach for her hand when she frowns.

"Yeah, I hope so."

"Caz, whatever support you need, I'm here for you and Rae."

Shaking her head, she says, "No, Jason. It's not your job to be in charge of our finances. We'll be okay. Fortunately, the summer's been busier, so the tips have been better."

"I know it's not my job, and I'm not saying I'll take away your freedom, but I'm here for you." This isn't about money. She may not realize it, but me buying them lunch helps with her finances. This is about her knowing she's not alone. She has me to be a partner with her.

"Thank you." She nods and goes back to her lunch.

Once we're done eating and the table is clean, Rae shows me her arts and crafts as I sit on the couch with Cassidy Rae, a box of tissues between us.

"Hey," I whisper. Cassidy Rae looks at me with raised eyebrows. "Get over here." I hold the box of tissues with one hand and lift my other so she can curl into me.

"Are you okay? Besides the whole being sick thing?" I ask her once she's settled.

"Yeah." She nods once.

"They say when you lie, your nose grows," I tease and she giggles, pushing her hand against my chest.

"I don't want you to get too much in your head about what I said while we were eating. I wasn't talking about money. I want you to know you can count on me and talk to me about anything. You're not alone, and you don't have to deal with things alone." We may not have known each other for a long time, but there's no doubt in my mind that I will do anything for her and Rae. I want her to trust me.

"Thank you." Cassidy Rae kisses my jaw. We sit like this for a bit, Rae humming from her favorite spot on the floor in front of us as she colors.

Cassidy Rae hugs my arm to her as I move my fingers around her shoulder with my other hand. It's perfection, despite the sore throat and runny nose.

"Can you sing us a song, Jason?" Rae looks up at me.

"Sure. It might sound a little funky today." I clear my throat and choose one of our older songs, something more upbeat.

I sit up on the couch, keeping hold of Cassidy Rae's hand, and begin to sing.

Open road, windows down,
Don't need 'nything else
but you by my side,
Singing along to my radio,
Holding my hand in yours

Swimming in asphalt
And drownin' in you,
I've got nowhere to be,
I've got all I need
Driving with you

I catch myself strumming my fingers, as if I had a

guitar. Old habits are hard to break. Mid verse, Rae stands and begins to dance. I chuckle, but stay on beat.

I look over at Cassidy Rae and wink as I sing the words to her. Half way through, I mix it up and transition to another song of ours—smoother and slower. Rae continues to dance, causing Cassidy Rae to giggle and look between her and me, her eyes gentle.

I stand and put my hand out for Cassidy Rae to take it. She takes her time to stand, and I dance with her, still singing.

You're sunshine and honey,
You're whiskey on my lips,
Warm and sweet
You're a slow-down ride
And back road trail,
Getting lost in evergreen

I twirl her around, and before she can come back to me, Rae has taken her free hand. Spying her other hand, I hold it and the three of us dance.

I start coughing as I drag on the ending of the song. "Whoa."

"Okay, maybe we should rest." Cassidy Rae looks as if she reached her dancing limit as well.

We sit back down, Rae humming to the beat she heard me sing.

Spending the weekend with Caz and Rae was great. I'd get sick all over again to have Cassidy Rae in my arms. We're going to dinner tonight, the three of us, when we're done working in Cash's house.

"Are you in a hurry?" Ryder asks.

"Kinda." I look at my watch again.

"You taking the lady out?"

"We're going to dinner."

"You two, or her daughter as well?" Cash inquires.

"The three of us." This is a like a spitfire round of questions.

"So are things serious?"

"They're getting there. If you're asking if we've made it official, we have."

"Good for you," Cash smiles.

"When can we meet her?" This from Cole.

"Not yet. She takes a little to warm up to people, and I want to focus on us before all of you bombard her and Rae." First, I'm going to take my sweet time falling for Cassidy Rae and making sure she falls for me, and then I'll introduce her to my friends. I want her to see the potential we have, as a couple and a family. It's unorthodox, me thinking of us as a family, but that's what Rae and her have.

I'm bulldozing my way into their nucleus, and I'll be grateful when they finally welcome me wholeheartedly. Rae already has. She has been comfortable around me from the beginning, and I've seen how she's shy around some strangers.

My ringtone interrupts the conversation. When I see Cassidy Rae's name on my screen, I smile and move away from the guys.

"Hey, gorgeous."

"Hi, I hate to do this, but I'm going to have to cancel dinner."

"Is everything okay?" Her voice is panicked.

"I need to go see my parents. My dad called. Mom's not doing well."

"I'll pick you up."

"You don't have to." Her voice shakes.

"Are you home? Don't you dare move until I get there. I'm driving you."

"I'm home," she mumbles.

"Listen to me, baby, everything will be okay. I'll take you over there, and I'll pick you up when you're ready." Once she agrees, I hang up and tell the guys I need to go.

Chapter 14

Cassidy Rae

I PACE THE SMALL SPACE in front of the television. As soon as I saw my dad's name pop up on my screen, I knew something was wrong. Although Jason insisted on driving me, I'm not sure if I want him to. I'm so overwhelmed that I'm becoming numb.

"Mommy," I hear Rae say, but don't respond. "Mommy?" Her voice is far away. "Mom."

"What?" I yell and turn to her, one hand flying in the air.

Big tears well up in her eyes. She tries to hold them back, but they roll down her red cheeks.

"God. I'm so sorry, baby girl." I drop to my knees in front of her. I hold her face, kiss her forehead, and pull her into me. She settles on my lap as I hug her, my own tears threatening to spill.

"Are you sad?" Rae looks at me with the paths of her

tears still covering her face.

"I'm sorry I yelled at you. Yes, I'm sad. I'm worried about Grandma."

"It will be okay." Her small fingers tickle my cheek.

"I love you, baby."

"I love you, too, Mommy."

I run my hands down Rae's hair, soothing her. She's always the one that calms me, though. Her love is something I never understood or thought I'd experience. There are no words to label what a mother's love is like.

"Jason's here," I whisper. "Are you ready?"

"Yeah. I wanna see Grandma and Grandpa." I trace her jaw.

"I want you to remember that Grandma is very sick." I feel the need to remind her, since I have no idea what condition we'll find her in.

"Okay."

As soon as I open then door, Jason wraps me in his arms. With his scent enveloping me, I cry.

"Shhh…" He rubs my back. "It's okay." He kisses below my ear, my temple, and the crown of my head, his lips landing where they can.

I squeeze him tighter, and feel when he removes one arm, only to have a little body pushed into me. Rae holds my hand that's wrapped around Jason's back.

I stare out the window as we drive in silence. The mood in the vehicle is somber, an air of uncertainty–different reasons for the three of us. Rae hasn't said much after seeing me so upset, but I know she's nervous. She has this need to take care of people. Sometimes I think she forgets she's a child, especially when we're at my parents' house.

Then, Jason is driving next to me with a tick in his jaw. He hasn't said anything since we got in the car and I gave him the address to my parents' house. The tension is there, and if I know him at all, I'd say he's struggling with how to make this right. It's something out of his element, and one thing I've learned about Jason Stone is that he likes having a handle on situations. He's said it in the past, pursuing me is one of the most spontaneous things he's done. I'm sure joining the band comes first.

As for me, I'm all over the place. I keep thinking how things would be different if I had never left. Then, I remember the challenges of a newborn and the confusion it could've caused my mom and realize I did what I thought was best at the time. It doesn't wash away the guilt, though. At this moment, the fire of guilt has been lit and intensified with lighter fluid. I'm burning in it.

I tense when Jason pulls into my childhood neighborhood. How will I find her? How will my dad be? He tends to take all the stress on himself, rarely allowing someone else to take the load off him. If I know him, he hasn't slept.

"It's that house on the left." I point to the house with faded beige siding and an unkempt front lawn. The ground is dry and brown on both sides of the driveway.

My heart stammers, my breathing falters, and I feel like I'm going to have a panic attack. I lean my head back and gasp for air, one hand on my chest. Jason puts his hand on my knee.

"Breathe, Caz." I nod, trying to do as he says. The air fills my lungs in short spurts, enough to keep my heart beating, but it's not enough for me to relax.

"Hey." Jason's eyes are full of worry. He gets out of the car and comes to my side, opening the door and undoing my seatbelt. He turns my body to him, forcing my feet to land on the driveway.

Squatting before me, he pulls me into a hug, a hand rubbing my back. I grip onto him, afraid of what letting go will lead me to.

I finally inhale a deep breath. I go for a second one, taking in as much oxygen as I can get. I'm greedy to the air that keeps me alive.

"Cassidy Rae?" I look up at my dad with tears in my eyes.

"It's okay," Jason whispers.

I move away from his hug and run to my dad. I look back at Rae, still buckled into her seat, stunned silence overtaking her. Slow tears trail down my face.

"Cassidy Rae." My dad's voice cracks, feeling like a sucker punch.

"Hi, Dad," I choke out.

"I'm so glad you're here." His voice is thick with emotion. I nod, the cry moving inside me on a jagged breath. My chest vibrates with the incoming assault of tears.

My dad hugs me back, and the tiny bit of control I was clinging onto evaporates with the fire of the guilt burning holes through me.

I wipe my cheeks with the back of my hands when I feel Jason and Rae behind me. My dad looks over at them, a soft smile.

"Hey, Grandpa."

"Hi, sweetie." He hugs Rae when she reaches for him. "How you doing?"

"I'm okay. We're a little sad 'cause Grandma's sick."

"I'm a little sad, too, but she'll be happy to see you."

"She will?" Her eyes look up at him in surprise.

"Of course." Rae stands back and peeks into the house before walking in.

"Dad, this is Jason. Jason, this is my dad." I finally introduce them.

"It's nice to meet you, Mr. Pressman." Jason extends his hand.

"Nice to meet you, young man. Why don't y'all come in? I've probably been out here longer than I should." The meaning of his words puts the purpose of our visit back as the focus.

"I'm going to go." Jason squeezes my arm. "It was great meeting you," he nods to my dad and shakes his hand again.

Jason turns to me. "Call me. Doesn't matter what time it is." He kisses my cheek.

With Jason gone, the weight of this day crushes me. I follow my dad into the house. Everything has always remained the same as it was when I moved seven years ago. The cherry coffee table sits in front of the television with the old green couch opposite it. Frames full of memories sprinkle the home, just like when I was a kid.

"Looks like someone already found her Grandma." My dad's voice is light. He looks at me with a smile and reassuring nod. Rae is sitting next to my mom in the kitchen, telling her about our trip to the zoo.

I halt as soon as I see my mom. I swallow down a cry and stare. The woman, who was always put together no matter her age, now sits in a nightgown with her hair matted to her. She looks more worn than I imagined.

Empty eyes look through me.

"Hi," I whisper and kiss her cheek as I take a seat at the table next to her. Rae smiles.

"I'm telling Grandma about Jason. I think she'd like him. Did you like him, Grandpa?"

"He seems like a nice man," my dad nods.

"Hi, Mom." She looks beyond me before turning to her face on me. I think I see a glimmer of recognition, but it may be wishful thinking. She slants her head and stares. I look at my dad, who continues to encourage me.

Silent tears stain my face. I listen to this little girl, who is my entire world, speak to her grandma as if all was right in the world. My mom looks at Rae and grins. My head snaps to look at my dad, whose face is beaming. I don't remember the last time I saw her smile.

I exhale and listen as Rae continues to talk to my mom. She's silent, but slight expressions occur.

"I'm going to prepare supper. You'll stay, right?" My dad looks at us.

"I lost track of time. Do you want to stay for dinner?" I ask Rae.

"Yes!"

I smile at her excitement and look at my dad. "I'll call Jason to let him know we're okay."

"You do that, and Rae and I will start getting everything ready. Want to be my chef helper today?" My dad looks at Rae.

"Duh," she shakes her head, and the both of us laugh at her sassiness.

After I talk to Jason, I join them in the kitchen.

Dinner is quiet. Rae does most of the talking as usual. I can't stop looking at my mom. She's frail.

After dinner, my dad sets my mom in their room and comes back into the kitchen. The muffled sound of the show Rae is watching in the living room mixes with the gurgling coffee maker as it brews. Rae has been so patient and well-behaved, she deserves a million cookies.

Smiling at how amazing my girl is, I inhale the soothing aroma and fill two mugs.

"Hey." I fold my hands on the table.

"I am so happy you're here." My dad takes a seat, lines of worry a clear sign on his face of the years that have passed.

"What's going on, Dad?" I tuck my lips into my mouth and bite on them to prevent from crying.

"She had a decline. The doctor said it was normal, considering the circumstances. I called you right away."

"What can I do to help?" I sip my coffee, waiting for his response. The warm bitterness brings pause to my galloping heart.

"Being here helps, sweetheart. Thank you for coming."

"Of course, Dad. I'm sorry we couldn't make it earlier. I didn't want mom to catch our cold. Now that I see her, I wish we had." The image of my mom staring motionless when I walked in fills my mind. Although she wasn't exactly active a few weeks ago, she at least fed herself.

"It's okay, sweetie. I think it was a good decision to wait." He reaches for my hand and squeezes.

"Hey, no tears. This is a happy day. I have you and Rae here. That girl is something else."

"She really is," I agree. "How bad is mom's condition?" I dare ask.

"The doctor suggested hospice, but…" He shakes his head, looking at an invisible spot on the table.

"I know, Dad." I reach over and hold the top of his hand.

"Since she can no longer move without assistance, they say having someone to care for her is best. Hey, no frowning allowed in this house." I think back to all the times growing up he made sure I'd be happy instead of upset. Whether it was something at school, at home, or simply hormones, my father always made it his job to make me smile.

"I'm sorry." I look down, my emotions high-strung.

"Listen to me, you did what you had to do for you and your girl. And you come to see us as often as you can. You didn't leave us, you moved on with your life like any child would do." My father reads the guilt on my face.

I nod. I know he's right. I visit as often as I can, we talk almost daily, but it still hurts. "I can move back in, find a job near here and help you. It has to be exhausting. With how I see her today, you can't do it all alone."

"Your mother is the love of my life. When we said our vows, we promised in sickness and in health. I never once doubted my role in her life, illness and all. She gave me you, my greatest gift. I do it because my love for her is stronger than my moments of grief."

Hearing him speak makes me realize how strong their love is. Truth is, my mother did have spurts of aggression around the time I got pregnant. Once, she almost knocked me over because I wouldn't allow her to leave the house alone. Memories like that overshadowed the good when I realized I was bringing a baby into this world.

As I sit in the kitchen, the Formica counters identical to when I was young, I remember it all—the good, the bad, the difficult. I'm grateful my mom was able to experience my high school graduation, but soon after the symptoms became more noticeable.

"How long does she have?"

My dad shakes his head. "Time will tell. She sits on the wheelchair because I move her, but if not, she'd be bed ridden."

The lines in my dad's face are more pronounced. Not only is he older, but the stress of caretaker has woven its way into his body, wearing him down.

"Mommy?" I look to the entrance of the kitchen. Rae's eyes are small and her hair disheveled.

"Come here, baby girl." I open my arms to her, waiting to embrace her and sit her on my lap. "I was just talkin' to Grandpa."

She snuggles into me and smiles at him, her eyes heavy.

"Do you want to go? I can call Jason."

"It's late. You're welcome to stay. Your room is there for the two of you." I check the time and realize it's much later than I imagined. Jason must be losing his mind.

"Do you want to stay?" I ask Rae. She responds by tightening her arms around my neck and cuddling deeper into me.

"We'll stay. I'll have to call Jason and let him know. My phone's been in my purse, and he's probably worried."

"I'll get a fresh pair of sheets set up and you can call him."

"I'll get it. Get some sleep, Dad. We'll figure the rest out tomorrow."

He smiles and says goodnight.

I carry Rae and grab my purse from the living room. I somehow grab the sheets as well on the way to my old room. Opening the door is like being hit with a tidal wave of the past.

I set Rae down and get to making the bed. Then, I look through the drawers. I still have clothes here. I find a small shirt and change Rae. It's still too big for her, but it's better than nothing.

I lay her down, running my hand down her back. "Are

you okay here a minute?"

"I think so."

"I'm just going to run down and make sure Grandpa got to bed. Okay?"

"Mmhmm. And call Jason," she mumbles. I kiss my sweet girl on the forehead and go back into the kitchen.

"Dad, go to bed. I'll clean that in the morning." I grab the soapy dish from his hand and rinse it, handing him the dish towel.

"I like doing this."

"Then do it in the morning. It's late, and you need to rest. Please," I plead.

"Okay, okay." I make sure he goes into his bedroom before closing the door to my room.

I scavenge through my purse, finding my phone. I have a few missed calls from Jason and text messages. I call him back and wait for him to answer, hoping he's still awake. I need to hear his voice.

It's surreal how quickly you become accustomed to someone. A month ago, Jason was a stranger. However, I know how easily a stranger can become much more. I look at Rae.

"Hello?" Jason clears his throat.

"Hey." My heart thumps.

"How are you?" He becomes more alert.

"You were sleeping."

"No, I'm okay."

I giggle. "Yeah right."

"Do you want me to come get you?"

"I'm going to stay the night here. Rae's asleep," I whisper.

"How was it?"

"Intense. Overwhelming. Emotional. Too many different things," my voice falters.

"Hey, it's okay," Jason soothes. Is it crazy to miss him? Tonight, I wish we were back on the couch, snuggled together.

"It's difficult seeing her like this." I tell Jason every detail about our afternoon and evening.

"I don't know what to do. How can I help them? I told my dad I'd move back in if that helps, but…" What happens if I move back here? Besides losing my job and the only home Rae knows, I'll be further away from Jason. Will I have time to see him? Will our schedules work out? Then again, how long does my mom have to live?

"Baby, everything is going to work out. Don't worry about me. You and I are here for the long haul. If you want to move back there, I'll support you. It's the same county, it's not like you're moving across the world, and even then, we'd make it work."

I lean back on the bed, lying down, careful not to wake Rae. "I wish you were here. I could use a Jason hug."

"I'll give you as many hugs as you want."

"Is it crazy to say I miss you?" I place the phone between the pillow and my ear.

"I miss you, too. We had a whole weekend together, you get used to that kinda bonding. It's not every day I spend a weekend sick with a woman," he teases.

Jason and I talk for a while, until I'm mumbling nonsense and he makes me hang up with a promise of seeing me tomorrow. I sleep, holding my daughter, and dream of the past.

Chapter 15

Cassidy Rae

My fingers stroke Rae's hair as she sleeps. I've been awake for some time, but I haven't had the courage to get up from this bed. I spent the first moments after waking up looking around this room. My eyes wander to picture frames holding snapshots of my life and the jewelry box I've had since I was a little girl. The dolls I kept stare at me as if shaking the memory of who I am from their empty heads. The books I loved as a child and teen are collecting dust in the corner shelf.

When my stroll down memory lane overwhelms me, I take comfort in holding Rae. She's the reason I am where I am in my life, and she is worth the tears, worry, and days of uncertainty. Thanks to her, I truly met Jason. She may only be six, but this tiny girl is more powerful than anything else in this world.

Her body shakes as she moves closer to me. Her dark

blonde hair is a mess atop her peacefully sleeping face. Her small hands hug me as she mumbles something in her sleep.

Sleep did not bring the clarity I was hoping for this morning. My mom's condition is far worse than I imagined. I'm glad my dad is here all day to help her, but it can't be easy. He must not have a moment to rest, and his age requires that.

We can move here, or I can work fewer hours and be here on certain days to help. My concerns about the move are for Rae. She had a great school year, and although it's summer, I'm not sure how long we would be here for.

Through research, I know the actual illness won't kill her, but complications due to it can.

"Hey," I whisper when Rae grumbles and stretches. "Did you sleep okay?"

"Yeah." She brushes the hair from her face and sits up. Her eyes do their own inspection of the space. She gets out of bed and walks around. Rae sits on the chair at my desk and smiles at me. "I like your desk."

"My dad built me that desk one weekend and we stained the wood, so it would match my dresser." I point to the wall adjacent to it. That weekend was DIY weekend. We built the desk and I helped him fix a few things around the house while my mom baked apple pie.

Rae grabs one of the frames and stares at it. I walk to where she is. Although we've visited since she was a baby, my main focus has always been to help my dad and care for my mom. We never make time to come in here and talk about my life.

"That was my high school graduation."

"Grandma and Grandpa look so different here." I smile sadly. She's only ever known my mom as a sick person.

"This was ten years ago. They were a lot younger, and Grandma wasn't so sick then."

"Oh." She places the frame where it was and turns in the chair, kneeling so she can face the backrest. "What are those?"

"They're a few ribbons from when I played volleyball in high school. Nothing special."

"They look special." Her wide eyes look up at me, pride shining in them.

I show her everything in my room—pictures of friends, clothes, decorations, and the dolls. I tell her everything that is tied to those items. This is a part of her momma she's never seen before.

"Are you sad you left here?"

"Yes and no. I've missed my parents a lot, but I needed to start a new chapter in my life that included you."

"And we wouldn't have met Jason," she stares at me.

"You're right. We wouldn't have, and he's pretty great, isn't he?"

"Yeah. He's going to teach me to play the guitar." Her smile is vibrant.

I show her more things around my room and she asks a ton of questions about my life before she was born. I've always been honest with her, within the appropriate parameters, so I answer every question truthfully. When I ask her if she wants the dolls for herself, her head moves like a bobble head doll.

"Are you ready to go see Grandma and Grandpa?"

"Yeah." She jumps on both feet.

She puts on the clothes she wore yesterday and I change as well. I should've brought a bag with clothes and a few necessities, but I never imagined we'd spend the night.

"Good morning," Rae sings as she walks into the kitchen. My dad smiles at her, the wrinkles around his eyes deepening. This girl brings sunshine into any room. What would normally be a heavy mood is switched with happiness.

"Good morning, Rae." He bends downs to speak to her. She tilts her head and gives him a lopsided grin. "Go say hi to your Grandma."

"How is she?" I ask my dad as Rae walks over to her wheelchair.

"Same as yesterday, sweetheart. Not much will change overnight."

We look on at Rae, who is talking to my mom, no worry in the world that it's a one-sided conversation. My mom offers a small smile, her eyes still distant and disconnected.

"What?" Rae leans into her. My eyebrows gather. Rae looks at me, her mouth open wide and her eyes gleaming. "She said your name." She points at me.

"What?" I shake my head. "You said she doesn't speak much," I turn to my dad.

"She doesn't, a few words or phrases every so often."

"She said it again." My mom's hand barely rises, but she reaches for Rae's face, her thin fingers touching her face.

My breath becomes ragged and I walk to them. "Mom?" Her eyes turn to me.

"My baby." She looks back at Rae.

With my eyes welled, I bend down next to Rae. "This is my baby," I whisper. "She's Rae."

"Cassie?" she mumbles.

A sob travels through me like a bursting pipe. I bury

my face in my hand a moment, willing myself to stay calm. Soft petting tickles my back. Rae smiles at me as her hand moves up and down.

"Why don't you sit and talk with her a while and I'll get some eggs cookin.'"

"I can help, Dad."

"No. You sit and spend time with your momma." I sit on a chair at the table and talk to my mom. Rae takes a seat on my lap, staying as close as possible. Her smile never falters.

I tell her about my life and my job. I even mention Jason. Rae tells her how much she loves drawing. A few expressions are seen on my mom, but her eyes are what impress me. A void fills them, as if she were in another world. However, there's still some reaction to what we're saying, and although her mobility is limited, her hands move.

I'm surprised when she holds my hand and mumbles something inaudible.

"She tries to express herself, but it's difficult. Mostly, she'll say names from people she hasn't seen or spoken to in years," my dad explains.

We spend the morning like this. We eat breakfast together, and I assist my mom with her meal, offering to help as much as I can. When we finish eating, I clean up the kitchen while my dad takes my mom outside with Rae. She loves sitting out there in the mornings. I wonder if she's aware that she's not well, and feels trapped by the disease. A part of her core is still present in her, but it's as if she can't release that part of her. As if the power of Alzheimer's is greater than her will to be herself.

Dishes washed, I call Jason.

"How are you?" his voice is laced with worry.

"I'm okay." I sit on the same chair at the table, so I can have a partial view of the patio. "Emotionally tired. I may be in shock."

"Anything you need, Caz, you tell me. I'm here for you. How's Rae?"

"She's fantastic," I chuckle. "I have no idea why I was blessed with such an amazing child, but she's brought happiness into the situation. She's sitting outside with my parents now."

"I'm glad she's getting this time." The tenderness in his voice moves me. "Are you sure you're okay? You sound as if you're pretending."

I groan. "How can you tell?" He's perceptive.

"Because I can tell when something's not right. Talk to me, babe."

"I feel like I'm going to lose it at any time. I've been trying not to break down, and the more I resist, the more difficult it becomes. I'm scared, Jason." Tears begin to fall like autumn rain, gentle and expected.

"It's normal to feel scared. You have to trust and have faith that things will work themselves out. Be grateful you can be with them and spend time with her and your dad."

"Thank you. You're pretty amazing, ya know." I smile through my tears.

"Nah. You're the amazing one. I'm in awe of you. I'm assuming Joyce gave you some time off?" he inquires.

"She did. She told me to take time to care for my family. She also said that I've worked hard enough in the last seven years to deserve time off. She's paying me while I'm away. It won't be as much as when I get tips, but I can't thank her enough for still helping me in what way she can." I wish Jason were here. I wish I were talking to him in person. Difficult times reveal to us those we care about and want next to us. Jason is that person.

"You deserve that, Caz." His voice is sweet.

"I think I want to spend a few days here. At least until I decide what to do." I haven't made any decisions yet, but I want—need—to spend a few days here.

"I can pick you up when you're ready, so you can grab stuff from home," Jason suggests.

"Thanks. I'd appreciate that."

"I'm serious, Cassidy Rae, anything you need. I'm here for you. I don't care what time it is or if I'm working. Don't feel like you can't call me because of some lame excuse. Call me. Text me."

"You're not just pretty amazing. You're the most amazing. I'll let you know a time in a bit?"

"Perfect. I'll have my phone on me. Bye, baby."

"Bye."

I stare at my phone, unsure of how I found someone like Jason to accept us and the chaos in my life. To accept everything about my family. I close my eyes and offer a prayer of thanks for bringing him into my life and for surrendering my stubbornness to see the great man he is. I pray for my mom and dad. I pray for Rae, and I pray for me. Then, I walk outside and spend time with my family.

Rae is showing my parents her dance moves as my dad claps to a beat and my mom smiles and sways her head. I sit next to them, smiling, and join my dad in clapping. Once Rae is done, she takes a bow.

"Now guess what animal I am acting like," she calls out.

Rae begins to act as different things, my dad and I calling out animal names. My mom has more energy in her today than last night. I'm sure the evenings are exhausting for her. While my dad and her watch Rae, I look at my mom. She was always so lively, so energetic, despite being older.

Her hair always had to be perfect. I laugh inwardly. I was always the opposite—subpar hairstyles, undone nails, and sneakers over heels. Had I known this would be her destiny, I would've begged her to teach me to do a French braid when I was younger. She loved braiding my hair, and I always took it for granted.

"Mom, can you guess this one?" Rae tears me away from my memories.

"Let me see."

Rae extends her neck, her mouth in an exaggerated frown from the force. She gets on her tiptoes and takes long steps. I giggle as she imitates this animal.

"Hmmm… a cat?" I play along.

"Nope," she giggles and continues to walk.

"Oh! A giraffe?" I wink at my dad.

"You got it!" she exclaims and runs up to me. "How did you guess?" I love the innocence of a child.

"They are your favorite."

"They are." She crosses her arms and slants her head, swaying her body. "What's your favorite animal, Grandpa?"

"A horse. They're strong animals."

"I like those, too." Rae nods. "How about you, Grandma?" She turns to look at my mom, who still seems to be humming a song.

"Her favorite animal is the elephant," my father responds for her.

"Like you, Mommy," Rae yells.

"Yes, baby."

I got a lot of things from my mom despite the lack of

fashion passion, and my love for elephants was one of them.

Jason arrives a few hours later. My dad was on board with Rae and I staying a few more nights to help with what we can. We will have to come up with a plan, so I can support him. Maybe tonight once Rae is in bed and my mom is sleeping he and I can chat.

"Rae, let's go grab some stuff from the house and we'll come back."

"I wanna stay," she demands.

"Rae," I warn, widening my eyes.

"Please, Mom," she begs, joining her hands and lacing her fingers together.

"We'll be back in no time."

Her eyebrows scrunch and she frowns. "I want to stay with Grandma and Grandpa."

I sigh. She doesn't understand that my dad has enough trouble having to care for my mom.

"Let the girl stay, Cassie," my dad says. "She'll be my helper. Ain't that right, Rae?"

"Yes! I'll be a super-duper helper. I promise, Mom." She looks up at me with puppy-dog eyes. I hate when she does that. It gets me every time.

"Dad, are you sure? I don't want her to stress you out."

"That girl couldn't stress me out if she tried. She's sunshine." He smiles and winks at Rae, who is already jumping up and down for getting her way. "You have some time with that young man," he juts his chin toward Jason, who is standing in the entrance of the kitchen.

"Thanks, Daddy. If you need anything, call me. I'll grab what we need and come right back."

"Don't rush. We'll be here," he says.

I take a seat in the passenger side and stare at the house as Jason makes his way to the driver's side.

"Hey." He reaches over, and his hand holds the back of my neck. I turn to look at him. The crease between his eyebrows is like a river in a valley as he looks at me.

"Thank you." I can't seem to stop thanking him.

"She'll be okay," he reassures.

I nod. "I know Rae will be okay. It's adding that extra responsibility to my dad that worries me."

Jason moves so both hands are holding my face. He kisses my forehead, and I close my eyes, soaking in the warmth of his lips on my skin. With the stress of the last twenty-four hours, seeing him is like a streak of light, piercing through a dark tunnel. Not knowing what the right decision is has been pushing me back and forth. I owe it to my parents to stay and help, but is that the best thing for Rae? She's my priority.

Right now, she seems okay there. Maybe the school I went to still has a good reputation. I can get information. I would be further away from Jason, but my family comes first. I hate to even think that, because I like him. I like what we're building. It won't be impossible to continue growing together. Difficult, yes.

Jason drives to my house. The tick in his jaw is repetitive and his scruff is a little longer than usual. We're both quiet as we ride the streets of Tennessee, but his hand remains firmly in mine. I welcome the comfort and allow it to take me away like a whimsical hot air balloon ride. Eventually we'll land in reality, but until then, I'll bask in the soothing rub of his fingers over mine.

Jason parks across from my home, giving my hand a squeeze before he releases it. I walk into my house and go into my room, stuffing clothes for a few days for both Rae and me in an overnight bag. The shoes we're both currently wearing are okay, so I won't need that extra baggage.

I walk into the bathroom and peek at Jason sitting on the couch, staring at the wall ahead of him. I shake my head and grab our toothbrushes, toothpaste, shampoo, conditioner, and anything else we'll need. I'll let Abigail know we'll be away a few days, so she can keep an eye on the house.

I called Joyce after I spoke to Jason this morning and told her my plan, which she encouraged me to do.

After I have everything I think we'll need, I walk into the living room and sit next to Jason. With my feet tucked under me, I look at him.

"You okay?" I trace the outline of his jaw.

"Yeah," he sighs.

"Liar," I challenge.

Jason's eyes are clouded when he looks at me. "I don't know how to help you. I feel your worry, yet I'm not sure how to ease your pain."

I smile and relax my shoulders. On an exhale, I lean my head on the crook of his neck and reach for his hand. Fingers linked, Jason rests our hands on my bended leg. I kiss the underside of his jaw.

This man has provided me with a different perspective of life. I once thought I was a mother and nothing more. I believed I had no space in my life for anyone or anything else besides the wheel I kept turning. Now, I see that I can have more. He's taught me that. Rae has taught me that by approving my relationship with him. She's so strong.

"This, right here, is all I need. Hold me. Comfort me. Be present. I don't need more than that. My life is about to get tossed up and thrown around. I'm worried I'll make a wrong choice. I'm worried I'll uproot Rae and undo the grasp she has of her life. I'm scared that in doing that, I'll lose what you and I could be."

"What we are."

"What?"

"We're not a could be. We are a real thing. In this moment. We won't lose that. I promise, Cassidy Rae."

I lift my head and look at the sincerity in his eyes. "Can you make that promise, though?"

"I can, because you're what I've been looking for my entire life. With every woman I've met, I searched for you. Now that I've found you, I'm keeping you. Call me greedy. Call me insane. I don't care. All I care about is keeping you and Rae in my life." Jason kisses my lips.

Tears are rolling from my eyes in a silent escape. He kisses my tears. With a gentle tug, he pulls me over to his lap.

"The only result from this situation is death. She's not the same person, but she's my mom," I cry.

"Shh… it's okay, babe." Jason pulls me into him, encasing me in his arms as I cry into his neck.

I break down, the control I had kept in front of my parents and Rae dissolving. I clasp the sides of Jason's shirt. Seeing my mom in such a vulnerable state is heartbreaking. Witnessing her lack of power is overwhelming. Watching my dad care for her devastates me. He's older than she is. He has his own health to care for.

"I want to move back home to help." I lean back and look at Jason.

"Okay."

"I can get a part-time job, so I'm around more. Not

having to pay rent will help alleviate the financial stress. Once school starts, Rae can be enrolled in the same school I attended. I'll have to look into it."

"That's what we'll do." Jason speaks as if the decision is his as well. In a way, it affects him, too.

"I'll have to talk to Joyce and the landlord. Make sure I can end the lease in a month. Tonight, I need to sit with my dad and talk to him. We need a plan, and I want to know as much as I can about the advancement of my mother's condition."

"Start with that. We'll figure things out. I'll help you move your things."

"I still want to have time for us, but…" I don't dare finish that thought.

"We will. It's not far. Other couples have a longer drive to see each other. We'll make time. We'll have a plan."

"I have no idea where you came from, Jason Stone, but I want to keep you." I hold his cheeks and kiss him straight on the lips.

"Well, Cassidy Rae Pressman, it's a good thing I want to keep you, as well. We got this, baby." He kisses me back with more passion than the other kisses we've shared in the last few days.

Jason's tongue sweeps mine and I sigh, leaning into him. I shift my body so I can face him straight on, and return the kiss with as much fervor.

"Baby," Jason murmurs against my lips.

"Mmm?"

"Come on," he taps my behind.

I keep my eyes shut, enjoying the closeness we're sharing before reality settles. I'd love nothing more than to get lost in his kiss for hours.

"If we don't stop, this trip will take double the time it

should," he groans. I can feel his reaction underneath me, and I'd be lying if I said it didn't affect me. A man hasn't touched me since the night I got pregnant with Rae. And that was less touching and more humping. Drunken sex isn't good sex. It's been even longer since I've been kissed the way Jason kisses me.

"Don't get me wrong, I'm very fond of this position," he winks with a mischievous smile.

I give him a hard kiss and stand. I giggle as he takes a minute before he gets up from the couch.

"Did you eat?"

I shrug. "I had some breakfast. Eggs. I wasn't that hungry, though."

"You hate eggs," he states.

"Not hate, I just prefer something else."

"Let's grab a quick bite on the way over."

"Would you mind stopping at the grocery store on the way as well? I want to grab a few things for the house," I ask.

"Of course not."

After we eat lunch, we stop at the grocery store. I'm filling the cart with ingredients to make different recipes. Jason walks with me, rolling the cart while I stop every few minutes to debate if I need a certain item. I'm a pro at shopping on a budget, so I scan the aisles for sales. I keep in mind that softer foods are easier for my mom to eat and grab a few soups.

Once I'm done, we wait in line to be rung up. As I bring out my wallet, Jason places his hand on mine and shakes his head.

"Let me."

"No." I'm adamant.

"Please, Cassidy Rae."

"This isn't why–"

"I know it's not, but I want to. It's a way I can help."

My breathing becomes labored as I try to hold in the pulsing need to weep. He doesn't have to pay for us, and I'd never have asked him to bring me if I knew he would. However, seeing his pursed lips and scrunched eyes, I concede. I nod and move away, surrendering to someone's help.

Chapter 16

Cassidy Rae

IT'S BEEN A WEEK SINCE Rae and I moved back into my parents' house. She was on board with the decision, saying she's been a great help to Grandpa. Jason stayed true to his word and helped us move all of our things. His care has split my heart open and welcomed him in.

I spoke to my landlord and explained the situation a few days after Jason and I went to pack a bag, she allowed us to finish off the last month and move. I paid her for the month, but we moved right away. Leaving Abigail and Blake was hard, and a lot of tears were shed in the process of saying goodbye, as well as a lot of promises to keep in touch and visit.

Joyce reluctantly let me go. Reluctantly, because I know she loves Rae and I, and will miss us. She told me if I ever needed to go back, a job would be available for me.

In the week I've been here, I haven't seen Jason, but

we talk each day. Rae has adjusted better than I imagined, and my dad seems relieved to have us around. My mother's condition remains the same.

"Dad, go get some rest," I tell him as I watch him nodding off.

"I'm okay."

"Go rest. I've got it covered here. If I need anything, I'll wake you." I've been memorizing my mom's schedule. Everything is planned out as per the doctor's suggestion. With my mother barely mobile and her lack of communication, bathroom breaks are important.

It's midmorning, so she's already had breakfast, sat outside, and used the bathroom. I can handle some time on my own, so my dad can take a nap. He's up real early with my mom.

"We've got it covered, Grandpa," Rae echoes me. I giggle. She is an angel. If I ever thought my daughter was special before, now I know she's the kindest human in this world. In a time when she can be a rebel, become emotionally unattached, or angry, she is still the happy, supportive girl.

"Okay. If you need anything at all, let me know." My dad yawns and walks into his bedroom.

I sit by my mom, her wheelchair next to the couch.

"How are you feeling?" I ask her. The first thing my dad told me was to speak to her as if she were fully present. It's important to keep them feeling safe and comfortable while maintaining that connection, make sure they still feel loved. Rae is somewhere in the kitchen.

"Do you remember when we used to bake cakes together? I do that with Rae now. She loves being in the kitchen. She says she wants to be a pastry chef when she grows up." I smile at my mom, memories from childhood invading my mind.

"You'd let me lick the spoon when we were done, and Dad would tease me by trying to grab it away from me." My mom reaches for my hand, her lips twitching. I hold her hand with both of mine and continue to talk to her.

"I met a man, who is pretty amazing. After I had Rae, I didn't think love was in the cards for me. I love her so much. No wonder you and Dad were determined to have a baby. His name is Jason. He was here helping us move our things. Dad seems to like him. I'm sure you would, too." I wipe a tear with the back of my hand.

"He's patient and kind. He cares so much about Rae, you'd think she's his daughter."

I stretch the hand I'm holding with care. Without movement, her joints become stiff, so massaging and moving them helps. I repeat the action to the other hand. Then, I grab a photo album on a shelf and sit back down.

I open the album and look through the pictures. Decades of my life, and some before my time, are placed in this book. We look through the pictures as I recall events in my life. It helps me to remember her that way, so full of life and vibrant.

The days have passed, and we've entered a routine. July is half way done, and Rae is enrolled in her new school. She'll begin come late August and I've spoken to the principal about our situation at home. Turns out, she's the same principal from when I was in school, a lot older, but strict as ever.

As for Jason and me, we haven't had time to see each other since I moved in. It's been almost three weeks, and it's starting to worry me. This new normal is stressful. I've taken it to heart, leaving no time for anything else. I haven't even had a chance to find a part-time job, which I need to do, because as frugal as I've been, the little money I had is disappearing.

"Hey, Cassidy. It's been so long." I look at the woman in front of me in the grocery store. The familiarity in her screams at me, but it takes me a second too long to recognize her.

"Don't tell me you don't recognize me. You'll make me self-conscious." She pats her hair down.

"Oh my God. Bronwyn?"

"Yes! Where the hell have ya been? You just disappeared overnight and no one ever heard from you again."

Bronwyn and I tended the bar together before I got pregnant. I glance behind me in panic, hoping Rae takes a minute longer than necessary to pick out the cookies she wants.

"Um, I've been good. Working at a diner outside of Nashville."

"We should catch up. How long are you here for? Not that Nashville is a far drive away." She chuckles.

"Yeah, definitely. Are you still at Wilde Fire?" I ask her about my last place of employment.

"Nope." She shows off her ring and squeals. "I'm engaged!"

"Wow. Congrats." My eyes are wide. "That's wonderful."

"Thanks."

"Mommy," I hear behind me, and my eyes fall closed. I can't ignore her. I turn to my daughter and smile. "I got the cookies I want." She beams, the happiness coming from her causes me to smile, almost forgetting the woman standing with us.

"Who is this?" Bronwyn leans down. "Hi."

"Hi," Rae shyly wraps her arms around my waist.

"Well, I gotta go." I try to race out of there.

"You have a daughter," Bronwyn states as if Mommy was a term used for anyone. I nod once and hold Rae's hand.

"That's wonderful, Cassidy. How old is she?" My work friends never used my full name, always resorting to Cassidy.

I bite down hard, my teeth grinding. "Six." I know I can't lie because it will just throw Rae into asking more questions.

"Oh." I see Bronwyn's mind working. She's calculating the years since I've left. "I didn't know you were seeing anyone."

"I'm not." I try to find a way out of this situation.

"After you left," Bronwyn leans in to whisper. "This guy kept coming in asking about you. I thought he was just a patron with a crush, but…" She angles her head to look at Rae. "Could it be?"

I shake my head. "I don't know. It's not my proudest moment."

"Oh, well. It's not like we would even be able to track him down," she chuckles.

Thank God for that. I don't know anything about Rae's father. I didn't even catch his name. But, what if someone did know him and told him about Rae. Would he want to take her away from me? Could he sue me for not reaching out to him? I should know the laws in relation to this.

"I really do have to go. My dad's waiting for me, but it was good to see you. Congrats again on the engagement." I walk away before she can speak again. I forgot that this community was much smaller than Nashville.

"Who was that?" Rae asks.

"I used to work with her when I lived here."

"Her hair was too yellow."

I laugh, thankful she can lighten the mood and calm my nerves. At the checkout line, I hear someone else call my name. *Can't a girl catch a break?*

I turn to see a man behind me. I squint my eyes. "Oh my goodness, Ben?"

"I thought that was you. How are you?" I look at one of my best friends from high school.

"I'm okay. How about you? God, it's been years." I smile.

"I know." He looks down at Rae and smiles. "Is this your daughter?"

I nod. "This is Rae."

"Hi, Rae. Are you in town? I heard you had moved."

"Yeah. I actually moved back in with my parents. My mom isn't doing too well, so I'm helping my dad care for her."

"I'm sorry to hear that. Hey, we should catch up. Let's have coffee."

"Sure." Ben and I were great friends growing up, but we became better friends in high school. My other friend, Sara, and him were always there for me. Sara moved away for college, and I lost touch. Ben would come by the bar every so often when I first started working until school started.

We exchange numbers and I say bye when I need to pay for my purchase.

"Who was that?" Rae looks at me.

"That was Ben. He was one of my best friends when I

was younger."

"Like a boyfriend?" She scrunches her nose.

"No, silly." I tap the tip of her nose. "Girls and boys can be friends without being boyfriend and girlfriend."

"Oh." She shrugs.

The sound of yells stops me as soon as I open the door.

"What's going on?" I rush into the house.

"Nothing. It's okay. Stay there."

Rae and I stop, and I see my dad holding my mom as she screams. I can't make out what she's saying, but she seems stressed.

I turn to Rae. "Baby girl, stay here. Don't move, okay?" She nods, her eyes wide as she looks on at her grandparents.

"What's going on?" I repeat with a calm voice.

"She seems to have gotten agitated. I can't tell why, but my assumption is pain somewhere in her body. She started to rock, and almost tipped in the chair." My dad had moved my mom from the wheelchair to a chair in the kitchen as part of her routine.

"Hold her, and I'll see where the pain can be." I rub my hand down my mom's back in case it's muscular. I check her arms and hands. I move down to her feet, and notice her calf is cramped up.

I tell my dad and begin to massage her leg. Her cries subside, and her face begins to unscrew. Finally, she relaxes into the chair. I slump down on the floor and look up at her. I look at my dad. His eyebrows are pulled in and his lips are flat.

"Thank you," he slumps.

"Are you okay?"

"Yes." He sits down on a chair and breathes heavy. Rae and I got here right on time.

"Come here, baby girl." I call Rae over. She sits in my lap on the floor.

"Is Grandma okay?"

"She is now," my dad answers.

"Good. I don't want her to feel bad." Rae places her head on my shoulder. I smooth her back.

"She's okay." I comfort her. "I have an idea. Why don't we sit outside and watch the sunset?" I suggest.

"That's a great idea," my dad responds with a smile.

"What do you say, Mom?" I look at her. She's in a daze after her burst of pain, but I think she'd like that.

Rae and I sprint to put the groceries away, so we can catch the sunset.

Once we're done, my dad and I help my mom back into the wheelchair, and Rae helps me wheel her out into the back porch. Nature is healing, and spending time together is nourishing. I hold my mom's hand as we sit outside, Rae keeping her permanent spot on my lap.

"How is that young man doing?" my dad asks.

"He's good."

"You should make time to see him," he points out.

I nod in silence.

"I miss Jason," Rae adds.

"I know, baby. We'll see him soon." Having him come over here is challenging. Maybe we can go to lunch or dinner with Rae. I miss him, too. I know he's respecting the time I have with my parents. He's being patient, but it's not fair to have him on standby.

"I'll call him when we go back inside." He mentioned he would be performing at Riot tonight, and I wish I were in a situation where I can go and surprise him. I'll catch him on the phone before he goes on stage. We spoke last night, but I miss his hugs and his forehead kisses.

Even though I haven't seen him, our conversations alone are enough to make me fall a little more for him each day. When I lie at night, worried, he comforts me. Some nights he'll sing. Today, I want to see him, smell his musky cologne, feel his arms around me.

Once the evening begins to set, we go back in to prepare dinner. My dad calls Rae to help him, so I can call Jason.

"Hey, beautiful," his soft voice answers.

"Hi." I lean back on the headboard of my bed. "Are you busy?"

"Never too busy for you, Caz." I smile upon hearing the nickname Rae and he gave me. My parents are the only ones who ever called me Cassie. At school I was always Cassidy Rae, and at the bar, Cassidy.

"At what time do you have to leave for Riot?" I ask.

"I've got about two hours. How are you?" The meaning in his question is heavy.

"I'm okay," I sigh. "It was a hard day."

"Tell me about it."

I tell Jason what happened with my mom when Rae and I got home from the grocery store. "Rae was scared."

"I can imagine. How's your mom now?"

"She's okay. After I massaged the cramp out, she calmed. The four of us sat outside to watch the sunset before I called you." I scoot down on the bed and turn onto my side. "I miss you," I confess.

"I miss you, too. I like our talks, but I want to see you. Make sure you're really okay." I smile as a couple tears run down the side of my face. I got lucky with him, and we haven't had a chance to fully develop our relationship.

"Are you okay with this? With us not able to see each other as much?" When I first decided to move here, seeing each other seemed like an easier option than it has been. I'm on the clock twenty-four seven to make up for lost time.

"Babe, I want you to do what you need to do. I'm here to support you. Yes, I want to see you. I want to hold you and comfort you, especially days like today that were hard for you. I also know how important this is to you. You have guilt about moving away, although you shouldn't. You made what you thought was the best decision for you and Rae."

"I know," I whisper. "Thank you."

"I'm here for you. We'll see each other soon. How about we go to dinner Monday? I'll pick you up."

"Yeah. I'd like that. Although, I'm not sure we'd get away with leaving Rae behind. She's been asking about you."

"We'll bring her with us." Jason doesn't hesitate.

"You're an angel," I tell him.

"Not quite, but when it comes to you I want it all." He's been more vocal about his feelings in the last few weeks. Jason and I talk for a little longer until I have to go down and help with dinner. He promises to call me when he's done at Riot.

I walk into the kitchen to oldies music blaring from a radio, Rae and my dad dancing as they cook, and my mom's head bobbing as she smiles. I realize moving back was the best decision. Rae needs this time with my parents as much as I do, and my parents need her. She's been a light in my dad's day since we got here as well. I'm not sure how much time she'll have with my mom and how much it will hurt Rae when she's gone. Every morning I wake up wondering if my mom has survived another night. So far, she has, but the uncertainty lingers close by.

Rae spots me and grins with all her teeth. She comes up to me and holds my hands so I can dance with her. I move with her, twirling her and tilting her back. Her giggles are better than the music playing. My dad winks as he holds my mom's hand. The love he has for her is admirable. Anyone else would have placed my mom in a home and visit her when they could.

As I twirl Rae in the kitchen, I dance over to the stove and stir the pasta before checking if it's almost cooked. Seeing as it still has a few minutes, I pick Rae up and dance. She tilts her head back and laughs. I love this girl with my entire heart and more. It's the kind of love I can't describe. It's the kind of love I didn't know humans were possible of having.

The smile on my mom's face is visible from all angles. It makes me proud to be a part of this moment.

Chapter 17

Jason

I SCRUB MY EYES AS I yawn while stopped at the red light. I had one beer at Riot last night before leaving. I wanted to talk to Cassidy Rae, but by the time I called her she must've been asleep already. I've given her time, although it's been difficult. I am at a loss on how to be there for her when I know being present isn't an option.

Cole questioned my decision to drive over to her parents' house today instead of waiting for dinner tomorrow. When I heard Cassidy Rae talking yesterday and the stress with what happened with her mom, I knew I had to be there. I want to be there. Even if we only get a few minutes, I'll take it.

The car behind me honks, taking me out of my reverie. I couldn't sleep. When she wouldn't answer my call, I began to worry. I know the rational reason is she was sleeping, but negative thoughts caused me to stay wide awake in case she would call. In case she would need to talk to me.

When I finally woke up, later than planned, and checked my phone, I still hadn't heard from her. I decided jumping in the car and going to her would be my best option. Now, I'm barely awake as I maneuver through the streets.

I make a sharp right, causing the car behind me to deafen me with his horn. The sign of the coffee shop beckons me like a neon light to a broken-hearted fool. I park in the only spot available and walk into the shop in hopes that the caffeine will kick in by the time I make it to Cassidy Rae's.

The line is long and the tables are full. I look at the menu, wondering if Cassidy Rae and her dad would want coffee. Rae would love one of those vanilla frappuccino things with whipped cream. Deciding to grab just black coffees for the three of us, I look around the interior. Small, square tables are littered throughout with different coffee wall art hung on the walls.

I freeze as I look at the details. I squint my eyes and cross my arms. My jaw clenches as my heart accelerates. I tilt my head and continue to stare until she sees me. Her eyes widen as they land on me. I shake my head so slow I don't know if she notices.

Fuck coffee.

I turn and walk right back out through the doors that led me into my worst nightmare.

Fuck. Fuck. Fuck.

I slam the top of my car. I don't care if it dents. I hope it does. I rub my eyes with the heels of my hands to keep from losing it. My heart is threatening to race out of my mouth, causing the back of my throat to burn.

"Jason?" The surprise in her voice doesn't help the

situation. I keep my back to her, wondering why she'd do this. Not even my dream woman could get away with not disappointing me. Call me a pussy, but my heart got tore up.

"Hello?"

I turn around and pin my stare on her. She leans back.

"What are you doing here?" Her voice is laced with her own emotions.

"I could ask you the same thing, Cassidy Rae," I spit.

Her eyebrows scrunch as she looks at me. "I came to apply for a job."

"Oh, yeah. It looked like that was exactly what you were doing."

She crosses her arms. "What do you think I was doing?"

"That was no fucking interview. You don't laugh that way with a potential boss. Are you playing me?" I accuse even though I ask her.

"Are you fucking kidding me? That," she points behind her, "was a friend of mine. He and I went to middle and high school together. Yes, I did come to apply for a job, and I ran into Ben. We were best friends growing up. He asked if I wanted to have a quick cup of coffee and I almost said no. Not because I thought it would betray you. I know if I'm crossing lines and that was nowhere near it. I needed a break. I needed five fucking minutes to myself out of that house, so I took him up on his offer to catch up."

"It's my job. It's my responsibility to give you time like that. I'm the one who is supposed to make you smile. Me." I point at my chest, my voice eerily low. I'm looking at everything from the outside.

"He's an old friend from high school, nothing more. I

was telling him about you. How I…" She looks down at her sneakers.

"How you what? Landed the rich musician?"

"What? No." Her eyes snap up to me. "You know this has nothing to do with your money."

"The fuck am I supposed to think, Cassidy Rae? Where's Rae?"

"She's with my parents."

"Your dad has enough taking care of your mom." It's a low blow, but I'm angry.

"Hey, don't make it sound like I dumped her on him. I asked her to come and she wanted to stay." I scoff. "Forget it. I'm going home."

She walks away from me, digging through her purse.

"Where are you going?" I reach her.

"Home. You show up here, accusing me of cheating on you, when all I had was coffee with a friend." Tears fill her eyes. Is she telling the truth? I'm a fucking idiot if I jumped to conclusions without talking to her like an adult.

"I'll drive you."

"You don't have to, Jason. Go back home."

"The fuck I will."

"Why are you even here?" Her tone knocks me back.

"I missed you. I didn't want to wait until tomorrow." I look over her head, avoiding her; vulnerability is difficult for me.

Cassidy Rae sighs. "You look tired."

"So do you," I respond. Her eyes are sunken and sad. She sniffles, and I know she's trying not to cry in front of me. She's trying to be strong.

I take a step toward her and reach for her hand. "Is he just a friend?"

"Yes. I saw him at the grocery store the other day and when I ran into him today, I thought I'd sit for a few and drink a cup of coffee with him. Ben and Sara were my two best friends. Sara moved away for college and never came back. I lost touch with Ben a little after I started working at the bar," she explains.

"Jason, you can't assume like this. You know how they always say not to believe everything printed in the tabloids?" I nod. "You shouldn't believe what you make up in your head. I thought you knew me better than that. You can relate. If I saw a photo of you with a woman in a magazine, I'd ask you about it before yelling that you're cheating on me."

"That's because you're the sane one out of the two of us." She's right.

"I know you've been hurt in the past, but I am not going to repeat those betrayals."

"Rationally, I know that's true. I reacted before any other possible reason crossed my mind." I pull her into my arms and inhale her scent.

"You have to trust me." She rests her chin on my chest and looks up at me.

"I do."

Cassidy Rae arches a brow and I laugh. "I promise, I do. It caught me by surprise to see you sitting at a coffee shop as if you had no worries in the world. I should know if you need a break. I should be able to sense that and come to you or call you."

"You did, though. You're here. You took that initiative. You are that person for me. How could you even think anyone else comes close?" Her honesty surprises me. She gets on her toes and kisses my lips. Hugging me again, she mumbles, "I missed you, too," into my chest, and we both relax. "But we also have our own lives and people in them we can't ignore because of jealousy."

"I know that. I'm sorry."

"Do you want to come to the house?" Her brows furrow, unsure after the argument we had.

"I was headed that way. I stopped here to get some coffee because I didn't sleep well. I didn't want to get there and be yawning nonstop."

"Do you want to grab a cup before leaving?" Cassidy Rae loosens her hold around my waist.

"Nah. I'm pretty awake now."

She frowns, and I kiss the tip of her nose. "Having you this close definitely wakes me up," I whisper into her ear. She shivers as I press my hand on her lower back and bring her close to me again. I look down at her with a raised brow and one side of my lip tilted up.

Cassidy Rae sighs. "Let me stay like this a minute before we leave."

I lean my chin on the top of her head, taking in her scent and holding her with both arms. She draws designs on my back with her fingers as if she were comforting me, instead of the opposite. She's my perfect southern princess. I'm an ass for second-guessing her, but it hurt to see her sitting at that table with someone else when she needed me.

We need a new plan. I can come over every so often and help her. I can help her dad, do anything they need. I can no longer support her by staying quiet and away. Of course, that's if it's okay with her parents and her.

"Follow me?" She angles her head up.

"You drove?" I ask, leaning back.

Cassidy Rae giggles. "Don't sound so surprised. I can

drive; I just don't own a car. I used my dad's."

"Oh, okay. Yeah, I'll follow you." I kiss her full lips and walk her to her car. She smiles when I open the door for her.

"I'm so happy you're here," she confesses with a blush.

"I got you, baby."

The drive to her house is shorter than I thought. I wasn't as far away as I originally imagined when I stopped for coffee. I pull in behind her and take a deep breath. My heart is racing at the unfamiliar situation. The control I usually have a grasp on is nonexistent today.

I startle when she knocks on my window. When I turn to look at her, she's bent over laughing. I climb out of my car with a smile.

"I'll get you back for that," I tease.

"Jason!" A tiny head of blonde hair tumbles toward me. I hug Rae and lift her up over my head before placing her back on the ground. Her fit of giggles causes me to smile. "How come you're here?" She looks up at me.

"I came to surprise y'all."

"I found him in the coffee shop," Cassidy Rae winks at her daughter.

"Did you get the job?" Rae asks.

"I don't know yet, baby girl. They will call me for an interview."

"They'll give it to you. You're good at making coffee" she compliments her mother as she looks on at her with admiration. The relationship these two have is surreal. My sisters get along with my mom, but this is a different level. Their situation created a deeper bond. I'm lucky they're allowing me to enter it.

"Let's go inside." Cassidy Rae leads the way. "Dad, you remember Jason, right?" Her dad is sitting at the kitchen table reading the newspaper. He lowers it and smiles.

"I sure do. Hello, young man." I shake her dad's hand and greet him.

"How'd it go?" her dad folds the newspaper in half and places it on the table.

"Time will tell. Where's Mom?" Cassidy Rae looks around the kitchen.

"She's resting a bit in the bedroom."

"Oh, okay. Is she okay?"

"Yeah. Nothing to worry about, she needed to lie down and get some shut-eye. Why don't you go somewhere with Jason while your mom rests?" Mr. Pressman suggests.

"That's okay, sir. I came over to offer help and support any way I can."

"We're okay," her dad nods once. I see where Cassidy Rae get's her self-sufficiency and stubbornness from. "While my wife sleeps, I relax a bit."

"We can hang out here, Dad," Cassidy Rae suggests.

"No, no. Take the girl to the park. You remember which one, right? Your mom will be in there for an hour or so."

"Are you sure?" Cassidy Rae looks at her dad with squinted eyes.

"I promise. I'll call you if I need you to come back sooner. I'm sure Rae would like to go to the park." He leans over and winks at Rae. Rae nods her head, not saying a thing until the adults decide.

"Are you okay with that?" Cassidy Rae turns to me.

"Yeah." I nod.

Cassidy Rae bends in front of Rae and asks, "Do you want to go to the park?"

"Sure," she smiles.

"Dad, anything you need, even if we just left, you call me. Okay?"

"I will. Now go off and have some fun."

Cassidy Rae hesitates a moment before grabbing her purse. Rae hugs her grandfather and kisses his cheek. Then, she comes to hold my hand. I observe in awe of the amount of love they have for each other and the calm despite the heavy reason they're all here.

I pull into a parking spot, Rae practically jumping from the car.

"There's a merry-go-round," Rae exclaims from the backseat.

"Yup. That was my favorite as a kid," Cassidy Rae tells her.

As soon as we're out of the car, Rae runs to the merry-go-round. I hold Cassidy Rae's hand and smile. "She's happy."

"She always is. That girl has been our savior during this time. I see the same relationship she has with my dad that I had with him at her age."

"That's great, babe."

"Yeah," Cassidy Rae sighs.

Rae tries to spin herself around before she calls for us to help her.

"Hold on tight," I warn.

Rae squeezes her hands around the bar and I chuckle. Grabbing one of the outer handles, I begin to push the merry-go-round. Rae's giggles echo around the park.

"That's not fast," she challenges.

I turn to Cassidy Rae with raised brows. When she nods with the go-ahead, I begin to spin faster.

"Yessss!" Rae's yells are amplified.

Warm arms wrap around me from behind. I smirk as I spin again once the merry-go-round begins to slow. Cassidy Rae remains behind me, a soft kiss lands in the center of my back. I place my hands over hers while I take a break from spinning Rae. This woman owns me. It happened so fast that I didn't have time to judge it. As I stand here with her and her daughter, I realize that I want this to be my life. I want her to be my family.

"Don't spin it anymore," Rae calls before I have a chance to grab the rail.

"Okay." I respond and watch her begin to slow. I grab Cassidy Rae from behind me and hold her to my side. She wraps both arms around me, hugging me, as we look at Rae.

"Can I play in the different things?" Rae asks once she hops down. She tries to walk, but staggers from all the spinning. Cassidy Rae giggles and I grab Rae's shoulders to stable her.

"Dizzy?" I tease her.

"Yeah." She widens her eyes and leans her head back. I chuckle, and Rae joins me.

"Ready to walk?" I ask her. Rae nods and I release her shoulders. She runs over to the jungle gym and begins to climb the dome, hanging upside down when she reaches the top.

"She has so much energy," Cassidy Rae comments. "Thanks for being here. I know it was a rough start, but I'm so happy you came."

I look at my girl straight on and smile. "Sorry for being an ass. I should've talked to you first."

"You're forgiven," she mocks.

I pull her into me, tapping her behind without a second

thought. "Behave." Cassidy Rae's soft moan surprises me. "Fuck, babe." She blushes and hides her face in my chest. "Hey." I grab her chin and tilt her head up. "Don't hide from me." I give her a chaste kiss.

Cassidy Rae nods and pinches her lips together in a smile.

"Trust me, you affect me in the same way," I tell her. Our situation is unconventional. She's a single mom, so it's hard for her to get a lot of time alone, and with being at her parents' house, taking care of them is her priority. "We'll get there," I assure her.

"No man is this patient."

"You're wrong. A man who wants a woman in his life for the long haul is patient and understanding. You're not just sex, Caz. Yeah, I want that with you," I lean into her for emphasis. "But, I'm here for everything."

"I don't know how long this situation will last. It could be months or…" Her voice trails off.

"Don't think about that. Part of the reason I wanted to come was to talk. I have nowhere to be, so I can wait until you're done with what you have to do to talk."

"Good talk or bad?"

"All good, babe."

Cassidy Rae nods, and we take a seat at a bench as Rae plays. I haven't been in love in a long time, and I don't think young love is the same as when we're older. Looking at Rae play and holding Cassidy Rae next to me, I question if this is love. I never want them out of my life. With Cassidy Rae, the order I've always had in my life seems boring. My straight-laced self doesn't understand, yet it urges me to take a leap of faith. I've taken one risk in my life before and joining Rebel Desire was worth it. The value of having Cassidy Rae in my life is infinitely more.

We leave the park an hour later, and I suggest picking

up lunch so they don't have to cook. We stop at a deli not far from their house and grab subs, chips, drinks, and a soup for her mom.

Back at the house, we set the table and Cassidy Rae helps her dad move her mom onto the wheelchair.

"You didn't have to buy lunch," her dad says.

"We wanted to," Cassidy Rae responds.

As we eat, her dad asks me about the band and my job. The conversation is easy with him, jumping from that to sports to housework. His laid-back personality must be one of the things keeping him strong.

Rae tells her grandparents all about the park and how fast she spun. "Then, I got super dizzy and couldn't walk," she giggles before taking a bite of her sub.

"Sounds like fun," her grandfather responds. "Did you thank Jason and your mom for taking you?"

"Thanks, Mommy. Thanks, Jason." Rae's face lights up.

"You're welcome, baby," Cassidy Rae tells her as she helps her mom eat her soup.

"You're welcome, Rae Rae," I tell her.

"That's my nickname," Rae explains.

"A very pretty one," her grandfather compliments.

After lunch, Rae sits with her grandmother and reads her a book. She's taken the role as seriously as the adults. Cassidy Rae tells her dad to rest, and I sit with her in the kitchen.

We're silent for a bit, the distant sound of Rae reading a book traveling from the living room. I hold Cassidy Rae's hands from across the round table.

"I know you're stressed," I begin. "I've given you space to fulfill your responsibilities, but I also assured you you weren't alone. I feel like I have left you alone by not being more present. I want to be here helping you when I can. I want to see you and hug you when you're upset or scared. I don't know if you're okay with that, or if your dad is. I can come help you on the weekends or some evenings."

"You have so much going on and your own life and family, it wouldn't be fair."

"Right now, you're my number one. Supporting you is my priority. This isn't easy for you." I squeeze her hand and lace our fingers together, kissing her wrist.

"I appreciate it, although that wouldn't exactly give us time alone. We started a relationship with a *huge* roadblock in the way. How do we balance my personal life with our relationship when this is taking up most of my time?" She waves around the house.

"You said we could go to dinner tomorrow. We make time. We make it a point to carve time for us."

"You make it sound easy." Her eyes water.

"Baby, it is. We complicate things in our mind. Once your mom goes to bed and Rae is settled in for the night, we can grab dinner. We can find ways to spend time together without overdoing it. It doesn't have to be extravagant. Extravagant isn't your style anyway. I'll give you the best, regardless."

"Have I told you how happy you make me?" She bites her bottom lip.

"You make me happy, too. Rae makes me happy. Having you in my life is not what I envisioned, but it's so much better."

"I really want to kiss you," she whispers. I lean over the table, giving her what she wants.

"Okay," Cassidy Rae says when I sit back down. "We'll make this new plan work."

Chapter 18

Cassidy Rae

JASON STAYS WITH US ALL day. He helps me around the house and joins Rae as she reads more books to my mom. Seeing him here, unhurried, spending time with my family, it makes me fall deeper for him. He's insistent that we can make this work, yet I'm not sure. What I didn't express yesterday is that when the time comes for my mom to pass, which is inevitable, I still have my dad to care for. I can't leave him alone in this house.

"Mommy, come 'ere!" I finish drying a plate and put it away.

When I walk into the living room, Jason is sitting on a chair with his guitar propped on his lap. Rae and my dad are sitting on the couch next to my mom.

"Jason's going to sing for us."

I smile and stand behind them as I watch Jason wink at me and begin to strum the guitar. Knowing he brought it proves his intentions were clear about cheering us up and doing what he can to support us.

His soft voice begins to sing the words of one of my favorite songs. It's the same one that was playing in the diner the day we met. He has a beautiful voice and I wonder why he chose to play the bass over singing.

When he starts the second song, Rae stands and walks to me. She hugs the side of my body and sways to the rhythm. I pick her up and move with her, earning myself a mega smile. Jason looks on at us as he sings. When I peek down at my parents, my emotions become raw as I watch them hold hands.

I have no idea what will become of my father once my mom is gone. Rae and I will make sure he still has his family.

Jason puts the guitar down after three songs and we all clap. He wears a sheepish smile as he looks at each of us.

"It's almost time for supper. You'll stay to eat with us, right, young man?" My dad asks Jason as he picks himself up from the couch.

"Um…" Jason looks at me.

"I won't take no for an answer. You've been a great visitor, offering free entertainment and all."

"Thank you, sir," Jason responds.

"I want to help cook," Rae scurries into the kitchen.

I walk up to Jason and he tugs my arm so I fall onto his lap.

"Thank you." I hold his face.

"You're welcome. I'm happy to be here. Your dad is great."

"He is. He's always been one of my favorite people." Jason touches his lips to mine for the briefest of moments. I place my head on his shoulder, his hand running up and down my leg.

"I need to assist my mom in the bath. Are you okay out here with my dad and Rae for some time?"

"Of course. Do what you have to do. I'll help them in the kitchen." He squeezes my knee.

I've questioned if he's real. This all seems like some kind of dream. When I found out I was pregnant with Rae, I knew I wouldn't have a complete family or loving relationship with her father. I don't even remember his name. What I never imagined was meeting someone who could give me that, although he's not her biological father. I keep wondering if I'll wake up to a stark reality that this was all a dream.

I kiss Jason's cheek and wheel my mom into the bathroom so I can help her into the tub. Having this role with my mom is humbling. It has put life into perspective. She always took care of me, and I never imagined we'd be in a position where she would be reliant on me to care of her.

It was smart of my dad to invest in this tub with a side door. I'm glad someone thought of creating something that would be beneficial to the senior community. I open the door and help ease my mom onto the built-in bench. I make sure the water is warm and help her wash up.

She's frail. Each week I see her slowly slip away. The doctor said it's a good sign that she's still able to move, even if it's with our help. It's important for the skin so it won't tear or bruise, since that causes her to be prone to infections, which could be deadly.

After I finish bathing her, I brush her hair and hum. It's kept short, but I take my time caring for her.

Dressed and refreshed, I bring her out into the kitchen. Jason, my dad, and Rae are all singing to the song on the radio as they each tackle a task in meal prepping. I place my mom at the table in her chair and join them.

"Chop some garlic." Jason hands me a knife and cutting board. I work on the garlic, the aroma potent and delicious. I'm a firm believer that garlic makes every meal better. My dad is stirring a pot with cubed potatoes in it and Rae is measuring milk.

"Mashed potatoes?" I ask Jason.

"Yup. I seasoned pork chops and they're cooking in the oven."

"Special recipe?" I tease.

"Always." He winks.

Once the food is ready, we eat together, conversing and laughing.

"I have a surprise for dessert," Rae announces. She skips to the pantry and brings out the box of chocolate chip cookies. Then she opens the freezer and pulls out the vanilla ice cream. My mom loves ice cream and it's one of the foods that sits well with her. Go figure. She hasn't lost her sweet tooth.

I collect the plates and ask Rae if she needs help. She shakes her and instructs me to sit back down. She balances four plates and a bowl with spoons in it. Then, she brings over the ice cream carton and the cookies. As soon as she takes her seat again, she serves a scoop of ice cream in the bowl. "Can you pass that to Grandma?" She looks at me with focused eyes. I nod and smile, doing what she's asked.

After, she begins to assemble ice cream sandwiches, handing each of us a plate with one.

"Thank you," Jason says. "You should open an ice cream shop, Rae Rae."

"Ohhh! That would be fun!" She bounces in her seat.

Ice cream shop. Bakery. Restaurant. My girl wants it all.

"This is delicious," my dad compliments. Rae is all smiles as we each enjoy our dessert.

After my parents are in their room and Rae is in bed, I sit with Jason on the couch.

"I can't thank you enough for today." Our morning was rough and I was angry for his assumptions, but this man holds my heart. We need to talk things out.

"It's the least I can do. Are we still on for dinner tomorrow?"

"Yeah, I think so." Jason lifts a brow. "As long as everything is okay here, yes. I want to spend time with you."

Jason brings my legs onto his lap and runs his hands up and down them. "I admire you. Not only are you an amazing mother, but you have the heart of an angel. Watching you today showed me just how special you are."

I roll my eyes. I don't take compliments well. "It's my job."

"No, babe. You could've stayed at home, visited when you had a day off, and done what you could. You changed your entire life around selflessly."

"They're my parents. They did that for me time and time again. They deserve it."

"Exactly. Your compassion is boundless." He leans forward and kisses me. The scruff on his face is a combination of soft scratching and tickling on my skin. I welcome the sensation and wrap my arms around his neck. We stop before it gets too far, leaving me breathless.

"I hate to end this kiss, but it's not the right time," Jason says, running a hand through his hair.

"I know."

"I'll pick you up tomorrow at eight-thirty. Do you think that's a good time?"

"Yeah."

"Good. I'll look up places not too far from here for us to go to."

"Oh, there's this place I used to love. It's nothing fancy, and I'm not sure it's still open."

"What's the name? I'll check," Jason offers.

"Buns. It's a burger joint, and they're greasy, but so worth it." My mouth is watering. "And their milkshakes were the best. And their onion rings. Oh God, I sound like a fatty."

Jason chuckles. "Nope. I like that you eat greasy burgers the same way you eat salads. Sometimes we need the comfort of something familiar."

"Yup," I smile.

"I'll call you tomorrow." I walk Jason to the door, wishing he could stay. "Goodnight." He cradles my face and kisses me again. I hug him to me, hesitant to release him. Having him here today has been wonderful. It's helped me feel more grounded and all of us were in a better mood.

"Goodnight," I tell him once I release him.

I drag myself to bed, wondering how we'll be able to build a stable relationship in the situation we're in.

Jason arrives right at eighty-thirty and everything in the house is settled, for the most part. Rae isn't in bed yet. She asked me if she could stay up to see Jason and then promised she'd go to bed.

"Hey, Rae Rae." Jason bends down and hugs her.

"Hi." She yawns as she attempts to smile. "Mommy

said I could say hi before going to sleep."

"I'm glad you waited up," he rubs the top of her head, causing her to giggle. She's holding tight to an old stuffed animal of mine. She's grown attached to the elephant.

"I'm going to tuck her in and I'll be right back," I tell Jason.

"Take your time," he nods.

Back in the room, Rae hops into bed and I tuck her in. I kiss her forehead and wish her a goodnight.

"Have fun, Mommy. I love you."

"I love you, too, baby. You'll be okay here?" I rather leave her sleeping than awake. Now that the evening arrived, I'm nervous about leaving her here. My dad is in his room, but it's not the same as when she's being watched by Abigail, who solely cares for her.

"Yeah," Rae yawns. Her eyes are small as she shifts in the bed. She'll be asleep before we walk out the front door.

"Remember to call Grandpa if you need anything."

"Mhmm," she replies.

I close the door behind me and tiptoe back to the living room. "She's out."

Jason holds my hand and kisses my cheek. "She'll be okay," he comforts me.

I nod. She will be, but this is new for me and she's my baby girl.

We pull into Buns' parking lot, and we're seated almost immediately when we walk in. The memories of my teen years jump out at me from the old, black and white photographs on the wall to the vinyl seating. "The barbecue burger was the best," I tell Jason.

"You weren't kidding when you mentioned this place. They have a ton of options."

"I know." I scan the menu, although I know I'll order the barbecue burger with a side of onion rings. Jason orders a bacon double cheeseburger with fries.

"I got a call from the coffee shop today," I begin.

"You did?" His eyes light up.

I nod. "I'm going tomorrow to meet the manager for an interview."

"That's great. Congrats, babe."

"Thanks. I'm staying level-headed, but seems like they need an extra hand in the summer."

"I'm proud of you."

"Let's not celebrate yet. Coffee is new to me. The most I've done is run a normal coffee maker at Joyce's. Espresso and fancy coffees are different, but I'm a quick learner."

"I have no doubt you can do it," Jason praises.

"How are things going with the band? All we talk about is my family, and I want to hear about you."

"We're good. We got details for the movie soundtrack and began working on a song."

"Tell me more about this movie." I think it's amazing that they will be creating music for a film.

"It was a no-brainer for us to say yes. Besides the fact that we respect the hell out of our service men and women, Bri's husband was a solider who died while serving our nation. He was a buddy of ours, too."

"Wow, that's admirable. Wait, aren't Bri and Cole…?" Jason nods. "Was that awkward at first, if y'all knew her husband?"

"You have no idea," he chuckles. "Cole also wasn't the

most, um… not the kind of guy to settle… if you catch my drift. He had a bit of a reputation."

"So he slept around?" I say.

"Oh, yeah." Jason runs a hand through his hair and laughs. "A lot."

"And now he doesn't," I add.

"No. Actually, I didn't notice, but he had stopped fooling around once Josh passed away. Their start was rocky, but they're in a good place now."

"They live together now, right?" I remember him mentioning that.

"Yup. Happy as two peas in a pod." Jason's smirk is lopsided, and I'm attracted to it like a mouse to cheese.

The waitress interrupts my ogling when she brings our dinner. He's told me a little bit about each of his friends. When I meet them, I won't go in so blind. *When I meet them.* It's okay to assume I will, right?

Jason takes a bite of his burger and nods his head. "You were right. This place is good."

I smile. "Told ya. We'd hang out here when I was in high school, but I've been coming here since I was about Rae's age. I'm glad it's still around."

Jason and I share our fries and onion rings as we eat our burgers and continue the conversation. I tell him more about growing up in this area and my favorite things to do.

"Do you have room for a milk shake?" Jason asks.

I rub my belly. "I should say no, but it's too tempting. Want to share one?"

"Works for me. You choose, since you're the Buns pro."

I giggle and look at the menu for any new flavors. I keep it traditional, asking him, "Oreo shake?"

"Perfect." Jason waves the waitress down and orders the shake as she clears the table. Then, he stands and walks around the table. He takes a seat next to me in the booth and puts his arm around me. "Better."

I bite down a smile. Jason leans in for an innocent kiss, resting his free hand on my knee. Once again, the waitress interrupts us as she places the milk shake in front of us, smiling.

"You're not worried about being noticed?" I ask Jason before taking a sip of the sweetness.

"Nah. I'm spending time with you, not worrying about other people."

"I needed this. Thank you." I kiss his cheek. He moves his arm from around my shoulder and sneaks it in behind my back to wrap around my waist. He squeezes my hip and smiles.

"I'm glad we had this time," he whispers into my ear.

As we walk out of the restaurant, I hear, "Hey." I turn around and see a guy stand from one of the tables closer to the entrance. He's sitting with three other people. My eyebrows furrow as I look at him.

"I know you," he says as he approaches us. Jason turns as well and looks down at me with a raised brow.

When the man gets closer, blurry memories begin to surface. My heart kicks into overdrive, and I clamp down on Jason's hand, causing him to jolt.

"It's been a long time. We met on your twenty-first birthday. Cassidy, right?" The man tilts his head and looks at me. My eyes are wide as I stare at him. Jason looks at him as well.

I nod my head.

"How are you? I went back looking for you some time

after, but you were gone."

"Oh, um… hi. Yeah, I'm good. I gotta go." I fumble over my words. Flashes of the one night that changed my life rush through the front of my mind.

He looks at Jason, who seems ready to pounce on him. I tug his hand to drag him away, desperate to leave. How the hell did my past catch up to me? I was certain it never would.

As I race out of the building, I gasp for air and release Jason's hand so I can lift my arms and breathe.

"Cassidy Rae?" Jason's voice is eerily quiet. Tears burn my eyes. He knew my name. How the hell do I not remember his? Tequila shots, that's why.

I ignore Jason, who is rooted to the ground, as I fight back the desire to puke the meal we just ate. I move away from the door, so I don't cause attention. Jason follows, giving me space.

"Was that?" He looks from the building back to me. "She looks like him."

I shake my head. No. Rae always looked like me. The only difference was her eyes. She can't look like him. She can't. If he sees her, he'll know. What happens then?

"Baby, I need you to talk to me." I look up at him, tears staining my face. I tremble.

Jason rushes to me, holding me tight. "It's okay. I need you to breathe so you can talk to me calmly."

My breathing is ragged as I try to fill my lungs. Somehow, Jason guides us to his car and opens the door for me, sliding me into the passenger seat. When he sits on his side he turns to look at me.

"Cassidy Rae." I look at him. "What's going on?"

"That was…" I can't admit it.

"I know." He intertwines our fingers.

"He remembered me. I was drunk. I assumed he was, too. We were all drinking together. If he finds out about Rae, could he take her away from me?"

"Shhh…" Jason coos as I cry into his shoulder. "I'm not familiar with the laws, but I don't think it's that easy. You don't even know if he'd want that."

"He came back to look for me."

I look at Jason. If Rae's dad came back to look for me, that means he was looking for something. Had he known I was pregnant, would he want to have been in Rae's life? Did I take that chance away from him and Rae by not staying or seeking him out?

"What am I supposed to do?"

"I don't know." Jason carves paths through his hair with his fingers. The lines on his forehead are etched with worry.

"If he sees her…" The idea of losing Rae or having some kind of custody battle sickens me. She's mine. She's been the one thing I'm most proud of.

"We don't know anything."

"Am I supposed to tell him? If you were him, would you want to know?"

"I don't… I'm not sure."

"I'm sorry. I'm sorry. That's not fair. This isn't fair to you." I lean back on the passenger seat and close my eyes. I can tell him and let him decide what he wants to do, or I don't tell him and pray we never run into him again. That could cause more problems.

"Look at me, Cassidy Rae," Jason demands.

I turn my head and stare.

"You do not have to make a rash decision. I will talk to my lawyer tomorrow. I'll get the facts and we'll go from there." Hearing him say *we* provokes my emotions again.

This is on me, yet he's taking a part in it. I want to tell him he doesn't have to do that, but I don't have a lawyer I can consult. I don't have anyone with legal background I can approach about this, so I nod.

"Give me a few days." Jason's hand holds the back of my neck, his thumb massaging me.

"She's my baby."

"I know. I don't see a reason for you to lose custody. You're a great mother. You've worked hard to keep her safe, nourished, and clean. You have people who could speak up for you and offer testimonies."

I listen to Jason talk about all this and I'm distraught with the thought of going to court.

"He'll need a paternity test," Jason continues.

"He's her father," I confirm.

"I know, but the court will want that evidence. It will buy you time."

"He may not even care," I sound unconvincing.

Jason smiles. "Exactly."

The words, *I went back,* continue to play in my mind and I remember what Bronwyn said when I ran into her at the grocery store.

We get back to my house and Jason parks the car. "Come here." He undoes my seatbelt and pulls me over the center console onto his lap. My legs extend onto the seat I was just occupying.

Jason cradles my face, his fingers lacing into my hair. "I promise to find the answers for you. Don't let this bring you down. You're so strong." He kisses my dry lips. "After we have the facts, if you want to find him and tell him, we will. I want your mind clear when you go to your interview tomorrow."

"Okay." I had forgotten about the interview. I need

this job.

"I don't think you realize how much I care about you." His blue eyes burn into mine. I swallow hard and hug him as much as I can in the confinements of his car.

"I do. No man that didn't care would stay. You're still here, comforting me and solving my problems because I can't even think clearly. I don't know why or how you got to the diner that day. I don't care to understand it. All I care about is that we're here, together."

Jason's lips skim over my jaw in route to my lips. He gives me a closed-mouth kiss first, taking his time. When his tongue sweeps across my lips, I open my mouth. Our lips mold and tongues move together. Jason's hand wanders up and down the side of my body as his mouth continues its exploration, like a desperate man in search of gold.

I match his need, gripping onto him. I've been independent for a long time, but feeling the comfort and security in this man's arms has sparked a desire to have someone tackle life with me.

"Damn," Jason leans his forehead against mine and murmurs.

I tilt my chin up and brush my lips against his. "Thank you. Lately, you're doing a lot more than you need to for my family and me."

"You're mine. We work through things together."

"I feel like I know nothing about your family and you're spending all this time with mine."

"Your family needs us more right now." I swallow back my tears and nod. If I start crying now, I'm not sure I'll stop.

When I saw Ben at Drink A Latte, the coffee shop, he asked if I was seeing anyone and I told him about Jason.

It was nice to speak to someone openly, who is an adult. It's not appropriate to talk to Rae about him, and my dad has enough things to think about other than my love life. I confessed that I was falling in love with Jason but didn't understand how when we've only known each other for a couple of months.

Ben told me that the older we get, the more serious we become in relationships. We remove the games and teasing. When he pointed out that Rae was probably a big factor in that, I had to agree. Being a mother doesn't allow me to date liberally or waste my time. I let in a man I was serious about getting to know.

After witnessing Jason with my family yesterday, I knew that the feelings are real.

"I want you to get rest. Call me tomorrow. I'm going to talk to my lawyer, but I want your main focus to be on the interview."

"Thank you." I withhold my confession.

As soon as I climb into bed, I pull Rae into my arms and hold her tight throughout the night.

Chapter 19

Jason

LEAVING CASSIDY RAE LAST NIGHT was fucking hard. I've never seen her so weak. I wanted to kiss away her fear until the sun rose, but that's not an option. Instead, I woke up early and called my lawyer. I gave him the information I had and hung up with a promise he'd contact me as soon as he had some information.

"Hey, babe," I answer my phone when it rings.

The guys raise their eyebrows as they overhear my greeting. I flip them off and walk out of the studio to talk to Cassidy Rae.

"Hi."

"How are you? How did the interview go?"

"I got the job," her voice is flat.

"That's great! Congrats. We'll celebrate this week."

"Thanks."

"Now tell me how you're feeling."

"Like crap. I pretended everything was normal this morning, but I'm losing my grip on my emotions. I need to stay strong, so I can take care of my mom, but I can't stop thinking about the worse case scenario."

"Focus on your mom for now, and let's wait to hear from my lawyer. I'm almost positive the mother's custody weighs more, especially since you've been caring for her all these years."

"You're right."

"Are you driving home?" I ask. I lean my head against the wall, one of my legs crossed over the other.

"Yeah. I wanted to share the news with you. It may not be the greatest job, but I'll be happy to have an income. Since it's part-time, my schedule is flexible as well. I'll be working mostly the morning shifts, and a couple afternoons. I start tomorrow with the afternoon shift. My evenings will be free, which will be nice."

"So date nights are still a possibility?"

"Even if I worked nights, we'd make this work." Her response makes me smile. Cash comes out and signals for me to return. "I gotta go back to work, Caz. I'm proud of you. Everything will be okay. I promise."

"Thank you."

"I'll call you later. Go share the news with your family." I hang up when she says bye and exhale, glad she got the job. If Rae's biological father wanted to fight for custody, having a stable job is a plus for Cassidy Rae.

Being at work today has been pointless. I'm not here with the guys. It's not fair to them, but my mind is preoccupied with Cassidy Rae. This has to be eating her up, clawing its way through her system.

"All good?" Cash asks when I return.

"Yep. She got a job." I haven't told them about last

night. It's not a story for me to tell.

"That's great," he responds.

We get back to work, discussing numbers, sales, and projections. All stuff I should enjoy. We work with our team to perfect the lyrics for the movie. This is a different process than creating our album. The movie producer has certain requirements and expectations. It's not the easiest feat, staying within those parameters. The four of us strive on breaking away from limits, so we work a little harder at this one.

By the time we're done, I want to race to Cassidy Rae's house. Instead, I grab a quick bite to eat alone because all my friends have wives or girlfriends to go home to. As much as I want to call Cassidy Rae, I know she's currently having dinner with her family.

I'm annoyed I can't come home to her. I'm frustrated my lawyer didn't call me back today. I'm worried this fucker will try to steal my girl away. I saw the way he looked at her. I heard his words when he said he went back searching for her. She doesn't know him, so we can't trust him. What if he hurts her or Rae?

I grab my phone and send Cassidy Rae a text message to call me once Rae's in bed. Then, I turn on the television and watch the sports channel.

"Jason." I look in my rearview mirror and raise my eyebrows.

"Yeah, Rae Rae?" I picked her up after calling Mr. Pressman, so we could surprise Cassidy Rae at the end of her first day at work. Daisies are sitting on the passenger seat, wrapped in paper and plastic. Rae picked them out at the grocery store.

"Do you think Mommy will be surprised?"

"Super surprised."

Rae cheers and dances in the seat. That girl always finds a way of winning you over. It didn't take long for me to care about her. It hasn't taken long for me to fall in love with her mom, either. I just need to find the right time to tell her, and with Rae's dad popping up, I want to make sure Cassidy Rae is in the right state of mind for that.

These Pressman girls have me wrapped around their fingers.

I may not be Rae's biological father, but I can provide the love of a father, even if her real one wants nothing to do with her.

"We'll walk in quietly and wait for her if she's still working, okay? We can't make a scene," I explain to Rae.

"Okay. Can I carry the flowers?" she asks as I park the car.

"You sure can." I get out of the car and open her door. She smiles as she holds the flowers in one hand and my hand with the other.

It takes me a minute to spot Cassidy Rae when we walk in. Rae runs to her before I can hold her back. I try to reach for her arm, but she's already crashing into her mom's hip.

Cassidy Rae looks at her with wide eyes and up to find me a few feet away, my fists clenched and eyes just as wide as hers. She tries to shield Rae to no avail when she hands her the flowers and says, "Congrats," louder than necessary. This was not the plan.

I walk up to them, overhearing the man ask Cassidy Rae how old Rae is. I stand next to Cassidy Rae, my arm around her shoulder and a kiss on her cheek.

"Ready to go?" I say through clenched teeth.

"Mmhmm," Cassidy Rae hums. "I gotta go. Sorry."

She better not be fucking sorry.

As I try to usher her out, the guy calls out. "Is she?" he pauses. Cassidy Rae turns to him, eyes cast down. There's no denying Rae's age and similar features. "We need to talk, then."

"Not now," I shake my head. I don't bother to look around. I try to be as subtle as possible, considering this is Cassidy Rae's new place employment.

"I'll come back tomorrow," he states. I turn and walk away.

As soon as we're outside, Rae asks, "Who was that?"

"An old friend, sweetheart," Cassidy Rae bends and hugs her. "Thank you for the flowers. They're beautiful." Her voice cracks.

"You're welcome. I picked them out," she beams with pride.

"What are you doing here?" Cassidy Rae stands and looks at me.

"We wanted to surprise you when you finished your first day. I'm sorry. Had I known, I wouldn't have brought her." My hair has been receiving a beating over the last twenty-four hours. I tug at the roots before dropping my hand.

"Don't be. You had no idea. I was getting ready to leave and I saw him."

"We'll talk later," I whisper as I hug her.

"Please tell me your lawyer got back to you."

I nod. "That's the other reason I came. I spoke to him. It's pretty good news. We'll talk about all this after." I nod toward Rae.

"Thank you." Cassidy Rae touches her lips to mine and then carries Rae. "How was your day?" She holds her as high as she can. "You're getting too big for me to carry."

"No I'm not," Rae whines. "Pick me up again." She holds her arms up. Cassidy Rae picks her up and pretends Rae is flying. She swooshes her through the air quickly as Rae bursts into a fit of laughter. I watch them both, needing this to become permanent.

"I told your dad I'd grab dinner on the way home. Your mom was having a good afternoon and resting. He looked good, too."

"You're the best." She smiles, although the worry lines around her eyes are still present. I'm sure the last thing she wants to think about right now is cooking dinner.

"What should we eat?" I ask.

"Pizza!" Rae yells.

I look at Cassidy Rae with a quirked brow. "Works for me."

"Great. How about I grab it and you head home?" I offer.

"Can I go with you?" Rae asks.

"I think your mom could use the company right now. Spend some time with her." I wink at Cassidy Rae, who sighs and begins to relax.

This morning Rich told me Cassidy Rae shouldn't have a problem keeping her full custody, but the father may have a right to visitation. He said they could settle outside of the courtroom if they find a way to peacefully discuss Rae's custody. It's good news that Cassidy Rae won't lose her, but her biological father has a right to build a relationship with his daughter if he wants one.

It's fucked up, but I'm hoping he doesn't. Yet he said they needed to talk after meeting Rae. He doesn't seem like the kind of guy that would want to stir things up, but people are deceiving. All I know is that I need to protect my girls.

Cassidy Rae

I RUSH TO BUCKLE RAE in the car and over to the driver's seat, locking the doors before I start the car. The need to break down is high, but I have to remain strong. When Scott–he finally told me his name–came up to me, I froze. He said we didn't have much time to talk on Monday and wanted to get together. Apparently, he did come back asking about me. He was interested in dating me back then. I kindly told him I was seeing someone, and that's when Rae ran up to me.

His eyes bugged out when he saw her, and then realization dawned on him as she looked his way. I have enough worry with my mom to add Rae's biological father coming into the picture. There's no escaping this now, though. He saw her and he wants to talk. As soon as we eat, I need to hear what Jason's lawyer said.

"Did you like your new job?" Rae asks.

"I did, baby." I keep my voice even. "The people are nice and it's fun to make different kinds of coffees. The flowers are beautiful." The bouquet of daisies lay on the seat next to me as I drive. Rae knows me well to choose these flowers. They're some of my favorite.

"I'm glad you liked them. As soon as I saw them I told Jason they were yours. I think he loves you."

My breath hitches. "What?" I squeak.

"Yeah. Boys that love girls give them flowers."

I giggle. "You think?"

"Yup. One day, Bobby gave flowers to Jenny at school

and that's what he said." I laugh, snorting. Relationship advice from kids.

"It's a little different for adults," I respond.

"Why?" Her voice raises.

"Because we have more responsibilities and have to make sure that you want to spend a long time with that person. You take time to get to know them."

"But you already know Jason," she points out.

Yup, and what I'm feeling is love.

"I do." There's not much more her mind will understand at this point. "Tell me how you helped Grandpa this afternoon?" I needed to go back to work, but I missed spending the entire day with Rae and helping my dad.

"I helped Grandma eat and I read her a book while Grandpa cleaned the kitchen. She smiled while I read."

"Thank you for doing that."

"It's fun," I watch her shrug through the rearview mirror.

We soon arrive at my parents' house and I find my mom and dad in the living room talking. Well, my dad is talking, and my mom sits next to him in her wheelchair.

"Hi." My dad looks up at us. "How was your first day?" I feel like I'm a kid again going back to school after a long summer.

"It was great."

My dad eyes the flowers. "Those are pretty."

"I picked them out." Rae sure is proud of that.

I put the flowers in water and let my dad know Jason is bringing pizza. In the pantry, I find a boxed soup for my mom. As soon as I get my first paycheck, I'm going to make her real chicken soup.

Jason and I sit on the couch after everyone's in bed.

"You seem better," he states.

"I am." I inhale. "Rae helps with that. Her innocence always brightens my day."

"She's a special one." Jason holds me close.

"What did your lawyer say?" I hesitate as I ask the question.

"Good news is that as the mother and sole caretaker, you shouldn't have a problem keeping that role. He said you would keep custody unless you were mistreating Rae or neglecting her, which isn't the case. Now, if her biological father–"

"Scott," I interrupt him.

"What?" His eyebrows pull in.

"His name is Scott."

"Oh." Jason frowns.

"We might as well call him by his name."

"Anyway, if Scott wants to claim his rights as her biological father and have custody, he could petition it. I don't think you will lose yours. You'd just have joint custody or whatever agreement you decide upon and the court approves."

"Okay." I digest that information. "So I'd have to share her?" I look up at Jason.

"It's hard, but it could be much worse. It's not like he could take her away from you just because. You have everything going for you, and Rae can speak for herself."

"I don't want her involved unless absolutely necessary." I refuse to throw her into some kind of legal battle.

"I understand."

"I don't even know him." I chew on the inside of my bottom lip. "I can't just send her off with him, even if he is her real father." The ugly truth is that I screwed this guy–drunk one night–without knowing his name or where he came from. I've raised Rae. She's *mine*, and I'm not sure I can put her in a situation where she goes off with a stranger, even if they share DNA.

"You won't have to. I think the best approach would be for Scott to spend time with Rae when you're present. I'd like to be there, too. We can see the kind of person he is and get to know him. My lawyer doesn't work directly with family law, but he has a partner that does. You'll want to have someone to defend you. He could be a nice guy, Cassidy Rae, but I'll be damned if you don't do this legally." Jason stares at me with intensity. His blue eyes gaze into mine, his mouth in a straight line.

"I agree. I'm not putting my daughter in jeopardy, nor my maternal rights."

"Good."

I touch Jason's cheek and scoot closer. "What's going on?"

"Nothing," he shakes his head once.

"You may be a talented musician, but you're a terrible liar," I tell him.

"Cassidy Rae…" he warns.

"Jason Stone," I use my mom voice. He flinches and turns to me. "Don't you dare try to warn me off. I think we're past that in our relationship." I sit taller, crossing my arms.

"I'm fine."

I arch a brow with my head angled away from him. Jason chuckles.

"Don't look at me that way."

"Why not?" I demand.

Next thing I know, Jason's hands are grabbing my hips and pulling me onto him.

"Because it makes me want to do this." His lips crash on mine, his tongue is forceful in its entry as it desperately seeks mine. One of Jason's hands is tight on my hip and the other is tangled in my hair, holding my head in place. I tense at his boldness until I feel his tongue sweep mine.

A low moan travels up my throat, only to be silenced by Jason's mouth.

"You're mine," Jason declares. "I may not be able to claim Rae as my own, but I can claim you. No one takes you away from me unless you want to walk on your own."

I don't have a chance to respond because he's back to his attack. The hair on his face scratching me only amplifies the rawness in his kiss. He's always been gentle with me, but at this moment, Jason is carnal and in control. When he thrusts his hips, I groan. On the second thrust, I kiss him back with the same amount of force, grinding into him. We're like two horny teenagers, but the friction feels so good. Seven years of abstinence will make you feel like an out-of-control, hormonal kid, ready to explode.

Jason grips my hips, stilling me. He leans his head back and looks at me. His breathing is labored and his chest rising at the speed I want to be dry humping him to. I look at him, my own breath struggling to fill my lungs. When his fingers move under the back of my shirt and trace my skin, I shiver.

"I want nothing more than to continue this, naked, but not here. Not with your family in this house and not on your parents' couch."

I shut my eyes. My body is tingling, sensations I haven't

felt in years awakened. "I know." Jason continues to move his hands around my back.

"I want to take my time with you. Make love to you when the moment is right, not because I'm jealous." He closes his eyes and sighs.

Make love. I smile at his choice of words.

"You're blind if you don't realize that I don't want anyone else but you. You don't have to go all caveman, claiming me. Although," I look away. "That kiss was intense." I feel warmth taking over my neck and face.

Jason holds my chin and turns my head. "I enjoyed every second of it. Don't be embarrassed, baby. If the situation was different, we wouldn't be having this conversation."

I don't know when the situation will ever be right for us. Between Rae and my mom, I won't even be able to spend a night with him. That would be irresponsible. But, I want to.

"I don't want you to be jealous. You have no reason to. I want to be with you. I want this to work." I link my fingers with his and raise our arms out to the side.

"It will work."

"As for Rae, I know she cares a lot about you, even if her biological dad comes into the picture."

"You two have become my world," he confesses.

I release his hands and cup his face. My lips brush against his. "And you've opened ours."

"I'm in love with you, Cassidy Rae."

My body relaxes, and my eyes soften as moisture clouds my vision. I hug Jason, a few tears rolling down the side of my nose. "I love you." I look up at him.

"You do?" His wide eyes make me giggle.

"Yes. I've been feeling it, and watching you with my

family on Sunday sealed the deal. Any man willing to do all you did is worthy of my love."

He kisses me much softer this time, no jealousy or worry laced in his lips. I cling onto him, dreaming of a day we can live a full life together.

Chapter 20

Cassidy Rae

I PARK THE CAR AND take a few deep breaths. Jason should be arriving soon, but I'm already late and don't want to make a bad impression.

As promised, Scott went by the coffee shop the day after he saw Rae with a mile-long list of questions. He hesitantly agreed to wait until Friday to talk, since I don't work and wouldn't have to leave my dad alone for so long. He caved when I told him about my mom.

It's now Friday and I'm not prepared for this conversation. I'm grateful Jason insisted on coming, too.

I jump out of the car and walk into the pizza parlor. It's an odd place to meet for this kind of conversation, but Drink A Latte is off limits since it's my place of work and I wanted somewhere public.

As soon as I walk in, I see Scott sitting at a table. He looks up and smiles awkwardly.

"Hi." He stands.

"Hey," I reply. I created a human with this man and I don't really remember him. I thought this stuff only happened in movies. I sit when he signals to the chair. I look around the restaurant as I wait for him to speak. I'm not sure how to begin besides stating the obvious.

"So… you got pregnant." He raises his eyebrows. His eyes are as brown as Rae's, though his hair is chestnut. He's lean and good-looking in a preppy way. I twist my fingers together and nod. "God, I'm sorry." It's clear his discomfort is as high as mine.

"Don't be. Rae has made my life amazing. It's been challenging, but she's the sunshine in my life."

"I could tell that day she ran up to you."

"Yeah."

We both stay silent, looking around without making contact.

Scott finally looks at me and says, "This is stupid. I asked to meet with you and I'm acting like an idiot. I'm her father." His voice trembles a bit.

"I'll be honest. I don't remember much of that night. I didn't even know your name until Tuesday afternoon. You're a stranger to me, but you're my daughter's father." I shrug. "Please understand that Rae is my life. This is difficult for me. I always assumed I'd never see you again, so I'm struggling a little bit with you wanting to meet her." I figure honesty is the best approach.

"I don't know you," I shrug apologetically.

"I'm not a bad guy. I have a stable job and come from a good family. That might be empty words to you, but I have people you can talk to. Take it as testimonials."

I shake my head. "I think the best thing is to get to know each other. Rae might be confused at first. She's asked a lot about her father, but I think she's kinda chucked it to the side, thinking she'd never meet him. She's smart and mature for her age, but she's still a child. Her heart is vulnerable."

"I get that. I have a niece who is four. I see how sensitive children can be. When she doesn't get the color she wants for something, all hell breaks loose," Scott chuckles. I laugh along with him because I know exactly how that situation could play out.

"Hey." I turn to see Jason. I smile and stand to give him a hug. He holds me with one hand, keeping his eyes on Scott. "I'm Jason." He extends his hand.

"Scott. It's nice to meet you."

"Likewise. Sorry I'm late. Work ran longer than planned." Jason sits next to me, keeping his hand on my knee.

"I was explaining to Scott the challenges that I face," I explain to Jason. "He has a niece that's four." I throw that in.

"What do you do?" Jason asks Scott.

"I work in sales for a food supply company. I've been there for a few years now." Scott doesn't miss a beat in responding.

"Did you go to college?" Jason shoots him another questions.

"I got my Bachelor's in Business."

"What are your intentions with Rae?"

I squeeze Jason's leg under the table, but he doesn't flinch. Scott looks at me. "Shouldn't these be questions she asks?" He points at me.

"Cassidy Rae and I are together, and I care about what happens to her and her daughter."

"I want to meet her. I want to get to know her. Imagine

you find out you have a child. Wouldn't you want the opportunity to at least try to build a relationship?"

"Fair enough."

"I would like a paternity test done," I speak up.

"My lawyer already suggested that," Scott replies.

"So you've talked to a lawyer?" I ask.

Scott nods. A knot in my stomach forms. "What exactly do you want?" I whisper.

"Like I said. I want to meet her and spend some time with her. I'm more than happy for you to be present. I'll take the paternity test, and after I receive those results and spend some time with Rae, I'd like to discuss custody."

I swallow the lump in my throat. My eyes water. I knew this was coming, but it doesn't lessen the strike. With my heart beating in my chest, I nod.

"I'll talk to my lawyer and we can set up the paternity test. I would like to wait for those results before you meet Rae," I say. "Like I told you, my mom is very sick and we're not sure how much time she has. Rae's overwhelmed, and it's a lot for her to process—moving to a new house, starting a new school next month, the stress about my mom's health.

"Meeting her father would push her. I know she'll need to go in for the test, but I rather wait before we make plans. That's all I ask. As soon as we have the results, we can take her to the park. I'll introduce you. You can talk, play, whatever you want." I blow out air.

"Okay." That was too easy.

"My schedule is a little weird since I'm working part-time and taking care of my mom, so I ask for patience when it comes to settling on a date."

"Look, I don't want to cause problems. I'm not here to take her away from you or anything. I rather work through this as quietly as possible. I'm not looking for drama."

"Thank you."

"I'll call the lab to see what days they have available for the tests and will let you know, so we can choose a date that works for you."

"Okay," I nod.

We agree to be in touch and Scott leaves. It was less stress than I imagined, but I don't know if it will remain that way.

"Are you okay?" Jason asks me.

"I think so?" I hold my face with my hands.

"Baby steps," Jason rubs a soothing hand across my back.

"Yeah. First step, paternity test. Although, I have no doubt he's her father," I state.

"I know." Jason purses his lips and nods.

"Hey, you're still our guy." I smile. "No one else can take the role of Country Prince." I use his words.

"A southern fairytale," he smirks.

"Do you want to have dinner with us? I believe it's taco night."

"Can't say no to Rae's famous tacos."

I lean in and kiss him. My dad is probably worried about what happened and I want to get back to tell him. He was shocked when I first mentioned it. He has enough preoccupations, and I feel like I'm adding to his list of things to stress about.

"How's your mom today?" Jason asks as we walk out, hand in hand.

"So-so." I tilt my head side to side. "It was harder to get her out of bed. The doctor says it's all part of the illness. Eventually, she may lose all mobility and become bedridden. She's been sleeping more, as well." I'm not blind to my mom's health. I see her weaken, yet I continue to take care of her as lovingly as I can. We all do.

My dad and I had a conversation a few nights ago. He had bought a plot in a cemetery a few years ago. He's realistic to what's coming, and I wish I could be as strong as him. Right now, I feel like I've been hit with a double whammy and I'm barely holding on.

With everything going on with my mom, meeting Scott has not come at the best time. A week and a half ago we did the paternity test. It doesn't help that Rae had a few questions of her own to ask when I mentioned the lab work. It's not exactly easy to tell her she needs to go to a doctor to get a saliva swab and not explain what it's for. I've never lied to her, and I wasn't going to start now.

We sat and had a conversation about the man she saw in the coffee shop. I explained briefly that we needed to do a test to confirm his paternity. I didn't exactly do the best job of explaining this to my six-year-old.

"Does it hurt?" she asked.

"No, baby girl. They put a cotton swab in your mouth, like the ones to clean your ears, and get a bit of saliva from the inside of your cheek."

"Eewww. I don't want something from my ear in my mouth."

I giggled at her reaction, so I took a cotton swab and practiced what I though the test would be like. It helped her relax, but it didn't quiet her questions. When she asked why we needed to do the test, when I should know that's her father, I was silenced by the embarrassment that I don't remember much about the night we conceived her. I remember flashes. I remember having sex. Scott's face isn't totally clear in my drunken haze.

"Are you ready?" I ask Rae. She nods, her body slouched. "What's wrong?" I ask as I sit next to her on the couch.

When the results came back positive, Scott wanted to meet Rae. I'm lucky I work four days a week, and the results came in on my last day of work for the week. My dad insisted he would be okay for a few hours and encouraged me to go with Rae and Scott to the park.

"I'm nervous." She bites her fingernails.

"It will be okay. I'll be there with you, and Jason will meet us at the park. Nothing bad will happen. Scott wants to meet you and get to know you. I know this is weird, baby. I'm sorry you have to go through this." Tears fill my eyes as I bring her to me in a hug.

"It's not your fault."

Yes, it is. She may be blinded by a child's unconditional love, but this discomfort is because of me.

"Scott is a nice person," I reassure her. We have spoken a few times. I was adamant to know a bit more about him before I exposed my child to his presence. He even got a letter from his employer and a few friends, who could be biased, but the effort spoke for itself.

Jason did some research on him as well, and everything came back normal. He wasn't listed on a sex offender log or anything of the sort.

"What if he doesn't like me?" Rae murmurs against my chest. I pull back and look down at her with my nose crinkled.

"Why wouldn't he?"

"I don't know," she shrugs. "What if I'm not funny to him or smart enough?" I hate that these doubts are creeping in. She has this need to be accepted–my fault for keeping her away–despite the confidence she expresses most of the time.

"You are the funniest girl I know, and you are so smart. Your teacher told me so. You're beautiful, caring, and you have the biggest heart I know. There's no way anyone would dislike you." I smile at her and kiss her button nose. "And you're the best baker in the world… and artist." I add.

"Are you sure?" She frowns.

"I'm absolutely positive." I tickle her ribs, breaking her into a fit of giggles.

"Okay. Stop," she laughs harder. "I believe you!" she yells.

Rae catches her breath, her cheeks pulled up with her smile. "I love you, Rae. You're always going to have me by your side."

"Thank you, Mommy." She wraps her arms around my neck and squeezes tight. I hold her for a few seconds before looking at my beautiful girl. "Do I have to call him Dad?"

"You call him whatever you want," I reply. I don't want her to feel obligated to say something she's not comfortable with.

"I think I like Scott better."

I nod. "That's perfect, baby. Are you ready to go?" I ask.

"Yeah," she lifts a shoulder.

"I've got you," I comfort her.

I take a few deep breaths as I grip the steering wheel. The park has a few people littered throughout with it being summer, and I spot Scott sitting on a bench, staring off. I wonder if he's as nervous as we are.

"Ready?" I call out in the car, not only for Rae, but as encouragement for me as well.

"Yeah," Rae whispers.

I turn off the car and walk to the backseat. Rae's hand tightens in mine as we make our way toward Scott. Before we reach him, a text message from Jason comes in informing me he will meet us soon and wishing both Rae and I luck.

"Jason wishes us good luck," I tell Rae.

"Is he coming?" her voice trembles.

"Yeah. He'll be here soon."

"Good," she sighs.

"Hi," Scott says as he stands.

"Hey."

Rae looks up at him silently, her grip around my hand even tighter.

"Hi, Rae," Scott squats down in front of her. I join him, keeping Rae's hand in mine.

"Sweetie, this is Scott. He's your dad," I add although she knows. I guess it gives a sense of reality to this and makes Scott feel included.

She offers a tight smile and leans into me. "She's nervous," I tell him.

"It's okay. I'm kinda nervous, too." He looks at Rae.

"You are?" she asks him.

He nods.

"Why?"

"Well, I'm your dad, but you don't know me. It's kinda weird, but I want to get to know you. Maybe you won't like me."

"Yeah," she looks down. "I feel the same." She plays with the dusty ground with the tip of her shoes.

"Can we talk? Maybe get to know each other?" He asks her.

"Okay."

I sit on the bench with Scott, Rae climbing on my lap. She holds onto me as Scott speaks to her.

"What do you like to do for fun?" He begins asking her questions. Rae keeps her head on my shoulder.

"I like coloring and baking."

"That's cool. I like eating baked goods," Scott smiles.

"What's your favorite?"

"Cupcakes. Do you know how to make cupcakes?"

"I do. My mom says they're my specialty." She looks up at me. I wink at her with a smile.

"Well, maybe I can try them one day. What's your favorite color?"

"Blue. Girls are supposed to like pink, but blue is more pretty."

"Guess what?" Scott leans in a bit. "That's *my* favorite color."

"It is?" Rae's voice rises a bit and she sits tall.

"Yup."

I sit back and watch them interact. Slowly, Rae is becoming more confident. Scott does seem like a decent person from what I'm seeing. He has been careful and clearly has a list of questions prepared. The more I see him, especially next to Rae, I can point out their similarities. Not only is the color of their eyes the same, but so is the shape. Rae's eyes are wider than mine, more expressive. She got that from Scott.

"Do you like to color?" Rae asks Scott.

"I haven't colored in a long time, but I'm sure it would be fun."

"Do you have a mommy and daddy?"

"I do," he smirks. "They're great parents."

"My mommy also has parents, but my grandma is sick," Rae frowns and casts her eyes downward.

"I heard. I hope she feels better. I've been praying for her." Rae and I both snap our heads toward him.

"You have?" she asks, surprised.

"Yeah."

"Thank you," I say.

He nods in acknowledgment, not saying more than that. "I also have a brother," he tells us. "He has a daughter that's a little younger than you, so you have a cousin."

"What's a cousin?" Rae looks at the two of us.

"It's when the sister or brother of your mom or dad have a child. It's almost like being sisters, but a little different." He looks at me, his mouth screwed. I nod, encouraging him.

This is surreal. Never would I have imagined a day like today. This was never an option I would have considered. My fear about this meeting is dissipating as I watch Rae and Scott interact. They laugh and ask each other different questions. I hope this bubble doesn't explode on us. I continue to stress the legal aspect, but maybe Scott will be flexible.

Realizing how much time has passed, I check my phone for any sign from Jason. He should've gotten here by now. I shield my eyes from the sun and look out into the parking lot in search of his car. It's not there. Worried, I send him a quick text message asking if everything is okay.

"Mommy, can I show Scott how I can swing?" Rae grabs my attention.

"Sure, sweetie." I remove my arms from around her and watch her skip to the swing set.

"Thanks for this, Cassidy." Scott's face is relaxed as he smiles.

"You're welcome. She seems to be warming up to you." I continue to wonder where Jason is.

"Is Jason coming?" Scott asks.

"Yeah. He should've been here by now. I hope he's okay."

"I'm sure he is. He's in that band, right?" I look over at Scott.

"Yeah," I nod.

"Is it serious?" My eyebrows furrow. "I don't mean to pry, it's just that…" Scott looks away. "We have a daughter together. Had you never run off, I would've found you. We could've been raising her together and maybe, who knows." He shrugs. I squint my eyes, my eyebrows burying deeper into my eyes.

"Scott," I start unsure how to continue. I take a deep breath. "I don't know what would've happened, but being with someone because of a baby isn't the right way to approach a relationship. I hope we can get along and become friends, especially for Rae's sake, but I'm happy with Jason."

He nods, pensive. "If he's in a band, will he be around for you and Rae?"

"Look, I get your concern, but that's between Jason and I. He's supportive of us and makes us his priority. Yes, he will travel when he's on tour, but that won't diminish my relationship with him."

"We could be a family."

I nod. "A modern family. I hope you understand." My lips flatten together.

"Yeah. Figured it'd be worth a shot. You left an impression on me."

"We met once," I state.

"Yeah, but we had a blast together. I'm not talking about the sex," he lowers his voice. "I mean, yeah that was good, but before that."

"I'm sorry. I don't know how things would be had I been there when you returned, but that's not how things happened."

Scott nods, focusing on Rae again, who is calling our names. I sneak a peek at my phone and haven't received anything from Jason. Nerves set in, thinking something happened to him.

Rae runs over to us, asking Scott if he saw how high she swung. He nods, telling her she's a big girl. She sits on my lap again, sweat sticking the loose strands of hair that fell from her ponytail to the sides of her face. I still don't have a word from Jason, but my attention is back on Rae as she speaks to us.

Chapter 21

Jason

I SAT IN MY CAR for fifteen minutes watching them. Rae was talking with her hands as Scott laughed at something she said. Cassidy Rae stared at her daughter in awe, consumed by whatever she was saying. It was hard to watch. Those are my girls sitting with another man, except he had them first.

He knows Cassidy Rae more physically intimately than I do and he had a hand in creating that little girl that makes me smile so much. Reality hits as I looked at them. I have no place there.

What am I? Some guy that fell for a single mom. Rae isn't my daughter. Although Scott just appeared in their lives, he has a right to be in it. When I saw the three of them laughing, I backed out of the parking spot and drove away. If I weren't in the picture, maybe they'd be a family.

I should walk away, even if it breaks my heart. See if this guy and her have something special. Let them have a chance at being a real family. The thing is, her and I have something special and can have our own kind of family.

A weight crushes my chest as I drive in the opposite direction of where my girls are. How do I compete with that? Eventually, I could be left. Cassidy Rae could fall in love with this guy. Obviously something attracted her to him years ago. That could still be there.

I look at my phone when it pings.

Caz: are u almost here?

I read her words, but I don't reply, unsure what to tell her. I drive around with no direction. I'm in love with that woman, and I promised her to always be there for her, except I'm not sticking to that now. I've always had a grasp on life. I always knew where the road was leading. Now, I'm lost.

When the sun blinds me, I realize I've been driving for hours. I go back to the park and see that they're gone. I drop my head onto the steering wheel. *I fucked up.*

With a killer headache, I drive to Cassidy Rae's house and see her car in the driveway.

I grab my phone and call her.

"Jason? What happened?" Her voice is shushed when she answers right away.

"I'm outside. Can you come out a sec?"

"Is everything okay?" The words rush out of her mouth.

"I just want to talk to you."

"Okay." She hangs up and a few seconds later she opens the front door and walks to my car. I turn off my car and get out, my hands in my pocket as I look at her approach me with worry marking her beautiful face.

"What happened today? I thought something

happened to you." Her body is tense.

"I'm sorry. I want to tell you I got stuck doing something for the band, but that's not true. I went to the park, and when I saw you three sitting on the bench, I felt like I didn't belong. I had nothing to offer in a situation like that, so I drove around for hours questioning what the hell I'm doing. Am I getting in the way of a family being together and happy?"

"No," Cassidy Rae interrupts me. "Jason, I kept looking for you. Rae asked what happened when you never showed. You're in our lives and very important to this process. Why would you think otherwise?"

I run a hand through my hair. "I feel like I should step back and let you guys work at being a family. Even if nothing happens between you and Scott romantically," I squeeze my eyes shut. "I'm getting in the middle of it."

Cassidy Rae frowns. I see the tears filling her emerald eyes. "Don't cry." I pull her toward me, but she doesn't hug me back.

"Are you breaking up with me?" Her words shake.

"No. I don't know what I'm saying. I feel like I'm preventing you from fully giving Scott a chance."

Cassidy Rae's warm hands hold my face. She gets on her toes to make eye contact.

"You listen to me, you stubborn man. "I love *you.* I want you. You need to get that through that thick skull of yours. I wanted you there today. I wish you were. There will never be another man for me. I don't care if I had a daughter with him. Rae will always care about you, even if her dad is in her life.

"I need you to believe that. I need you to trust me. I don't want to lose you because of this. I'm trying to do what's best for my daughter, for my parents, for you."

Tears slide away from her eyes. "I'm tired."

"I don't know where my place is in all of this."

"Your place is right next to me, where you belong. I know my life is chaos you're not accustomed to, but I don't want to lose you. I understand you have trust issues with what happened with Christie, but I'm not her," she hiccups.

I close my eyes. I can't lose her. "I'm going to need patience." I ask her for what she asked me in the beginning.

"Okay."

I give her a soft kiss. "I'm sorry. I shouldn't have put my issues on you. It's not fair. You're trying to do everything right by all of us, but again, who's taking care of you?"

"I understand this has to be so hard. If it's hard for me, I can imagine how difficult it is for you."

"You just don't need my bullshit with everything you have going on."

"I need you," Cassidy Rae emphasizes. "I have no idea what will happen when it comes down to dealing with lawyers, but I know I want you by my side."

"When will that be?" I ask.

"I don't know. We're seeing Scott again in two days on Saturday. I'd like for you to go if you're free. I think it would be good to get to know Scott."

"I'll be there. I can pick you and Rae up and we drive together."

"Yes," she exhales. I hold her waist, pulling her closer into me. She fits between my widened legs and snuggles into my chest.

"We need to go to LA on Tuesday for a few days. The band has a couple interviews and we have to meet with the music producer for the film. Will you be okay?"

"Yeah," she looks up at me, her lashes moist from her tears.

"I thought maybe I could take this trip, give you a break, and figure shit out," I confess.

"I don't need a break. You're taking a trip for work to LA, and you'll be back. That's normal for your career. Please, don't over think this situation."

"I won't." At least I hope I won't. I've always been pretty confident, but after Christie fucked me over I've felt insecure. Then, I meet Cassidy Rae, which I feel I'm not humble enough to deserve her love.

"Stop thinking." She places her fingers on my forehead, trying to smooth my skin. I chuckle at her attempt and rest my chin on her shoulder.

I'm being a pussy. I know it's not fair to force Cassidy Rae to try at a relationship with a man she doesn't care about, but there's that devil side of me telling me I'm not good enough when she can be with the father of her child.

"I'm yours, remember?" Cassidy Rae blushes. Fuck do I ever remember that make-out. We were like horny teens going at it on the couch. My dick hardens at the memory.

"I remember."

"I expect you to act like it." I love when she gets tough, demanding with me.

"Yes, ma'am," I tease.

"Good. Now, give me a kiss before we go inside."

"With pleasure." I lean down, greedy for her lips.

I close my eyes as we take off on our private plane. Traveling has become a lot fancier since we've become famous and the label has arranged all of our travel needs.

A few days in Los Angeles might help center me.

I spent some time getting to know Scott when we went to the park on Saturday. He seems okay. He has a thing for Cassidy Rae though, and I'm not cool with that. I promised I'd trust her, and I do. Scott is just an obstacle on the path I had planned.

She reassured me I'm who she wants and made me promise I wouldn't stress this. I made a vow to remind her of the person she was before she became a mother. I want to be the person that does that. I want to be the man that teaches her she can have it all, but I need to be able to balance what comes our way in order to do that.

"How are things with Cassidy Rae?" Cash asks next to me.

"Good." I keep my eyes closed.

"Not convincing."

I open my eyes and turn my head to my right to look at Cash.

"You do look a little banged up," Ryder comments.

I flip him off. "I hate when you two tag team."

"No tag teaming. What's going on?"

I sigh and tell them. No point in trying to play it off. We have a long flight, and Cash and Ryder won't let this go.

"Rae's dad reappeared. He found out Cassidy Rae got pregnant and now wants to be a part of her life. It's fucking crazy. She doesn't know this guy, and now they're doing play dates at the park. He's got a thing for her, too."

"The girl or the mom?"

"You're an idiot," I tell Ryder.

He laughs. "Bad joke?"

I shake my head and ignore him.

"Is he a good guy?" Cole asks.

"He seems it. I went with them on Saturday to the park. Cassidy Rae wants me to get to know him, too. I promised her I'd be there with her and didn't show the first time they met. I fucked up. I saw the three of them sitting together on a bench like a fucking happy family and drove away." I run a hand over my face.

"You're jealous," Cole points out.

"No shit," I deadpan.

"Look, at first it was difficult when Bri would mention Josh. We knew him and he's dead, but it still hurt. It was like I was up against his ghost, and I was losing. Until I decided I could stay and fight or give up. The situations are different, but it seems to me that you're Cassidy Rae's choice. You got two choices—give her up or stand by her."

"Bri really brings out your sensitive side."

"Fuck you," Cole responds.

"He's right," Cash speaks up. "Be there for her. She already has enough stress with her mom being sick."

"I know." I scratch my beard. "She's not doing too good either. The last few days she's barely gotten out of bed. They knew this would happen, but it's still hard on them."

"You gotta be there for her. You're the most levelheaded one out of all of us. Don't become a pussy like this one," Ryder lifts his chin toward Cash.

"Fuck you," he tells a laughing Ryder.

"Yeah, I think this trip will be good. It'll ground me."

"How's Rae with meeting her dad?" Cash asks.

"She seems okay. They get along. I'll admit, the guy seems like an okay dude, but I have his family and he may want it back."

"Nah, brother. They were never a family. He may be Rae's blood, but they're your family." Cash adds, "If you want them to be."

"I never thought I'd end up with someone who has a kid."

"I'm kinda enjoying seeing you go through this," Cole chuckles.

"You're another idiot." I'm taking turns insulting them.

"You were such an ass with the whole Bri thing that I like seeing you this way. Call me a dick, I don't give a shit. About time you get a taste of your own medicine and fall for a woman."

"I'm with Cole on this one," Cash laughs.

"I don't know why you guys make it so complicated. You like a girl, be with her. Communicate, fuck, make love, whatever. It's easy." We all look at Ryder. The son of a bitch got lucky with Jen.

"I blame the fact that you and Jen are both so easy-going that you never fight."

"We fight. Trust me, that tiny woman gives it to me hard—and not in the way I want—but the make-up sex is even better. We just talk it out, or yell it out, but it's our thing."

We all shake our heads. Those two definitely have the oddest, and most drama-free, relationship out of all of us.

"My advice, turn the hook-up into love. Worked for me," Ryder keeps talking.

"Anyway, I'm sure we'll be okay," I finish off.

"We want to meet her soon," Cash states.

"I'm not sure when that will happen. I want her to meet you guys, and Bri, Jen, and Liv, but I hate to say this, it'll have to be after her mom passes."

"Is it that bad?" Cole asks.

"Yep."

"Tyler's wedding is soon," Cash points out. "Might be a good time."

"We'll see." Tyler Hunt gets married at the end of August and we'll all be there. I'd love nothing more than to have her on my arm for that wedding. "Fuck, I want a drink." I ring for the stewardess to come and we all order something.

I'll make it back from Los Angeles and go straight to Cassidy Rae's on Friday morning. I'll show her that my jealousy the other day was due to feeling displaced, but that I'm one-hundred-percent in.

Chapter 22

Cassidy Rae

RAE IS OUTSIDE WITH MY dad, watering the lawn, while I sit in my mom's room. They gave me time with her when I got home from work this afternoon. She's been in bed most days since Sunday, and I'm worried this is the beginning of the end. Jason left for Los Angeles yesterday, and I'm wishing he were here more than ever. I can't tell him that because he's working and it wouldn't be fair. I know he's struggling with accepting Scott while trying to find his place in our lives. All of this is so confusing.

I scoot closer on the chair and grab the hand closest to me. I run my fingers through her hair, talking softly.

"Rae's dad, Scott, ran into me a couple weeks ago. When he saw Rae, he knew she was his. I never thought I'd see him again, Mom." I sniffle. "I didn't even remember his name. It was embarrassing." I continue to soothe her.

"We've met him twice, so he can spend time with Rae. Jason is jealous, but he shouldn't be. I'm not attracted to Scott. I've come to realize that the reason Scott and I slept together was so that Rae could enter my life. She loves you so much. I'm happy we moved back to be with you." I take a few deep breaths. I look around their bedroom. It hasn't changed. The same bed and decor. To this day I can't believe I moved out. I was selfish, or maybe I was protecting my child from a stressful upbringing.

"Anyway," I continue. "Things are complicated. Scott seems like a nice person, but I can't trust him yet with my daughter, even if he is her father. He asked if Jason and I were in a serious relationship. He wants to have a real chance at being a family, but I don't love him. I love Jason. I have no doubt in my mind who I want to be with.

"I'm worried that when we bring in the lawyers to settle custody, it will be a rollercoaster ride. You know I never liked those. I wish you were fully present to talk about this." I wipe my cheek with the back of my hand before placing it back over hers.

"I need you to tell me everything will be okay. My lawyer—thanks to Jason—has run background checks on Scott and everything has come out clean. He has no criminal record, he's never been in trouble with the law, and he seems to be loved by his family and friends.

"I can't help but think that this nice-guy persona will disappear as soon as we're in front of lawyers agreeing on our custody. Rae does like him. She told me he's nice." My breath is loud as I exhale. "Dad says things will work out."

My mom stares up, not moving. I sigh, staying quiet and continuing to brush her hair with my hand. Being here with her is nice, but I'm already grieving her loss and she's not gone yet. Seeing her bound to the bed, feeding her soup as we sit her up as much as we can, are all stark realizations that her days are numbered.

"Mommy." I look at the door when Rae whispers my name. I smile at my little girl, who has grown up a lot this summer. I wave her over and she tiptoes over to my chair. "Is she okay?"

"Yeah. She's tired. I was talking to her for a bit and combing through her hair."

Rae smiles and leans back on me. "I love her a lot."

"She loves you, too, baby. She may not be able to say it, but she does."

"Is she gonna die?"

I look down at my daughter and kiss her forehead. The sound of her giggle lightens the room. I nod. "She's very sick. We don't know when, but yes."

"I'm going to miss her." Rae pets my mom's arm.

"Me, too." I choke up. Rae turns to look at me.

"Don't cry." She hugs my waist. "We have Grandpa, too." I nod as I hug her. My tears are an uncontrolled mess as I weep my mother's inevitable death.

I feel a hand on my back and look up to find my dad standing next to us. I nod and catch my breath. When I stand from the chair, Rae looks at me with sad eyes. Maybe I shouldn't have lost it like that in front of her.

"I'll sit here for a while with Rae. Go take a break," my dad says. I nod and walk out of the room, grabbing my phone from the kitchen table. I still have two days before Jason returns and I miss him. I send him a message asking if he can talk, noting the time difference. I'm not sure what his schedule is like over there.

I answer my phone as it rings.

"What's going on? Are you okay?" His voice is panicked.

"Yeah. No. I don't know. I miss you. I… I wanted to talk. Hear you."

"I'm here, baby." I close my eyes as I hear his words.

"Thank you," I whisper and close the door to my room. I lie on my bed and talk to him. I tell him about my mom's condition these last two days.

"Scott wanted to see Rae again, but I told him we couldn't. I need to be here if anything happens."

"Do what's best for you and Rae right now. If he really is that good a guy, he'll be understanding." Jason still hasn't warmed up to the idea of Scott being in our lives. I don't blame him. If the tables were turned, I'd be insecure as well.

"I love you," I tell him so he knows I mean it. I've never been in love before. Not like this. This is a real kind of love. The love I feel for him makes me want to make promises that last beyond a lifetime. "I never thought I would," I admit. "I never thought I'd love anyone besides my family."

"I'm lucky you do. I miss you."

"What have you been doing?" I settle into my bed ready to listen to his stories about Los Angeles.

"We met with the music producer today. We had lunch with Ronan Connolly after—"

"The movie star?" I interrupt him.

"Yeah," Jason laughs. "Cash and him are friends, and he has a role in the film.

"Oh my God. That's so cool."

"He's a great guy. We also performed the song, did a bunch of business, which was boring. I keep thinking about you. I want to be there with you."

"You will be soon."

"Yeah."

Jason and I talk for a while longer. He tells me about the interviews they have coming up tomorrow and a guest performance for Musically Talented, one of the many song contests that exist. I relax as I talk to him, imagining him back soon.

When I hang up with Jason, I feel calm and ready to face the world again. Or at least my mom's illness. I give my dad and Rae more time with my mom and begin cooking dinner. It's the hardest on my father. They've been married for so many years, and soon she won't be here anymore. I can't imagine what that would feel like. He's lived the last ten years focused on taking care of her. Once she's gone, Rae and I will have to make sure to keep him busy.

I'm glad I'm only working a few days a week with this new job, so I can be here as much as possible. This week I work the first three days of the week, and then I have four to be home with my mom. The pay isn't a whole lot, but it helps that I don't pay rent at the moment. I have been less stressed financially since moving back here.

I roll out the dough I bought at the grocery store and shape it into something resembling a circle. I bring out the tomato sauce from the fridge and the shredded cheese. Pizza sounds perfect for dinner tonight.

I'm almost done placing the last pepperoni when Rae comes into the kitchen.

"You cooked without me?" She pouts.

I smirk and rub her head. "Here, help me place a few pepperonis." I carry her and sit her on the counter, handing her the container with the round meat. I let her add a few extra pieces.

"I love you, Mommy." Rae puts down the pepperoni

and moves forward to hug me.

"I love you, too." I tighten my arms around her, and carry her off the countertop, humming a song I used to sing to her when she was a baby. "You're getting big, Rae."

"You can still carry me though," she replies. I don't say anything else. I continue to hum, appreciating moments like this before they're gone. Soon she'll be too big for time like this with her Mommy. In the blink of an eye, my little girl will be a little woman, giggling with friends about the cutest boy in school.

I'm not looking forward to those days, but when I imagine them, I see Jason there with me.

"Cassidy Rae." I stir in my bed. "Cassidy Rae," someone is yelling my name. I pull the blanket under my chin and rub my eyes.

"Cassie." My eyes shoot open. Is that my dad? I throw the covers off me and run out of my room.

"Dad?"

"I need you." He sounds frightened. I run into their room and find him kneeling on my mom's side of the bed. I blanch when I see her.

"Dad?"

"Call the doctor. Call 9–1-1."

I nod my head, swallowing the lump in my throat. The sun hasn't fully risen yet, but I run to the house phone and dial 9–1-1 first. After I give them details, I call the doctor. Then, I wait with my dad for them to arrive.

I don't need a medical professional to tell me what I already know. When I touched my mom's hand, it was frozen. Her eyes were glassed over. She had no heartbeat.

I knew she was gone the moment I realized it was my dad calling my name. I lean against the wall as I watch the paramedics wheel her away. Two days ago I was sitting in this room telling her about my fears. I'll never have that opportunity again.

The heaviness in the room tumbles me down, until I'm on the floor, sobbing. My body wracks as I realize she's gone. This disease killed her even when the doctors said it wouldn't. Of course it would. Despite the disease itself not killing her, the result of it did. I hug my knees and bury my face in the space between my bended legs and body.

I should've accompanied my dad to the hospital, but they only allow one person to ride in the ambulance and Rae is still sleeping. I have no idea how I'm going to tell her what happened. At some point, my phone rings. I've lost track of time and should go check on my daughter.

I look at the name and consider hitting ignore, but I answer it.

"Hello?"

"Cassidy? What's wrong?"

I cry into the phone, unable to respond.

"Is it your mom?" Scott asks.

"She's gone," I manage to get out.

"Are you okay? Is Rae? I'll come over."

"You don't have to. Rae is still sleeping."

"I'm going to come. Give me your address."

"Really, Scott. You don't have to." I stretch out my legs and shake my head as if he could see me. He continues to insist until I mumble off the address.

When we hang up, I try calling Jason and get voicemail. He might be flying already. I send him a text message and hope he gets here soon.

A knock at the door startles me. Disoriented, I stand and glance around my parents' bedroom. The image of my mother lying on the bed, lifeless, is impregnated in my memory. I drag my feet to the front door.

"Hey." Scott's wide eyes stare at me. I try to smile, but instead a strangled cry comes out. He hugs me as I soak his nice shirt with my tears.

"Mommy?" I move away from Scott at the speed of lightning and look at Rae.

I go to her and pick her up, clutching her to me. I sit on the couch without releasing her. Scott closes the front door and looks around as he stands in the middle of the living room looking awkward.

"Please take a seat," I somehow remember part of my manners taught to me. He sits on the couch next to us. Rae looks at the two of us with her brows pulled into the center of her face.

"What happened?"

I close my eyes and chase the air that can help me speak. "Baby, this isn't easy to say." The waterworks are in full effect as I look at Rae's confused expression. "It's Grandma. She passed away this morning." I wait for her to speak. I give her time to process this information.

"She died?" Her voice cracks. I nod, unable to say another word without breaking down again. "Why?" she whines.

"Her heart stopped working." I shrug. There's nothing else to say besides that. The paramedics said it was most likely heart failure, but the hospital would have more information when they do an autopsy.

Rae crashes into me, her cries muffled by my pajama shirt. I run a hand down her back. I hate to see her like this. I hate feeling this way. I hate that this is how it all ends.

Scott reaches over and pats Rae's head. He's uncomfortable in a situation like this, but I have to acknowledge that he's trying his best to be here for her.

Rae looks up at me, her eyes puffy and nose runny. I kiss her forehead and move her hair away from her face. "Cry all you want, baby girl. I've got you."

"It's not fair," she complains.

"I know. I know," I agree with her on repeat.

Another knock of the door startles me. Rae is gripping my shirt, keeping me planted where I am.

"I can answer it," Scott offers. Seeing as there's no way to move Rae at the moment, I nod.

My heart stops when I hear Jason's voice. I get to my feet, carrying Rae, and walk toward the door.

"You're here," I cry. As soon as Jason sees us, he engulfs us in a hug. His scent comforts me. His body brings me home. Hearing his soft voice is a reminder of all I still have.

"It's okay," Jason whispers into my ear, kissing right above it. He rubs my back in circles, the warmth of his hand slowing my breaking heart.

One of Rae's arms moves from around my neck and reaches around Jason's neck. I look at her through my hazy vision and see her face dug into the crook of his neck. Her small body is trembling. I look up at Jason and he nods. I let Rae's other hand reach for him and loop around his neck. Jason hoists her up and reassures her that everything is going to be okay. He clasps my hand and smiles.

Scott is staring at us with his hands in his pocket. "I'm going to head to work. I'm sorry about your mom. We can talk later." He places a still hand on Rae's back. "Bye, Rae."

She turns her head and mumbles a goodbye.

When Scott extends his hand to shake Jason's, I look between them and take in their interaction. I relax when Jason grabs his hand in a firm handshake and thanks him.

"I'll be right back," I whisper to Jason, my hand on his shoulder. He nods, and I follow Scott to the door.

"Thank you for stopping by. I appreciate it."

"You're welcome. I really am sorry for your loss. I know you have Jason, but if you need anything, you can call me. I can watch Rae if you need time to sort through details. We'll have the evaluator with me, if you want. We need to finish that process anyway. I understand that you and I will never be more than friends, and I do hope we can be friends for Rae's sake, but I want a relationship with my daughter."

"It's hard to let her go," I confess.

"I know, but I want to get to know her. It's difficult to explain, but I love her already."

With tears in my eyes, I smile. "That's because you're her father." I think about my own parents and how much we mean to each other. How can I do that to Scott?

"I promise we'll speed up this process. I think we can come to an agreement with our lawyers and not prolong it. We'll do what we need to with the evaluator. Just give me a few days."

"We'll talk next week," he nods, conceding to the space I ask.

When Scott leaves, I walk back into the living room to see Jason sitting on the couch, Rae on his lap. He puts his finger over his lips. I sit next to him, placing my head on his shoulder, careful not to wake Rae. His hand finds mine, and we sit like this for a short time. The silence surrounds us.

Chapter 23

Cassidy Rae

JASON DRIVES US TO THE hospital to pick up my dad and get the information we need from the medics. Dad looks worn when I see him sitting in a chair with his head in his hands.

"Daddy." I sit next to him and hug him. We both cry, mourning the loss of my mother. The one thing I'm grateful for is that she passed in her sleep and didn't suffer more than she could have.

"Sorry it took us a bit to get here," I tell him. Rae is by the entrance of the emergency room waiting area holding Jason's hand. Her eyes are wide as she looks around the hospital. I nod her over and Jason brings her. He gives his condolences to my father before my dad hugs Rae.

"I already contacted the funeral home. They are squaring away the arrangements. What did they say here?"

My dad doesn't loosen his hold on Rae as he speaks.

"It seems to have been heart failure. Her heart stopped working." He lifts a shoulder. His red-rimmed eyes break my heart. I clutch his hand and attempt a smile.

"It's going to be okay, Dad."

He nods, his lips pursed.

As soon as we get home, Jason tells us to sit in the living room and rest. He goes into the kitchen, and all I hear is the sizzling of something and the clacking of other things.

I sit with my dad, comforting him. Rae fell asleep again, and I've decided that is how she's dealing with things. I put her in bed when we got back from the hospital and made sure the stuffed elephant she loves so much is with her.

"We'll have to clean her things out," my dad says absentmindedly.

"Are you sure you want to do that already?"

"Yes." It's a one-word response that tells me there's no fighting with him on this. "I feel stronger today than I will feel when we lay her to rest."

"We'll do it together after we eat." I want to make sure my dad remains strong during this time. At his age, a loss like this could weaken and depress him. I won't lose him as well.

"That boy in there sure loves you," my dad comments.

"Yeah, he does." I nod, and silently thank whatever god is up in the sky for bringing Jason into my life.

"Breakfast is ready," Jason pops into the living room. I turn my head to look at him.

"Thank you. Come on, Dad." I help my dad stand from the couch and guide him.

When we walk into the kitchen, my breath hitches at

the view. Jason has set the table, using a tablecloth and all. The plates and utensils are set perfectly with the food in the center of the table.

"You went all out," I tell him as the smell of eggs and French toast waters my mouth.

"I found eggs and bread, figured I'd get a little creative." He shrugs as if it's no big deal.

"You really can cook," I tease him.

His smile is wide. "Should we wake Rae?" Jason asks.

"I'm going to let her sleep. I have a feeling the weight of the last month is hitting her and I don't want her to be more affected than she is."

We sit at the table to eat; my mom's missing presence creates an eerie mood. My dad eats a little, which I'm happy about. I was worried he'd sit at the table and stare at the space my mom used to occupy. It will be hardest for him to overcome, and I will make sure I'm here to help him grieve.

After breakfast, I help my dad look through my mom's belongings. Jason promises to serve Rae breakfast when she wakes up, adding that if we need him to holler. I give him a chaste kiss before following my dad into the bedroom.

I look through her clothes and jewelry wistfully. She hadn't worn half of these things in years. I decide to keep a couple of items–special keepsakes for Rae and me to share. I keep most of her jewelry–the real gold pieces she owned–including her engagement ring. The small, round diamond shimmers on the gold band, and you can feel the love woven into it.

"Are you okay?" I sit next to my dad on the bed, where he's clutching a dress. His eyes are red.

"Your mother wore this the evening you were

conceived." He holds the blue, sparkly dress. I know how hard they tried to have a child and the significance of that memory.

"It's a beautiful dress." I put my arm around his shoulder.

"You should keep it." I nod, taking it from him and folding it.

"Thanks, Dad."

"I'm glad you and Rae are here," he squeezes my knee.

"Me, too." I kiss his cheek and link my arm with his. I've been crying on and off all day. I'm emotionally spent, but I want to be here to support my dad. We could've done this another day, but maybe this is his way of processing and accepting her death. Who am I to judge?

I wipe my cheeks when I see Rae peek her head into the room.

"Come over, sweetie." Her pace is slow as she approaches us. "Did you eat?" She nods. "Seems like the cat got someone's tongue."

She smiles and sticks her tongue out. "No, he didn't." She climbs onto the bed and nestles between my dad and me. We hug her, and my dad's body shakes softly. I rub his back in figure eights like he used to do to me when I was a child.

"I miss Grandma," Rae whispers.

"We all do, baby girl, but she's resting peacefully now."

"With God?"

"Yeah." I give her a lopsided smirk.

"He'll take care of her," Rae nods.

"Yes, He will, and she will take care of us. She's your angel now, so whenever you miss her, talk to her. You won't be able to see her, but she'll be listening for your prayers."

"Really?" Rae's brown eyes become rounder.

"Promise," I reply.

Saying goodbye to my mom was hard. It's been a little over a week since we buried her. It only took a couple of days to get things sorted with the funeral home. We didn't have a viewing, and my dad already had most of it organized, knowing my mom could be gone any day.

The days have been emotional, and my dad goes through spurts of sadness as the hours pass. I understand it's normal, but I feel helpless. I was given a few days off from work to mourn and be with my family, and Jason has been here everyday since. I'm grateful the band has given him some time to be with me, and I'll have to thank them personally whenever I meet them.

The burial was a peaceful farewell, although we cried the entire time. It was us and a handful of long-time friends. Abigail and Blake came, and it was great to see them and have them present during a difficult time.

My mom is finally resting, but my heart hurts not seeing her everyday. I feel empty without having her to take care of, and I can imagine my dad is feeling as if his purpose in life was buried with my mom.

Rae did stay with Scott during the burial, and he dropped her off when we were done. She wanted to go, but I told her this was something for adults only. I didn't think the emotional stress would have been good for her.

He's had a few visitations with her alone during the afternoons this week. Sometimes he'll take her to dinner. The court evaluator has observed us independently with Rae and interviewed us, along with Rae. We have each requested reference letters from people that know us. It's been overwhelming, but I promised Scott we'd speed up the process as much as we can.

Rae seems okay going with Scott and is always happy when she returns. I do believe it has helped keep her mind off of my mother's death.

"Hey." Jason places his hands on the counter, caging me. My skin pebbles as he drops a kiss on my neck. He has been incredible all these days, patient and sweet. He arrives with the rising sun and drives home in the moon's glow. I feel bad he spends all his days here, but it's given us more time together. When my dad and Rae go to sleep, we sit on the couch and talk for hours.

"Hi." I turn around.

"Are you okay?"

"Mhmm," I nod. My arms find their way around his back and I scoot close to him. "I was thinking about my mom and the situation with Scott. I'm overwhelmed."

"I know, babe. Let's go to dinner tonight, the four of us. I think it will be good for your dad." I set my chin on his chest and look up at him.

"He might want to stay home." He's taking his time overcoming this.

"We can ask." He shrugs.

"Okay."

"I love you so much." Jason's lips touch mine. I want longer to taste him, but it's not the best moment. Rae or my dad can walk into the kitchen any minute now.

"I think I'm always going to miss her."

"Probably, but the days will get easier."

"I love you, too, you know." I grin.

"You better, because I'm keeping you," he winks.

"You better," I echo and kiss his chest before moving away.

"Do you have anything else you want me to take to the church?" Jason asks.

We found a local church that accepted my mom's clothes for the women in the community. They have a group of women who live in shelters and accept donations. I was happy that they were going to a place that was in need of them.

"That's all that's left."

"I'll be back then." He kisses my cheek.

I'm grateful Jason offered to take the bags to the church. When he leaves, I look for Rae and my dad outside. Rae wanted to plant the seeds she saved from a tomato a few days ago, and my dad promised they'd do it today.

I see them both on their knees, patting down the dirt. "Did you plant the seeds?" I shield my eyes from the sun.

"We did!" Rae jumps to her feet, muddy knees and messy hair. My dad takes a bit longer to stand. Those two are quite the pair. I sit on one of the chairs out here and wait for them to join me.

"Jason went to drop off the donations at the church. He asked if we wanted to go to dinner. It'd be good to go out for a bit." I tilt my head and look at my dad.

"I think I'd rather stay. You and Jason go. Will you keep your old Grandpa company?" he asks Rae.

"No, Dad. We all go or we all stay."

"Cassidy Rae, that man has been here everyday since your momma passed. Bless his heart. Go spend time with him. It'll be good for the both of you, and your mom would want that."

"Are you sure?" My eyebrows wrinkle.

"Positive. What do you say, Rae? Wanna hang with me tonight?" I giggle hearing my dad use the term hang.

"Okay." Rae bites her lip.

"Are you okay?" I ask her.

"Yeah, Grandpa and I will have fun. Can we watch a movie?" She gives him her famous puppy-dog pout.

"You got it. I think we have some old movies your mom loved we can put in the VHS," my dad responds.

"What's a VSH?" Rae looks at us.

"VHS," my dad corrects her. "You're about to learn all about the old-time technology." My dad wears a proud smile, and I relax. This is will good for him. *My mom would want that.*

Life is supposed to go on, and I've seen that with Scott. In a way it's been helpful to keep moving forward. Next week I'm meeting with my lawyer, and we will talk about the custody process and review the agreement Scott's lawyer sent. He hasn't mentioned what is included, and I haven't asked. We've been amicable, and I would like to keep things that way.

I hear the sliding door open behind me and I turn to smile at Jason. The sunlight reflects on my damp skin. It's a gorgeous day, but it is hot. August tends to be the hottest month, and it's kicked off strong in the heat factor.

"Was everything okay?" I ask him when he grabs a seat and moves it next to me.

"Yeah, they were so grateful. Those women don't have much of anything."

"Thank you. I told them about dinner, but my dad says you and I should go out alone."

"Are you sure?" Jason looks at my father.

"Yeah, son. Rae and I will have a movie night. I'm going to teach her all about the VHS. You remember those, right?"

Jason chuckles. "Yes, sir, I do." He looks at me. "Are

you okay with that?" I nod and smile. I want to have time together like a real couple, without sadness lingering over us. He has taught me so much about enjoying my own life and not feeling guilty for doing so. It's too easy to get caught up in everyone else's needs instead of my own, but they're family and Rae *is* my life. I'm learning it's good for her to have her own life as well, and Scott has made that possible.

I yawn as I scoot back against Jason. We're lying on the chaise side of the sectional. We opted for a night in at his place. When Jason said he would cook, I suggested we pick up pizza instead and spend more time together.

"Are you tired?" He looks down at me. His hands rest on my stomach. It's the most comfortable I've been in weeks.

"This movie is boring."

"What?" The surprise in his voice makes me laugh. How can he like this stuff?

"It really is, Jason."

"Cassidy Rae, *Braveheart* is a classic."

"Great, it's still boring," I'm partly teasing him because he made a big fuss about finding my favorite movie. Truth is, this is not the kind of film I enjoy.

"What do you want to watch?" he asks.

"Nothing." The movie has been going for a good hour, and I stopped listening forty minutes ago. I've been focused on Jason's heartbeat near my ears and the comfort I feel being here.

"What do you want to do then?"

I move my body from side to side, scooting closer to him. "I just want to stay here for a while."

"Baby, you gotta stop moving that way." Jason groans as I settle between his legs. His hands have now snuck under my shirt and lay flat on my stomach. I shiver when he touches my skin. I love being with him like this, and it's nice to not have to whisper because people are sleeping. It's nice to disconnect a bit.

I jump when Jason kisses my neck, causing him to snicker against me. He continues his torment, his tongue joining his lips. My skin pebbles as he moves from the base of my neck up to right below my ear.

"Jason," I whisper-moan when he scrapes his teeth on my earlobe. One hand pushes into my stomach and the other moves to rest on my inner thigh. His mouth doesn't let up as he kisses random paths on my skin.

I turn my head to catch his lips. As my body turns to him, his hand moves to my back. Facing him now, my legs on either side of him, I kiss him how I want. My body flush against him as our lips meet and part to allow access to the other. My tongue sweeps against his and I'm lost in the feel of his kiss.

What starts as slow, builds in intensity and fire. My fingers graze the end of his hair as I settle on him. Jason hardens beneath me and my desire grows. We've only had the opportunity for make-out sessions like this, and I'm ready for more. I press my hips against his and Jason groans into my mouth. His hands are everywhere, desperate to touch me as we kiss.

His fingers glide their way up my shirt until they reach the edge of my bra. I sigh as I feel him slide his fingers from side to side. I arch my back, encouraging him. I'm being bold, but I want this. I want to be the woman I feel when I'm with Jason. The woman I thought was lost long ago.

He skims his hands over my bra and cups my breasts,

his thumbs running over my nipples. I shiver at the feel of him through the fabric. After a few times, he lowers my cups and touches me, skin on skin. I release the kiss and moan.

"Fuck, baby," Jason growls.

"That feels so good." My desire-laced voice sounds like a stranger.

"I'm going to make you feel even better." He throws my shirt over my head and I look down at my breasts spilling over my bra. I want to cover them and put my shirt back on, but Jason holds me and kisses me. They aren't perky like other women my age and they have some stretch marks from my pregnancy. I definitely have a post-pregnancy body, even though Rae is six-years-old, and it's not what I would define as sexy.

"So beautiful," he murmurs against my lips. His fingers pinch my nipples as his tongue invades my mouth.

His mouth leaves mine as it descends, licking my puckered nipples before taking one in his mouth. I push into him, taking in the sensations he's creating with his mouth and hands. I want more. I want to feel him everywhere.

I grind against him again and he stops kissing my breasts.

"Baby, I'm trying to make you feel good, but that movement is going to end this before we begin."

I giggle. "I can't help it. I feel you through our clothes and…" I trail off when he moves his mouth back to my nipples and bites softly. I cry out, making a noise I've never heard come from me before. I'm so sensitive everywhere.

Jason's hands sneak into the back of my jeans, resting over the top of my behind. I move his mouth back to mine, desperate to taste him again. I control the kiss, loving the way his short beard scratches my faces.

Grabbing the hem of his tee shirt, I lift it over his head and run my hands down his chest over the light sprinkling of hair. I grip his forearms and stand from the couch. I reach behind me and remove my bra.

Jason groans as it falls to the floor. "Stunning." He remains still. When my hands reach for my jeans, he sits up. "Let me." He unbuttons my jeans and lowers the zipper, removing my jeans. I stand before him almost naked and wanting.

"I want to touch you and make love to you. I'm desperate to do it all."

"Do it." My voice is hoarse. He kisses my belly and stands, hoisting me up. "In my bedroom." I wrap my legs around him as he carries me to his room. He drops me slowly with a passionate kiss before lifting his mouth and trailing kisses down my body. I tense, aware of his destination.

Jason looks into my eyes as his hand sneaks into my underwear and runs along my clit. I moan and lift my hips up from the bed.

"Fuck, babe," he groans and swallows my cries as he inserts a finger into me and begins to pleasure me with his hand.

I'm begging for a release by the time he gives it to me. "I love you," he murmurs against my lips.

I reach for his jeans in an attempt to get him naked, but he stands before I can. "Is this what you want?" He undoes a button on his pants. I nod. "You sure?"

"Yes," I croak.

"I'm all yours, baby. All of me belongs to all of you, and all of you belongs to all of me."

He steps out of his jeans and boxer briefs. I lean up on my elbows to look at him. Then I move to my knees and reach for him, gliding my hand up and down his shaft. I pick up speed when he doesn't stop me, never breaking eye contact.

Jason lengthens in my hand, the feel of him stirring a need inside of me that has been dormant for so long.

"You gotta stop now." He places his hand over mine.

"Make love to me, Jason."

He leans over me, bringing us both down on the bed and reaches over to the bedside table for a condom.

"I've been dreaming of this day for a long time, Cassidy Rae. You look even better on my bed than I imagined." He kisses me before I can respond and enters me. I tense until he puts his hand on my hip and massages me.

Jason moves in me, the feeling of making love to him overwhelming my emotions. I cling on to him, my mouth on his, and move my body to the rhythm he's set. We pick up speed, my orgasm building. The feel of his hand on my breasts adds to the waves crashing down on me. Jason moves his body in perfect harmony as I cry out his name and tremble beneath him. My orgasm extends as he continues to push into me and groans with a final thrust.

We're covered in a fine sheen of sweat and breathing hard. Jason leans his forehead against mine and closes his eyes. After a few beats, he leans down and gives me a kiss.

"Cassidy Rae Pressman, I'm so fucking in love with you." Jason moves next to me and kisses my shoulder before standing and walking into the bathroom. I scoot up on his bed, lying on my side. When he returns, he lies next to me and pulls me close. I rest my head on his shoulder, listening to his heartbeat. I want to stay like this forever. I want this man with me for an eternity if possible. He makes me feel as if I'm the most beautiful woman. He makes me feel special. He reminds me I'm more than a mom and a daughter.

I nestle my leg between his and drape my arm across his stomach. Jason runs his fingers through my hair as we both come down from our climax.

"I want you to stay here. I hate the idea of having to drive you home," Jason confesses.

I sit up and look at him with soft eyes. "But that's how it is." I shrug.

"It doesn't have to be." He sits to face me, his hand resting on my hip. "I want you and Rae to move in with me."

"What?" I gasp.

"Every time I'm here, all I can think about is what it would be like if you and Rae lived here. I picture her coloring books splayed on the dining room table. I imagine sharing a closet with you and Rae having a room full of toys and crayons. I want you in my life."

"Jason, living with a child is not as easy as it seems." I'm trying to wrap my mind around what he's saying.

"I know, but I want that. I want to be a family. We can build a small, one-bedroom in the back for your dad if you want. Like that he can be close to us."

I wipe a tear and shake my head. "You're insane."

"If this is something you want, we can talk to Rae and your dad together. I know we still need to finish the legal matters with the custody. All of that will be squared away soon. I want you here, in my bed and in my life, sharing a home together." He grabs my face and kisses me. His eyes are serious when he looks at me again.

I can't imagine not moving forward with him, but I don't know if it's too soon. I don't know if I can leave my dad, and he may want to stay in his house.

"Let me talk to my dad first."

"Is that a yes?" Jason smiles.

"A maybe. I want to see where he stands in all of this. I just returned and don't want to abandon him right after my mom died."

"I understand."

"It's not a no. Jason, I see that same life with you. I wasn't expecting it to be so quick, that's all," I reassure him.

"I'll accept that for now."

He kisses me and doesn't let up, kissing all over my body until it's time for me to go back home.

Chapter 24

Jason

IT'S BEEN A FEW DAYS since I asked Cassidy Rae to move in with me. Having her in my bed after making love to her was everything I wanted. I want her permanently there. I want to come home to her. I want to build a life with her and Rae and become a family. It might have been soon after her mom passed, but it felt right.

Every day I spend with her, I fall more in love. The way she laughs, how she pinches her lips when she's thinking hard, the love she has for Rae, all of those and countless other reasons are why I love her.

Yesterday, the court evaluator assigned to their case, interviewed me. I think I passed. She seemed happy with my responses and saw the home I live in. I asked her what would happen if Cassidy Rae and Rae moved in with me. In short, she said that it wouldn't be a problem unless Scott had issues with it and prohibited Rae from living with me.

I don't see that happening. He and I have gotten to a better place. After Mrs. Pressman passed away, I was surprised and angry to see him comforting my girls, but Rae is his daughter and I understood why he showed up. I kind of felt bad for the guy, when Rae reached for me instead of him. Compassion goes a long way in accepting someone and their place in your life. Scott's not going anywhere, and I think he realized neither am I.

I scratch my beard and jump in my car. We have a meeting with the lawyer today, and I'm picking Cassidy Rae up when she finishes her morning shift. Soon, the meetings will be over and we can move forward. It will be hard to see Rae spend time away from Cassidy Rae and me, but we'll get the hang of it.

Cassidy Rae is adamant that she remains the primary residential parent, with Scott being the alternate residential parent. I'm hoping the news from the lawyer is good today and Scott accepted Cassidy Rae's terms. It's been a bit of back and forth, but the sooner they reach an agreement, the sooner this is over.

"Try this on." I hold a dress up to show Cassidy Rae.

"That's too fancy," she says. I chuckle at her expression.

"It's not. Come on."

I hold the dress I picked from the rack, knowing she'll look gorgeous in it. We came shopping after the meeting with the lawyer. We have a few things to celebrate, and a dress to buy her.

Scott accepted the terms and the lawyers are getting to work, drawing up all the paperwork. Scott and Cassidy Rae will have to appear in court for the final hearing, but the lawyers both said it should be painless and fast since there are no disputes.

Cassidy Rae also agreed to go with me to Tyler and Mikayla's wedding in two weeks. I'm looking forward to introducing her to my friends and spending a night out. I'm also hoping she gives me a yes about living together soon.

"Just try it on. The wedding will be fancy," I plead.

"Are you sure? I've never been to anything like this."

"I'm positive." I grab her hand and walk her to the fitting room. I hand the attendant the dress. "One, please."

She raises her eyebrows and I laugh. "It's for her." I move my head toward Cassidy Rae.

"Good thing, or I'd be worried if I were her," the attendant jokes.

Chuckling, I reply. "Trust me, no worries in that department," I quip.

"Jason," Cassidy Rae scolds and pushes me into the waiting section of the fitting room. "Thank you, ma'am. Don't mind him," she apologizes.

"I have to make sure my reputation isn't tarnished."

Cassidy Rae rolls her eyes and I sit on the small bench right outside of the women's fitting room. A few minutes later, Cassidy Rae walks out. I catch my breath and stare at my beautiful girlfriend.

"It's too fancy and expensive." She runs her hands down the front of the dress.

"Quiet woman and let me look at you." I stand and whistle. "You look beautiful." The dress is strapless and has a slit where I can see her soft skin peeking out of. I hold her hand and pull her to me, swaying together. "It's perfect to slow dance in." I twirl her. "It has good mobility." I bring her back to me and tilt her back. "Good coverage."

Cassidy Rae giggles. "And it makes you happy."

"We'll take it," I call out to the attendant in jest.

"You're out of control," Cassidy Rae slaps my shoulder playfully.

"Nope. I'm in love," I kiss her perfect lips and slap her bottom before ushering her into the dressing room so she can change out of the dress before I tear it and embarrass her more than I have.

"You're in a good mood," Cassidy Rae says as we walk out of the store hand in hand. The dress is draped over my right arm in a garment bag. It was worth every penny.

"I'm happy that things worked out today in the meeting and that you're going with me to this wedding. My friends are dying to meet you. Now I just need to convince you to come to one of my shows at Riot and move in with me. I'm sure I can think of a few ways to be convincing," I whisper in her ear before scraping my teeth over her lobe.

"You're a terrible tease. I'm talking to my dad today when I get home. I think having things mostly squared away with Scott has helped me focus again. I want to be with you. I want all the same things you do, so please don't think I'm stalling."

"I know you're not, babe. I also know you have different responsibilities than my friends do. None are parents yet, and it's not easy leaving Rae so you can go to a bar and watch your boyfriend perform."

"I want to, though. Maybe Scott can keep her one night? Or my dad? When do you perform again?" The guys offered to take a short break, so I can spend time with Cassidy Rae, which I'll be forever grateful to them for.

"This Saturday," I tell her.

"As in three days from now?"

"Yeah," I look at her, amused by her counting skills.

"Maybe Rae can stay with my dad? It will be almost bedtime for her."

"Really?" My eyebrows pop up into my forehead. She smiles and nods her head. "I'd love that, but only if you really are okay with it. We won't have to stay after the show for too long." It's hard being in the celebration mood after her mom passed away.

"It will be like going out on a date. I used to leave her with Abigail. I'm sure my dad can watch her. It will be good to give him a role as well, some responsibility. It'll help with the lack of focus on my mom."

"That's a good idea," I kiss her temple. "Thank you." I finally feel like we're moving forward. Cassidy Rae will be more incorporated in my life, meeting my friends and seeing me do what I do.

"I love you, Jason. I want to make you as happy as you've made me and support you just as much. You've been incredible to me, and I want to offer the same partnership to you."

"You do."

"No. I haven't been able to. Before we had a chance to get there, I moved back into my parents' house. Now we're getting a real chance at us." She kisses my shoulder and smiles.

"Mommy! You're back," Rae runs to the door and slams into Cassidy Rae, causing her to step back with the force.

"I am." She picks Rae up and hugs her. "And we brought ice cream."

I hold up the paper bag and waggle my eyebrows. "I'm pretty sure we have a vanilla scoop with rainbow sprinkles and chocolate syrup." I dig in the bag until I find hers.

Rae worms out of Cassidy Rae's arms and grabs the ice cream. "Thank you, Jason." She hugs me and skips away with her ice cream. We both laugh at her enthusiasm. It's the little things that make that girl happy.

"We brought you one, too," Cassidy Rae sits next to her dad. "Pistachio with chopped almonds." She smiles at her dad.

"My favorite." He grins and gratefully takes the cup. "Thanks, kids. How did it go today?" He creases his eyebrows.

"Great." Cassidy Rae takes the cup I hand her and removes the lid. "Everything worked out. We'll have a court hearing to finalize it, but we've come to an agreement."

"I'm glad. It'll be good for Rae to have her dad in her life."

"Yeah," Cassidy Rae agrees, taking a spoonful of her plain chocolate ice cream. "I actually wanted to talk to you about something." I stand to leave, but Cassidy Rae puts her hand on my knee. "Please stay," she tells me.

"What's going on?" Mr. Pressman asks.

Cassidy Rae inhales and holds her breath before letting it go. "Jason and I are planning on moving in together. We have an offer for you. If you'd like, we can build you a small one-bedroom on his property, so you can have your space and still be close to us. In the meantime, we'd have a room for you in the house." She holds her breath as she waits for him to respond. I've learned all her quirks, all her reactions and ticks.

"I think it's wonderful that you're ready for that step.

I'm happy here. This is my home and it's where I belong."

"But—"

"No. I lived here for over thirty years with your mother. It's what I have left of her and I still belong here. I want you to go build your life with Jason and Rae." Her dad is holding her hand. "I'll be more than okay here, and you'll come visit. I'll go visit you as well."

"It's a big house for you alone," Cassidy Rae argues, but I can tell there's no changing Mr. Pressman's mind.

"I'm used to the space. I promise you, sweetie, that I'll be just fine here."

"I just got here, and I feel like I'm leaving you again just because Mom died." I had a feeling that was part of her hesitance.

"You're not leaving me. You're building a life. One day, Rae will go off to college or move into her own place. She'll still be a part of your life, but you'll learn that you need to give her space to fly with her wings."

"But, Daddy."

"Don't daddy me." He wipes her tears. "This young man and you deserve a life full of love like your momma and I had. Be happy, Cassie. I'm still Number One Grandpa, and that girl will have me in her life. Besides, I can play bingo in the Senior Community Center and meet friends."

Cassidy Rae nods. "We'll come over for dinner and take you out. You can babysit Rae."

She kisses his cheek and hugs her father. He shakes my hand. "Be good to her," he warns.

"I will, sir."

After dinner, Cassidy Rae and I sit with Rae.

"We wanted to tell you something," Cassidy Rae

begins.

"What is it?"

"You know everything worked out with Scott." Rae nods at Cassidy Rae's words. "Now, Jason wants us to live in his house."

I watch as Rae's eyebrows scrunch and her lips pinch. She's so much like her mother. "Are you guys getting married?"

"What?" My eyebrows jump into my hairline. "Um, no… I mean… not yet." I look at Cassidy Rae.

Laughing, she places her hand on my arm. "We're not, but we love each other very much and want to live our lives together," she tells her. It's not that I don't want to marry her, but I wasn't expecting that from Rae.

"Will I have my own room?"

"You sure will," I smile. This I can answer.

"What will my room look like?" Rae asks.

"Well, we have to decorate it. How do you want it to look?" I ask.

Rae's eyes widen. "I don't know. I've never had my own room before." My heart breaks a little for her. I will do everything in my power to take care of her and Cassidy Rae. They'll never have to worry about money or safety ever again.

"We'll go shopping and pick out the things you like."

"Really?" she whispers.

"Yup, Rae Rae." Her smile wins me over. I'd give that girl anything she wants.

"Well, not whatever you want," Cassidy Rae raises her eyebrows. I know I can get carried away. We'll talk about this later.

When she asks if she could go back to her old school,

Cassidy Rae tells her she'd talk to the principal. We both think it would be best for her to stay in an environment she is familiar and comfortable with. She's been through enough in the short span of a few months, and stability is the best for her.

"Are you happy about this then?" Cassidy Rae asks Rae.

"Yeah. I love Jason." I'm a man and I can admit I have emotions. Hearing her say she loves me chokes me up.

"I love you, too, kiddo." I squeeze her. I catch Cassidy Rae wiping her eyes and I wink. Fucking happiest day of my life. For now.

Once Rae and Mr. Pressman are in bed, I bring Cassidy Rae with me to the sofa and pull her onto my lap. Kissing her soft lips, I smile against her.

"I'm so fucking happy."

"Me, too." She tilts her head, her eyes smiling. As she holds my face, her eyes stare into mine. "You know I never thought I'd meet someone like you. I've piled so many things onto your plate and it isn't fair, but you wouldn't leave. You proved to me I could be loved through the good and the bad. Thank you."

"Caz, you deserve to be loved. I vowed to myself to show you that you are more than a mother. That you are a woman deserving of everything you want. I'll keep doing that each day." I kiss her shoulder.

"We'll have to talk about me getting a job at some point," she abruptly changes the direction of this conversation. I squeeze her hips and shake my head.

"I already told you, you don't need to work."

"You're not going to take us in and pay for everything. You already won't let me pay for a portion of the mortgage."

"Cassidy Rae, let me take care of you."

"You already do, but in order for me to be the woman you want me to be, the woman I am, I need to work. It's a need in me." She tries to explain the same thing she told me when she first agreed to move in with me. I want her to know she has support now. She doesn't have to do it alone or kill herself working.

"I'll work part-time only," she tries to negotiate.

I move her body so she's straddling me. "Baby..." I grip her upper thighs.

"Jason," she warns.

"I love you. I want you to breathe a little and relax. You've had some tough years and these last few months have been emotionally draining for you. Take a break. Spend the days with your dad while Rae is in school. Let me do this. In a few months, once we're settled, you can get a job. I don't want to take away your freedom, I love that most about you, but I want to be a partner in this. I need you to let me take care of you."

"You're too giving," she pushes down to kiss me. Having her in this position isn't going to let me think straight if she wants to keep discussing this.

"I want to give you and Rae the world. I know she has her dad, but I love that little girl."

"We love you, too. I'll take some time, and when Rae is back in school and we've gotten a routine, I'll look for a job."

"I'm glad we could come to an understanding. Now, about that kiss you're itching to give me..." I wink.

Chapter 25

Cassidy Rae

I TWIST MY FINGERS AS Jason drives. My heart has been racing since this morning and my stomach has been in knots. It's silly but I don't know what to expect from his friends. Do they think I've gotten in the middle of their work? Do they think I'm after his money? It doesn't help that Jason sprang on me that his sisters would be there tonight as well.

He reaches for my hand in the darkened car. "Breathe."

We'll get there early enough so Jason will be with me while I meet the guys and their wives or girlfriends. I think Bri is the only one not married. It doesn't help that his ex-girlfriend used to work at the same bar. I'm glad she's no longer there. He said something about her moving to Los Angeles. I wasn't really paying attention. Her loss was my gain.

"I feel stupid, but I keep questioning if they'll like me."

"They already do. I've told them all a lot about you. The girls are excited to meet you. You'll see. We're all one big family. We have been for years."

"And I'm the outsider intruding."

"Cassidy Rae," he chastises. "We're here." He pulls into a parking lot and parks the car. I walk out of the car when he opens the door for me. It's awkward at times, but I know he loves doing that, so I wait for him.

"Ready?" I nod. "I love you," he pecks my lips and guides the way into Riot. As soon as we enter I take in the space. It's a lot more casual than I imagined. A wooden bar is on the far wall with a stage to the left. The tables and chairs are against the walls so the center is open for people to dance. I'm sure people are standing and moving around while they perform.

He squeezes my hand and winks. I look forward and see Cash Knight. *Holy shit.* He's taller in person than he seems in pictures. Next to him is a brunette, laughing at something he is saying. Cole, and I'm assuming Bri, is next to them. I notice Cole elbow Cash. Suddenly four pairs of eyes are on us, and I'm ready to bolt.

"Hey," Cash says.

"Hey, guys." Jason says. "This is Cassidy Rae. Cassidy Rae, this is Cole, Bri, Cash, and Olivia. We call her Liv, though." He points each of them out.

"It's nice to meet you," Olivia says.

"It's nice to meet you all." I smile tentatively.

"We're sorry about your mom. We heard what happened. Hope you and your family are okay," Bri sympathizes.

"Thank you. We're doing alright."

"Are you excited about the show? It's your first time,

right?" Olivia asks.

"It is. This is really cool." I look around as more people fill the bar.

"Do you want something to drink?" Jason asks.

"I'm okay. Thanks." He leans into the bar and places his order.

"Oh, the girlfriend." I hear from behind me.

Jason turns around. "Ryder," he warns.

"I'm the jackass. It's nice to meet you, Cassidy Rae." I laugh at his introduction and shake his hand.

"I'm Mrs. Jackass, also known as Jen. So happy you came tonight." I'm taken aback when she hugs me.

"It's nice to meet you," I reply.

"Don't mind her, she's a hugger," Olivia excuses.

"I'm handsy," Jen shrugs.

"Yeah you are," Ryder jokes. Everyone groans, and I laugh.

"They're the perverted couple," Bri says.

"The things I've seen and heard," Olivia shivers.

"That's what you get for coming home earlier than you told me." Jen laughs as she puts her hand around Ryder. It's clear these two are crazy about each other.

"I should've kicked you out then," Olivia retorts.

"I'm your favorite cousin, you wouldn't have dared." Jen lifts an eyebrow. I smile as I watch their interaction.

"You're my only cousin," Olivia deadpans.

I giggle. "That's cool. You two are family and you married best friends."

"We did. She met Cash thanks to me," Jen says proudly.

"You sure did, Pajama Girl," Cash smirks at Olivia.

"I guess Jen is good to keep around." Olivia leans into

Cash.

"And I'm Olivia's best friend," Bri speaks up.

"Jason mentioned that. It's great." I smile. I really am an outsider.

"Here you go," Jason hands me a glass. I look up at him and then realize it's sangria.

"You like sangria?" Bri asks.

"Yeah." The chill from the cold glass moves through my body.

"You'll fit right in with us then," Olivia smirks. I relax, hearing her say that and get to know them as I sip the cocktail. I wasn't planning on drinking, but I'm glad Jason ignored my response and got me the drink. It helps me relax.

I tell them about Rae when they ask, and explain she's home with my dad. When the girls ask for pictures, Jason takes out his phone and shows them before I have a chance to. The only quiet one is Cole, and I'm thinking he's the hardest to crack. He's known Jason the longest and lived with him.

"We'll be getting ready to go on soon," Jason tells me. "My sisters aren't here yet and I wanted you to meet them before the performance, but they're always late."

"It's okay. I like them," I tell him as I lean in.

"They like you, too." He kisses me. "Look at me while I'm up there. I'll be playing for you." I nod and watch him walk away with the three guys.

"You're going to love their performance," Olivia says as she stands next to me. "It's fun to see them up there. The first time I saw Cash play here was a whole experience. I had seen him before at a music festival, but this show is more intimate."

"I can imagine. The space is smaller than I thought." I

take another look around. A lot more people are here now, claiming spots by the stage.

"Yeah. It makes for a great atmosphere."

The guys get on stage and I stare in awe as I watch them begin the show. It's amazing how they come together to play song after song. My eyes are glued to Jason as he strums the chords on his bass guitar. If Rae saw this, she would flip. She's definitely too young for a location like this, but I'd love to take her to a concert.

I sing along to some of the songs and notice Bri, Olivia, and Jen staring at the stage with the same admiration painted on their faces.

Jason spots me and winks, keeping in time with the music. That man is mine. Tomorrow I will be moving in with him and starting my life with him. How lucky am I to have met such an amazing person to share my ups and downs with? I used to question the reality of being in love with a person, and now I know it does exist.

They finish faster than I expected, and I'm left wanting more.

"What did you think?" Bri asks.

"That was so cool." I keep my eyes on the stage where they had performed.

"It really is," Jen says. "They're great at what they do." I nod in agreement, waiting for Jason to return so I can tell him how proud I am.

"Do you want another drink?" Olivia asks.

"No, thanks. One is usually my limit. I'm a lightweight," I shrug.

"Don't worry. We'll build your tolerance. Mexican and sangria nights are our specialty," Bri laughs. They have been so kind to me.

"That sounds like fun," I reply. I haven't had friends

my age in a long time. Let alone friends where I could hang out with outside of work.

"It is. Next time we have one, you'll have to come," she adds.

"Thanks."

"What did you think?" A sweaty Jason hugs me from behind. I scrunch my face and turn around.

"You were amazing. Sweaty." I lean back.

"Come on, gimme a kiss, Caz." I wrinkle my nose and smile, conceding.

"I'm so proud of you. I know it's not your first show, but you're a natural up there."

"Thanks, baby. Did you have fun?"

"I did. You were right. They're really nice." I tilt my head toward the women who have taken the time to make me feel welcomed.

"Big bro!" My head snaps to the left and I see two girls standing next to us.

"Hey, you made it. Cassidy Rae, these are my sisters, Reese and Taylor."

"Hi." My nerves kick in again.

"It's so nice to meet you," Taylor says. "Jason has told us a lot about you."

"It is nice to meet you. You're gorgeous. You did good, big bro." I laugh when she winks at him.

"Reese is the obnoxious one," Jason tells me. She slaps her brother across the head.

"Shut it. I'm not," she shakes her head. "Ignore him."

"Where's Mike?" Jason asks.

"Girl's night," Taylor smiles and holds up her drink.

"Mike is her boyfriend. They're practically married. I have to drag her out of the house and remind her she's only twenty-six," Reese rolls her eyes. "How old are you?"

"Twenty-eight," I reply and feel my eyes grow as I look between them. They look so much like Jason.

"Me too! We'll get along just fine." Reese links her arm with mine and I widen my eyes. Jason chuckles, running a hand through his hair.

"I should've warned you about her."

"Oh, please. What are you drinking, Cassidy Rae?"

"Oh, I'm already done. I'm a one drink kinda gal."

"Gasp." Reese places a hand across her chest. "I can't let that happen." She looks at Jason and nods. "Sangria it is."

I look at the other girls, who are giggling. I must look like a deer caught in headlights right about now.

Turns out Reese and Taylor are sweethearts. A little overwhelming, since they are Jason's little sisters, but they mean well. I finally get a chance to talk to Cole, and I got a smile out of him, so I take it as a good sign.

"Are you ready to go?" Jason asks. I nod, stifling a yawn. He reads through me and chuckles. "Let's get you home."

We say goodbye to everyone and walk out of Riot. I feel a lot more relaxed, but it could be because of the two sangrias I drank. Reese tried to give me a third one, but Jason interfered.

"Did you have fun?" Jason asks when we're in the car.

"I did. Your friends are great." I cover my mouth as I yawn.

"They liked you. My sisters loved you. Are you ready for tomorrow?"

"Yeah," I smile. I'm excited about living with Jason. Rae is beside herself. We picked out her bedroom furniture yesterday and they will deliver it tomorrow. My dad will come help us move. I want him to see where we'll be living and know he can always come to us. Jason made sure to tell him that. He can spend time with us outside of the house. He hasn't wanted to leave since the funeral, and it's important he goes out into the world.

"I'm ready to start our southern fairy tale."

"Me, too. I have the perfect country prince," I wink at him. Jason kisses my knuckles and smiles.

"Come tomorrow, I'm taking you home, baby. Then, I'm going to make love to you in *our* bed."

"It will be weird with Rae in the house." This is so new to me. When Jason made sure I knew that, from now on, he takes care of Rae and I, financially and otherwise, I began to refuse. He told me this is what we do in a partnership, and I argued that for a partnership to be equal both parties needed to bring in money. Eventually, I surrendered when he told me I needed to learn to accept help and love from people. He wasn't far off. I've been so used to being on my own with Rae, that I struggle to let others help me.

"Parents do it all the time. You'll just have to be quiet," he gives me a crooked smirk as he teases me.

"You're too good with your hands," I throw back.

"I'm even better with my mouth," his voice is thick.

"Tomorrow." It's a promise I intend to keep.

"You look beautiful, Mommy," Rae walks into the room where I'm staring at myself in the full-length mirror. I have never worn anything this elegant. Though simple, the way the dress fits speaks for itself. This isn't something I found at a second-hand store and bought for five dollars.

"Thanks, baby. Are you ready to go to your dad's house?" She nods. I still can't get used to the idea of Rae spending some nights with him, but I'm glad Scott could watch her tonight. We've been living here for two weeks and tonight is Tyler Hunt's wedding. Another milestone for Jason and I, attending a formal event as a couple.

"Can I have that dress when I'm bigger?" Rae asks.

"You sure can." I kiss her cheek. "What do you think?" I hold up a red lipstick.

"Yes!" She claps her hands.

Rae has become accustomed to living here. The first few nights, she snuck into our room and cuddled next to me on my side of the bed. She's shared a bed with me her whole life. We bought her a night light so she'd have some visibility if she woke up in the middle of the night.

"Are you sure you're okay staying at Scott's?" I've asked her the same thing the two other times she's stayed at his house. We have the hearing scheduled in two weeks, but we've decided to give the arrangement a go and see how it works out.

"Yeah. You'll pick me up tomorrow, right?"

"Of course," I tell her. As of now, she's stayed no more than one night at a time at his house. Their relationship is building, but it has taken a bit. I know Rae looks up to Jason a lot and in many ways sees him as a father. It's not fair to Scott, but it's how things have worked out.

Rae starts school on Monday as well, so I want to make sure she's home Sunday morning to get her ready for the new school year. We were fortunate the principal at her school had a spot available for her. She's happy to be back with her friends from her kindergarten class.

"Where are my girls?" Jason walks into the room wearing a tux. He looks so handsome dressed up.

"We're here," Rae replies on a giggle. He walks up to her and carries her.

I'll confess it's taken a bit for Jason to get the hang of having Rae around. He hesitated at first on disciplining her, unsure of what his role is. When I told him he is a guardian in her life and he could act as one, he began to get a better feel at this parenting thing. Although he's not her biological father, he's still a parent in my eyes.

"Doesn't your mom look pretty?" He asks her.

"So pretty," Rae sighs.

"Stop it, you two," I blush.

"Never." Jason leans in to kiss me. "Scott will be here any minute. Is your bag packed?" He asks Rae.

"Yeah. I put it by the door."

Jason kisses her cheek and places her on the floor. "We'll pick you up early tomorrow, okay? We'll go for brunch afterward, but eat breakfast with your dad."

"Okay," Rae nods eagerly. She loves brunch now. It's her new favorite thing. The echo of the doorbell catches our attention and we look at each other. Rae grabs my hand and leads the way to the front door. Jason follows us.

Scott stands there, staring. "Wow."

"Scott," Jason says with a nod.

"Hey. Are you ready Rae?" He clears his throat. I laugh inwardly. Scott and I have gotten to a place where we have formed a friendship. I know his initial feelings have dissipated, but Jason still tries to remind him of his presence every so often. He actually started seeing someone, but he's going to see where it goes before Rae meets her. I wholeheartedly agreed with that idea. Rae can get attached so easily. I would've done the same with Jason had I met him in a different situation.

"Yeah," she shrugs.

"Hey, we're going to have fun. Maybe not as much fun as these two," he jokes. "Kidding, Rae." He says when she screws her face up at him. "I've got big plans, kid. Movies, pizza, and ice cream."

"Yay!" Rae jumps up and down. She gives me a tight hug and then hugs Jason.

"We'll pick her up tomorrow morning," I tell him. "She starts school Monday." We agreed he'd come with me to the Parent Orientation the following week. I want him to meet her teacher and see where her school is. Fortunately, he was on board with her returning to her old school.

"We'll see you tomorrow."

I kiss Rae and watch them walk to his car. It still breaks my heart to share her, but I'm so happy that Scott did turn out to be a great guy. I know Rae is safe with him and he loves her so much already.

"Ready to go, Caz?" Jason whispers.

"You look very handsome." I kiss his lips and wipe away the red evidence. He bites my thumb as I do so and winks.

"You look stunning. I knew that dress was a great buy."

I grab my small handbag and make sure I have my phone and lipstick in it as well as my license. It's taken me a bit to adjust to Jason paying for us. He made me vow that I would let him take care of us, and that included financially. I agreed if he promised not to spoil us. I can't say he's kept that promise.

I wouldn't trade it for the world, though. Being at this place in our lives is perfect. I miss my mom every day, and I worry about my dad, but he's doing okay, getting by each day and I see him numerous times a week. I am looking into doing volunteer work with people who have Alzheimer's Disease. I want to honor my mom that way. If a part-time job is in my future like I told Jason, then I'll happily take it.

Life is good. I have a man I love by my side. My daughter is happy. Even Scott has become a good thing. My life could've gone in so many directions, but I'm so happy this is the path I took. I look at Jason and smile. "I'm ready." I'm ready for so much more with this man.

Chapter 26

Jason

CASSIDY RAE AND I SIT next to Cole and Bri. Ryder and Jen are on the opposite side with Olivia.

My woman is my every dream come true. Living together has been the best decision I've ever made, and I thank the stars that she agreed to love me. I hold her hand with both of mine as we wait for the wedding to begin. Her smile is bright, the red lips a gorgeous contrast against her blonde hair.

Tyler exhales by the altar and Cash puts his hand on his shoulder to calm him. Soft music starts playing, and we all turn to see Sam, Mikayla's therapist turned best friend, walk down the aisle with a simple bouquet.

The wedding is small, considering who Tyler is in the music industry. I think it's smart though. I know Mikayla and Tyler have had their share of challenges, and this is the perfect wedding for them.

When the wedding march begins, we all stand. Mikayla begins to walk down the aisle. She looks beautiful. Both Tyler and Mikayla are a part of our family. We got to know both of them better when we first went on tour with Tyler. Mikayla wasn't always mentally present, but we learned later she was struggling to overcome her past.

Thanks to him we are as successful as we've become. Mikayla is a great bonus. The love those two share is admirable. They are two strong individuals, who found the right person to overcome challenges with. It's an honor to be included in their day.

Tyler rubs his eyes as Mikayla joins him in front of the priest, and Cash smiles at her as he pats Tyler's back.

The ceremony is perfect, and I notice Cassidy Rae taking it all in. I spend most of my time watching her. One day, that will be us up there. I'll make sure of it. I told her a little about Mikayla and Tyler's history, and she seems as happy for them, as if she's known them for years.

After the ceremony, we drive to Cheekwood Gardens and Museum of Art, which is perfect since Mikayla is an artist. I walk with Cassidy Rae during the cocktail hour, which has an array of faux cocktails. With Tyler's history, they opted for a dry wedding, but the drinks are creative nonetheless. Cassidy Rae and I grab a glass of coconut lavender lemonade when offered and continue until I see my friends.

"Wasn't that ceremony beautiful? I loved their vows," Bri gushes.

"They were sweet," Cassidy Rae agrees. I wrap my arm around her waist and drink the lemonade. It's surprisingly good. I love watching her interact with my friends. I love having her here in my life. To think, I almost missed out on this.

Tyler and Mikayla arrive shortly after us and make the rounds, greeting their guests. When they make their way to us, I congratulate them both and introduce Cassidy Rae, both excited to meet her.

Before dinner is served, I steal Cassidy Rae away for a walk. The gardens, with art pieces and vibrant flowers, surround us as we take a stroll.

"I can't stop staring at you," I tell her. "It took us a little bit to get here, but look at us now. We beat the odds, baby," I pause. We may only have met a couple months ago, but what we've experienced together in that time feels as if I've known her for years. She's my forever. When you're sure the person in your life is meant to be, time is nothing but an excuse.

"I'm glad we did." She straightens my bowtie and places her hand on my chest when she's done. "You've taken us in and cared for us since the beginning. You're special." I give her what she wants when she puckers her lip. My tongue sweeps hers with a promise of more to come tonight.

When we notice people walking, we return and follow them to the courtyard for the reception. We're seated at a long table with Mikayla and Tyler. String lights, nature, and the soft humming of the outdoors surround us. I wonder if this is something Cassidy Rae would like.

Sam is sitting next to Mikayla. I introduce her to Cassidy Rae and she introduces us to Gabe, her boyfriend. Sam has always intimidated me when I've seen her, but today she looks relaxed. Her smile is a permanent feature.

When dinner is over, and the music starts, I lead Cassidy Rae onto the dance floor and hold her tight as the band sings a love song. We haven't had time like this. Our history is a little crooked, but I love it regardless. I love her. Inhaling the scent of her perfume, I hold her body flush to mine and move us to the music.

"This wedding is beautiful." Cassidy Rae sighs, her breath tickling my cheek.

"I'm happy you're here with me. If not, I'd be one of those losers by the bar with no one to dance with."

"I doubt that." She leans back a bit to look at me.

"It's true. I only want to dance with you the rest of my life. No one else would be good enough. You've made me a better man."

"You were already a great man. You had to be, in order to pursue a single mother and then stay by her side through everything."

"You're worth it. You have no idea how worth it you are, but I plan to show you for the rest of my life."

"Ditto." She presses her lips against mine.

Laughing and dancing, we spend the rest of the night having fun with our friends until it's time to leave. Cassidy Rae only checked her phone a handful of times to see if Scott or her dad had called, which is progressively better than other times we've been alone.

"Are you asleep?" I ask her as I drive home.

"No," she mumbles.

"Liar," I tease.

"I'm tired," Cassidy Rae complains. "It's way past my bedtime."

"Well, that's too bad. I had plans for when we got home."

"What?" She snaps her head front and looks at me. "Are we going to have sexy time?" I laugh as she waggles her eyebrows.

"You're too tired."

"I'm not." She reaches for my hand on the gear. "I'm never too tired for you."

"Well, I've been dying to peel that dress off you." I run my fingers over her exposed leg. Cassidy Rae trembles when I touch her, and I love that I get that reaction out of her. "We'll be home soon," I promise.

By the time I park my car in the driveway, Cassidy Rae is asleep. I look at her and smirk. She's perfect. I walk around and open the door, taking off her seatbelt, careful not to wake her. I carry her into the house. She mumbles something as I unlock the door with one hand. She's adorable when she sleeps. I love watching her at night as she cuddles closer to me and occasionally talks nonsense.

It's taken me a minute to process that she's here with me. That she lives here. I love every second of it. I love seeing her clothes in the closet and Rae's toys throughout the house. Looking back, Christie pulling the stunt she did was a blessing in disguise. I guess that's always the case. One disappointment leads to a whole new world of happiness. And being used by Christie led me straight to the woman I'm carrying in my arms.

I walk into our room and toe off my shoes before lying Cassidy Rae on the bed. I pull back the covers and remove her heels and dress before tucking her in.

"Baby," she murmurs.

"Shhh… go back to sleep." She rubs her eyes, spreading her mascara. She barely opens her eyes and pouts.

I laugh and undress. "Tomorrow," I whisper. Keeping my boxer briefs on, I lie in bed next to her and pull her to me. I kiss the top of her head and watch her sleep.

She's worth waiting for. One night of sex isn't going to make this moment better. She'll probably get mad at me tomorrow, saying we didn't take advantage of a kid-free night. That doesn't matter right now. Holding her in my arms is what I love best. Sharing these intimate moments together. I plan to make her permanently mine very soon, too. I don't want to waste another day.

I never realized how significant someone could become in your life. I had been in relationships before and enjoyed them, but this is different. The desire to share everything with Cassidy Rae is overpowering. It's a type of love that beats doubt and wins over fear. She's the person that threw order out the door and made it feel safe. Black and white is scary if her gray is gone. She's taught me to relax and trust whatever comes our way instead of counting on a plan, because life isn't a plan, it's a journey where you travel light and lose the map, so you can get lost in the best places possible. Cassidy Rae is my compass now, and all I need is her, Rae, and my music.

Epilogue

Cassidy Rae

Four months later

"THANK YOU SO MUCH FOR today," I tell Jason.

"I'm glad you liked it. Did you have fun, Rae Rae?" He peeks at her through the rearview mirror.

"It was awesome," she exclaims.

Jason surprised me with a trip to the elephant sanctuary where they moved the elephants from the Nashville Zoo. They have a small section for visitors to see some of the elephants. I was able to pet one. The experience was unique, and I was surprised when Jason showed me where we were going.

The last four months have been the best of my life. Things are settled, and Scott and I finally got Rae's custody legalized. He has his rights as her father, still remaining as the alternate residential parent. She spends every other weekend with him, but Jason and I are pretty flexible. The holidays will be difficult. She'll spend Christmas morning with us and then spend the afternoon with Scott and his family. Somehow, we've created a normal for us, and Rae is happy, which is my priority.

The hour and a half drive back home from the sanctuary flew. Jason is already pulling into the driveway and turning off the car before I realize we're home. Rae jumps out of the car first and races to the door. Jason laughs and follows her, unlocking the front door while I grab her bag from the backseat, shaking my head.

When I walk into the house, I see two matching pairs of cowboy boots with a bouquet of white daisies and eucalyptus leaves over the bigger pair. The scent of brown leather washes all over the house.

"What is this?" I turn to Jason.

"Every country princess needs her own pair of cowboy boots. We're living out our southern fairytale, Cassidy Rae. Every morning I wake up and thank the Lord that He brought you into my life. I thank Him for Rae, because she's as special to me as if she were my own." He places his hand over my stomach and smiles. "And soon you're going to bless me with my own."

We haven't told anyone that I'm pregnant, yet. We wanted to wait a few more months, when the pregnancy is more established. I wipe my face and laugh between my tears. Jason cried when I told him I was pregnant two months ago. He kissed me for a long time, made me promise I wasn't joking, and then made love to me. I had never seen him so happy before.

He guides me toward the boots. Pointing to the smaller pair, he says, "These are for my little princess," he smiles at Rae. "You told me a long time ago you wanted to be a cowgirl. Every girl should own a pair of cowboy boots to leave the boys in the dust."

"Those are for me?" Rae asks. Jason nods. She walks up to the boots and holds one up. "Mommy, we match."

She hugs the shoe and twirls around.

"We do, baby girl." I look back at Jason. "Thank you."

"I need to thank you for taking me as I am. I love you, Cassidy Rae." He waves Rae over. "I love your daughter."

Rae smiles at him. "I love you, too, Jason," she tells him.

"I've never wanted anything more than I want a life with you," he looks back at me. "All of you." He looks between us.

My hand covers my mouth when I realize he's getting down on one knee. "Cassidy Rae Pressman, will you fulfill the happily ever after of our southern fairytale and be my wife?"

I nod my head a bunch of times and cry yes. Jason holds the black velvet box open and I see the ring. I cover my mouth again, tears streaming down my face. Rae hugs my waist, witnessing it all.

Jason stands and kisses me, placing the ring on my finger. "It's a duplicate of your mom's, with its own uniqueness to it." I stare at the ring that does resemble my mom's and admire the additional baguette diamonds he added to each side.

Jason then bends down and looks at Rae. "I have something for you, too. I know I'm not your real dad, but I'd love to be your stepdad. I already consider you my daughter." Rae looks at him in awe as he pulls out a necklace with a tiny round diamond. He puts it on her and hugs her.

There is no point in trying to stop the waterworks. This is too much. The boots and the proposal. We're having a baby.

"Does this mean I can call you dad? Because I've kinda been doing that in my head."

Jason and I both stare at Rae.

"You have your dad, but if you'd like to call me that, I'd be happy. I do want you to remember Scott's importance in your life." If I thought I couldn't fall in love with Jason more than I already am, I was just proven wrong.

"I know, but it's like I have two dads. It's super cool." Rae touches her necklace. "Thank you." She kisses Jason's cheek.

When he looks at me, I see the same adoration I feel reflected back at me. I am going to spend the rest of my life loving this man and building our family. No one else could replace him. I wish my mom were here to witness this, but I'm so very grateful my dad is here to walk me down the aisle when the time comes.

"Congratulations." I turn my head toward the hallway that leads to the bedrooms and see my dad. I walk up to him and give him a hug. When I move away, I'm met with a bright smile.

"You're here." I link my arm with his and look at Jason.

"I wouldn't let him miss this. We're a family," Jason says. "And in a bit, we're going to celebrate with the rest of our family." Jason's parents and sisters have taken us in. They love Rae, too. His parents are kind-hearted people. It doesn't surprise me they raised such an amazing man.

I never believed in this kind of love, despite growing up with it with my parents. Once I had Rae, I knew my life was over and her life was my priority. I didn't think I would be able to balance the two until Jason stormed into my life and proved to me that I can give my daughter the best life while living my best life. It's not about sacrificing who I am to raise her. I need to teach her that I am my own person, so she knows to follow a path of individuality.

I want to show her that it's okay to accept our flaws and know that there are no mistakes, but lessons. She wasn't born out of love, but I'm showing her what love feels like. She has two homes where she is loved, and she can see through Jason and I what a loving relationship is like.

All those romantic movies I watched and compared myself to are dim in comparison to the real thing. Jason is my forever, and together we're building a lifetime of memories.

"Forever and ever," Jason murmurs against my lips.

Read a sneak peek of Hunter Daniels' story"
releasing fall 2018,

and add

Memories of Us

to your Goodreads:

www.goodreads.com/book/show/39349692-memories-of-us

Memories of Us

Hunter

I climb the fence and swing my leg over, settling down as I look out at the land my father worked hard to maintain. The land my grandfather built. I was supposed to follow their footsteps, but I threw it all to hell.

"Hey, girl," I run my hand down Addie's face. The mare juts her head in greeting. She was my favorite girl, until I found my other favorite girl. The second thing I fucked up in my twenty-five years.

"I can't believe I'm back here. Has he been cursing my name?" I ask the horse as if she'll answer. Releasing her, I look at the barn. Sighing, a wave of memories knock me down.

I'm cleaning the stalls, shoveling shavings while the radio plays Alan Jackson. I sing along as the words echo off the wood structure. I pay attention to the beat and rhythm the words create, picking up the different instruments that play.

"You singin' for an audience?"

I smile and turn around, leaning on the shovel. I look at her, eyeing her tight jeans and tank top, her cowboy boots hugging her legs.

"I am now." I sing louder, moving to her. I pull my favorite girl to me, twirling her around and moving to the music. I dip her low, hoisting her left leg up.

Her laugh vibrates around the space as I bring her back to me. She pulls my cowboy hat off and touches my forehead with hers.

"That's going to be you one day," she says.

"Only if you agree to be there with me."

"Always, babe."

Then, she puts my hat on and grabs the shovel I had leaned against the wall. "What do you need help with?" She begins to shovel shavings before I answer.

Adjusting myself, I walk behind her and hug her. "Baby, I need somethin' else right now." I push my hips into her, causing her to break into a fit of laughter.

"Hunter," she swats me. "We can't do that here. Your parents can walk in."

"Nah." I kiss her neck.

"Hunter Daniels, stop it right now." She shakes her body to rid me, but I tighten my arms, keeping her to me.

"I ain't ever lettin' you go."

She stops moving. "You better not." She turns in my arms, her kiss leaving me wanting more.

"Hunter Daniels! I never thought I'd see your ugly face around here again." I shake my head to clear the memory and look at Jack.

"Who you callin' ugly, dumb ass?" I jump down to meet my best friend.

"How you doin'?" He pats my back.

"Just takin' it all in, brother."

"You homesick?"

I shake my head. "Nah."

"How's the job? Rebel Desire, huh? You hangin' with the big dogs."

"It's been great. How are you? You have Julie pregnant yet?" I smile, sadness trying to pierce through me.

Jack chuckles. "Slow down. We got time for kids later.

We're still in the honeymoon stage."

"You been in that stage for over three years now."

He shrugs. "What can I say? That woman keeps me on my toes." He takes a step back to look at me. "You sure you're okay?"

"Yeah." I scrub my face. "Just weird being back here."

"Tell me 'bout it. Never thought I'd see you here again with the way you left."

"I couldn't tell my mom no." When my mom called to ask me personally to come to her and my dad's vow renewal, I couldn't say no. It's my parents' thirtieth anniversary and they're renewing their vows.

"She misses you. Talks to my momma about you all the time, what you're doing, the songs you're writin.' Maybe you should come visit more often." Jack adjusts his cap to cover more of his face.

"Can't. Work." I throw a lame excuse. "Besides, you turnin' into a chick now, worried about my momma?"

"Don't be a dick," Jack shoots at me.

"Takes one to know one."

"Glad to see your independence in Nashville has really matured you."

I sigh and run a hand down my face. I'm being a dick to him because it's easy. We've been best friends since we were in diapers, and our parents have been friends since before then. Jack is the brother I never had, which is why my leaving hurt that much more.

"What's really eatin' at ya?" Jack climbs the fence and sits. I join him, wishing I had grabbed a few beers and a cooler.

"Where do I begin?"

"Well, you ain't this tied about seeing your pops, so how 'bout you begin with the real reason you you're shakin' in your boots."

I smirk. Fucker.

"Have you spoken to her? Seen her?" I ask Jack.

"Nah, man." He shakes his head. "She up and left right after you, disappearin' into the night. Seems as you both have that in common."

I stare at him, jaw clenched. "I called. I said where I was going."

"She may have, too, just not to anyone related to you."

I hear tires crunching under the dirt road.

"Ready to face your pop?" Jack says with a smile.

Why is he still my best friend?

"Hunter!" My mom exclaims and rushes to me. I meet her half way.

"Hey, momma." I hug her, towering over her, but still feeling like a kid. I'm a Momma's Boy, and I ain't afraid to admit it.

"Been way too long. Are you eating enough? You need some of my chili and cornbread to fluff you up a bit."

"Mom," I laugh and shoo her arms away.

Before I can turn around, I hear mumbling and a door slam. Seeing as my father refuses to acknowledge me, I say, "I told you I could've stayed at a hotel."

"Over my dead body. It's about time you both reconciled. Now come on, I've got supper to make. You staying for supper Jack?" She calls.

"Depends. What are you making?"

I smile and shake my head.

"Get your ass in the house and call Julie and tell her to come over. We're celebrating tonight." My mom's voice sings and guilt washes over me. It's been three years since I've stepped foot on this land, always making my momma go see me in Nashville if she wanted to. Never inviting my father.

I came home one time after moving to Nashville. It was right after I left and it was to come get her. But she was already gone.

"Yes ma'am," Jack chuckles and follows us into the house.

I stomp my feet on the back porch before entering the house.

I grab a beer and hand one to Jack while my momma talks up a storm and cooks. She refuses help, saying we can help her set the table in a bit. My dad is nowhere to be seen, probably out by the barn tending the horses. Avoidance works best for us.

As soon as Julie arrives, I give her a big bear hug and catch her up on my life in Nashville. I've been trying to get them out to visit me, but their ranch keeps them busy. Being with them now, like old times, a pang in my chest amplifies. Not quite like old times. While Jack still has Julie sitting on his lap, mine is empty. I rub my eyes and gulp my beer. My one mistake. My one regret.

"I'll be right back." The chair screeches against the tile and I walk out to my truck to grab my bag. I need fresh air. I shouldn't have come. I could've made up some sorry ass excuse and said I had to travel for work. But I know how much this means to my mom. Her permanent grin all afternoon is evidence that it's been too long since I've been home. Being here is a reminder of all I fucked up.

I kick a rock with the toe of my boot and fling my overnight bag over my shoulder. Looking to my left, I see my dad shoveling shavings into a stall. Wasn't too long ago I was out there helping him.

I shake my head and walk back into the house,

whispers coming from the kitchen. "I can hear y'all," I holler and make my way to my old room, assuming my bed is still there for me to sleep in.

Dropping my bag on the bed with the same plaid comforter as when I was younger, I look at the medals hanging from the hooks. The one picture I have framed mocks me from the dresser. I put it face down and head back into the kitchen.

Acknowledgments

Writing a book can be a lonely process, but I'm so blessed that I have found people to join me on this journey that are kind-hearted and supportive.

Thank you to my readers, who have taken a chance on me and my writing and supported me along this journey. With each book I write, I tell you the same thing—without you, this would be an empty journey. I can write a million words, but if no one reads them, my purpose is futile. I hope you read these words, take from them what you need, and love the story as much as I do.

To my parents, thank you for understanding the need to feed this passion. Every time I release a book, my dad asks me for a paperback. He refuses it as a gift, and makes sure he (aka my mom) pays me for it. It was time I dedicated them a book. Thank you for always supporting me. It took me a while to see it, but it's clear now.

I am grateful to work with such an amazing team. Robin Bateman, thank you for taking the time to edit and make this book perfect for the world. I love your love of sangria. Amy Queau, your design skills astound me. You got me vision, and made it possible with this cover. Thank you! Tami Norman, working with you is a genuine pleasure. Thank you, thank you for always making the inside of my books beautiful.

Claire and Wendy from Bare Naked Words, I'm so glad I found you. You ladies are so helpful and keep me sane during a stressful time. I can always count on you, and that means so much to me.

My #SoapyThighsForLife girls—Rachel and Christy, no matter how many books we write, no matter what happens in the book world, I know I can always count on you. That's rare, and I'm so very grateful we have each other.

Joy, girl, you held my hand while writing this book. I talked your ear off while trying to get this story just right, and you listened and offered your best feedback. Thank you! I don't say it enough. You *finally* get to read the story you've waited so patiently for.

Veronica and Miriam, you pull through each time. I can't thank you enough for taking the time to read my books before everyone else, give me input, and support me throughout this journey. You've been with me from the beginning, not just with the books, but as friends.

Amber G, thank you for your guidance and help. I am so appreciative of your advice and tips.

To the After Hours Book House authors, thank you for your continuous support. We have a great group of strong women, who write badass books. I'm glad we have each other.

A huge thank you to my Fab Readers! You are a bright light in this career. Greeting you each morning and chatting with you makes my day. We have a true community thanks to you showing up and being true. Your support means the world to me.

Thank you to my review team for not only accepting to read my books, but also offer advice and input when I need it. Your motivation, love, and guidance matter.

Jennifer and Alicia, you ladies are always around, supporting me and encouraging me. I can't thank you enough for that.

To the authors and bloggers that unconditionally support me, thank you from the bottom of my heart. Working together, lifting each other, is what makes this book world (and the entire world) a better place. Kindness goes a long way.

About the Author

Fabiola Francisco loves the simplicity—and kick—of scotch on the rocks. She follows Hemingway's philosophy—write drunk, edit sober. She writes women's fiction and contemporary romance, dipping her pen into new adult and young adult. Her moods guide her writing, taking her anywhere from sassy and sexy romances to dark and emotion-filled love stories.

Writing has always been a part of her life, penning her own life struggles as a form of therapy through poetry. She still stays true to her first love, poems, while weaving longer stories with strong heroines and honest heroes. She aims to get readers thinking about life and love while experiencing her characters' journeys.

She is continuously creating stories as she daydreams. Her other loves are country music, exploring the outdoors, and reading.

Connect with Fabiola

Facebook ~ www.facebook.com/authorfabiolafrancisco

Fabiola's Fab Reads ~
www.facebook.com/groups/FabReads/

Website ~ www.authorfabiolafrancisco.com/

Twitter ~ www.twitter.com/authorfabiola

Instagram ~ www.instagram.com/authorfabiola